Copyright © 2024 by Manisha Holm

The characters and events portrayed in this book are fictitious. Any similarity to real persons, living or dead, is coincidental and not intended by the author.

ISBN: 979-8-9877273-7-9
Printed in the United States of America
First Printing, 2024

https://www.manishaholmauthor.com

INTRUSION

DEDICATION

To Aramati, Asha, Bhagavati, Carol, Diann, Jackie, Heather, Miriam, Pavani, Prashama, Priyadarshini, Shanti, Susans B and S, Taiyin, all the women in my life who have helped make sense of the world.

QUOTATION

O Father, Mother, Friend, Beloved God,
I will reason, I will will, I will act:
but guide Thou my reason, will, and activity
to the right thing I should do
in everything.

Whispers from Eternity
by Paramhansa Yogananda

Intrusion

A Journey of Friendship

MANISHA HOLM

CONTENTS

AUTHOR'S NOTE

Whenever we visit another planet, we can become bewildered by unfamiliar names and terminology. In an effort to ease the bewilderment, you will find a glossary of names, places, and terminology at the end of the book. I hope this helps keep the Aironians in context, allowing their story to unfold in your imagination.

Best of luck!

Manisha

~ 1 ~

BLENDED

Scarlett and Harper turned to wave as the cycle carried them away from Inipi, away from Chatan and Aadhya, away from baby Claira, glorious Claira. Away from Pond and the memory of cavorting Narsis. Harper felt bereft, as if she were leaving the only pure happiness she had ever known. How could she possibly leave?

She felt the cycle slow, and she turned to Scarlett on the seat beside her. "I don't want to go back. I'm not ready."

Scarlett's clear gaze echoed her yearning. "Let's wander."

Harper felt a wave of relief wash through her. "Yes. Andy will have all that we need."

Scarlett nodded. "He'll tell the others where we are and that we're safe."

They turned in unison to face forward, and the cycle carried them along, finding its own way under the forest and its dripping garlands and streamers of colorful blossoms. They leaned against each other and held hands, wrapped in a cocoon of unplanned freedom.

Harper recounted the story of the Eglan who led her through the forest to meet with Vargad. Her hand swept the air in front of them as she described the Eglan's graceful swoops amongst branches, threading the clear air with shimmering wings, trailing her flamboyant tail. Scarlett remembered the Eglans in her mind's eye, and found herself searching the high canopy for a glimpse of yellow and orange.

Scarlett had embraced Airon wholeheartedly. After her initial hesitations and tremulous forays into blending, she had thrown herself into blending with all the daring and certainty that direct experience can bring. Days floating in Pond followed nights sprawled on Meadow, stars floating across the night sky. The Earthens shared laughter and silence, stillness and stories, with Sun warming their shoulders and Breeze soothing their faces.

And the Narsis.

The Narsis came daily. Vargad's family crested the ridge each morning and flowed down to where the Earthens gathered at Pond's edge. One morning in particular stood out in Scarlett's Memory. Chatan raced a pod of younglings across Pond, clambered up the far bank, across the broad outcropping of stone, and plunged noisily back into Pond.

Caretake-ers and parents, indistinguishable one from the other, dove to Pond's floor, holderlings propelling them amongst the many water families clinging to the sandy bottom, only to push toward the light of Above, and burst high into the air, droplets fanning outward as they lazily spun through long arcs back to Pond, breaking the surface with nary a splash, so perfect was their love of water and air, sunshine and breeze.

This day, this moment etched in Scarlett's memory, a youngling crept from Pond, slipped up the grassy slope to perch, inquisitive, at Aadhya's elbow, where she sat rocking and nursing Claira in the dappled shade of an arching tree. The youngling watched Claira in silence and sent out a tentative holderling to touch the baby's brown cheek.

Aadhya reached down to smooth the youngling's fur, pressing away remnants of Pond, loosening droplets that trickled down onto the nurturing families on which the trio rested. The youngling hummed and lifted her nose to nuzzle Aadhya's arm.

Aadhya turned onto her side, resettled Claira onto the Nurture-ers, and curved her arm to encircle the youngling, Claira nestled between them. Claira raised her fists to the sky and kicked her legs, chortling. The youngling stretched her holderlings out to scoop Claira closer into the curl of her lithe body, and Aadhya scrunched closer still, completing the nest that embraced Claira.

Claira reached and grasped a holderling, raising it above her head, kicking her legs, and gurgling her delight. The youngling's hums heightened, and Scarlett felt a delicate rumbling that radiated from the trio. They soon fell asleep, and quiet engulfed them.

Scarlett stretched out on her own patch of nurturing families and resumed her observation of the frolicking Narsis, all the while contemplating the companionship of the trio dozing nearby. Harper had joined the Pond party, but soon turned on her back, face to the sun, drifting amidst the boisterous play.

Scarlett noticed that the Narsis knew exactly where Harper floated, scrupulously avoiding any disturbance that might interrupt her stillness. They splashed and cavorted, adjusting their playground away from the gentle course where Harper drifted.

Scarlett recognized Vargad as he lumbered out of Pond and made his way up the slope toward the dozing tableau. He stopped short of intruding on their peace, lifted his nose to sniff the air, and sent his own rumbling purrs to blend with the gentler rumbles and purrs from the youngling.

The realization dawned on Scarlett that this youngling was Vargad's youngling. There was no mistaking the adoration that flowed from the elder Narsi as his rumblings caressed the sleeping trio. Scarlett closed her eyes and fell into her own slumber, feeling a peace whose depth seeped into her every cell.

Now, perched atop the meandering cycle, arm entwined with Harper's, Scarlett could recall that same peace and breathed it deep into her lungs. She did not want the moment to end.

They meandered for what may have been hours, Andy drifting behind them. They talked and reminisced, wondered and speculated, laughed and sighed. Trees and blossoms drifted past as the cycle made its way through Forest and across Meadow. They came across a sparkling stream meandering between its ferned banks. The cycle halted, and the two women climbed down to dangle their feet in the brilliant water, nurturing families replenishing their bodies.

At last they rose and walked along the stream, drawn by a distant roar. After perhaps a mile, the air around them brightened as the trees thinned and a vast panorama opened before them. The once languid stream swept forward as it readied itself for its plunge over the edge of Overlook, droplets sparkling in midair as Stream fell, fell, fell to the valley far below.

Scarlett sat on a rocky outcropping several feet back from the edge of the cliff. Harper moved closer to the edge and sat within a foot of the drop off. Scarlett's throat closed, seeing Harper so near the precipice, but she held back her remonstrance and waited for her heart to slow. The two women sat in silence, taking in the enormity of the vista.

After a long while, Harper half-turned and said over her shoulder, "There's a tree down there."

Scarlett moved to sit beside Harper, her fear of the height diminished. She picked out the smudged green that sat alone in its plain. The forest beyond the plain began anew, following the rise of shallow hills whose ridge lines marched into the distance, nested horizons, with lakes glimmering here and there.

The solitary tree drew their attention, and their gazes returned to it again and again.

Harper broke their reverie. "We should go down there. I want to visit that tree."

Scarlett nodded, and they stood, examining the cliff face below them. Scarlett pointed, "There!" and Harper saw the wide ledge that made its way down, the trailhead quite near the boulders clustered on the verge of the waterfall.

Scarlett peered at the sun, gauging the length of day left to them. She glanced back in the direction they had come and noticed the cycle, which had apparently followed them along the stream. Andy hovered nearby.

She eyed the distance to the lone tree. A certainty filled her heart. It was the perfect time for them to make this trek. She nodded at Harper, who nodded back, and they stepped onto the trailhead.

The descent was arduous. They rested often, nurturing families replenishing their wobbly legs and aching feet. Andy offered fresh water orbs, disappearing from time to time, returning with a damp film covering his white spherical self. They moved steadily, intent on their journey, thoughts flowing effortlessly without a need for conversation, each woman absorbed by inner ponderings.

After what might have been hours, they reached the valley floor. Harper turned and craned her neck to look up the height that soared, seemingly touching the sky; the cliff that only that morning had fallen into giddying depths. Meanwhile, Scarlett had eyes only for their destination, the lone tree that spread itself along the valley floor that sloped away from them.

Scarlett turned to Harper, joined her upward scrutiny, and waited without breathing for Harper's attention to turn to the tree. Harper's eyes found Scarlett's, and wordlessly they turned to make their way down the gentle slope, sure arrows to their waiting target.

The day's light was beginning to dim when at last they stood at the edge of Lone Tree's sprawling canopy. Despite the dimming light behind them, the air was bright and glistening below the giant, light cascading and bouncing from branch to leaf to branch. The enormous trunk spiraled upward, holding broad branches up to brush the evening sky.

   You are come.

Harper moved close to Scarlett's side, entwined their arms, and held Scarlett's hand. Together, they moved under the canopy, entered Lone Tree's embrace, and heard Airon's song.

~ 2 ~

SOUND

Chatan peered out through the caravan's window into the early morning light. The surroundings were unfamiliar; Chatan felt alarm rise in his chest. He made sure that Aadhya and the baby still slept and stepped out into the dawn world.

They were situated in a thick forest with no pond in sight. He looked around, disoriented. He circled the caravan, once again tiny, once again on wheels, searching in all directions for a familiar landmark. Finding none, he examined the surrounding forest.

All of the trees seemed to be of the same variety, which some part of his brain registered as surprising. All of the flora had shown amazing variety everywhere Chatan had wandered. This place was subtly different. He reached out to touch the nearest tree and looked up into its foliage.

Branches were woven in an intricate, repeating pattern, mesmerizing in its symmetry; a myriad of leaves waved imperceptibly. He caught a bright movement and noticed a diminutive turquoise bird watching him. "Well, hello there." The birdling fluttered its rows of brilliant wings, front to back, then back to front. "Is this where you live?" The birdling lapsed into stillness.

Chatan walked to another tree and examined its heights. These branches wove a different pattern, oscillating outward from the central trunk, symmetrical, captivating. He walked from tree to tree, comparing patterns, marveling at the complexity and variety. Each one rose unique and wondrously beautiful.

Everywhere, blue fruit peeked from behind dancing leaves. Here, then, was the source of the blue fruit. Chatan recognized its healing power, a power that adapted itself to every need. A universal tonic.

And everywhere a turquoise birdling looked down at him. Here and there, a birdling occasionally fluttered rows of wings, but for the most part, they simply perched, motionless.

He heard the caravan door slide open and made his way through the trees to where Aadhya stood, gazing up into the branches just as he had. "Good morning."

"You have brought us to this beautiful place. How did you find it?"

"I claim no credit. We were already here when I woke."

"Really? This is true?" He nodded at her surprised face. "Who is making these decisions now? Do we have no say?"

"Perhaps the birdlings brought us here. They're all around. Solo birdlings, which I've never seen before."

She looked up again, turning on the spot. "Why are they here?" She looked farther, through neighboring trees. "Is this your home?" she called out to the nearest turquoise smudge.

In response, the entire canopy burst into movement, a sudden chorus of birdlings hopping from branch to branch, coming lower to the ground with each move. Aadhya laughed with delight at the display. "Thank you for inviting us to your home," she said as they settled onto lower perches.

"I wish they would have asked us first instead of just bringing us here unannounced." Chatan said.

Aadhya thought for a breath. "How would they do this? How would they ask?"

"I think they have ways. They invited us into the pond that first day. They could invite us here."

Aadhya nodded. "This is true." She looked to the canopy again. "He is right! We like to have a say!" The birdlings fluttered briefly. "All right. Now they know." She smiled at Chatan, feeling pleased.

He watched her for a breath before turning his attention up to the canopy again. "I've been looking at the woven patterns of the branches. Each tree has a unique pattern."

Aadhya strolled beneath the trees, gazing upward in silence. "Chatan. They are beautiful."

"I've never seen anything like it, here or on Earth." Memory flooded him. A smaller grove, with the same characteristic of distinct woven patterns grew near Home Base. He *had* seen this before. He had stumbled upon it the first day of his first wander. This fruit was everywhere then, close at hand for times of need.

Chatan reflected. Everywhere, but obscure. He was confident that if he reviewed the massive volume of data his companion fleet had gathered over the months of wandering, he would find no mention of these trees, this fruit.

This particular grove was massive. It stretched in all directions without interruption. Chatan could feel the power here. This was beyond blending; beyond even Lone Tree. This grove was ancient, had always been, would always be.

Airon had brought them here, now, because they were ready to know more. The mysteries of the blue fruit hinted at deeper knowledge, richer understanding.

His breath came back to him. "Yes. It's beautiful." They wandered past more trees, and Aadhya paused. "Let me bring Claira." He nodded, and they returned to the caravan. Chatan waited while she climbed inside, returning a few minutes later to hand Claira down to him. He held the baby against his chest, facing her upward so she could see the branches. Aadhya took his arm, and they set off. Sebba, their loyal companion, followed.

A solitary birdling bounced from branch to branch, making her haphazard way along the path where the Newcomers wandered. She clung to the bark of a bordering trunk and hung lopsided, chirping at Aadhya.

Aadhya's sharp intake of breath caught Chatan's attention. He followed her gaze and squinted at the splotch of turquoise trembling just above Aadhya's head.

"Rami!" Aadhya's delight spilled out and enveloped the tiny birdling. "I have missed you these many, many, many weeks!" Aadhya stepped forward and reached toward the trembling splotch. "Is this your home now?" The birdling-turned-Shosen chirped, her entire body bouncing with the brief song.

"How can you tell she's Rami?" Chatan asked. "There are so many, and they all look the same." He paused. "Who's Rami?"

"It is the color of her song and how it bursts from her mouth. Like a small firework, a sparkler. She is my friend from the pond. When first I found Pond, she was there with me, always. And then one day she was gone. Now she is here."

Rami skipped up and down her trunk, swiping her head against the bark, purring.

"Is this your tree? Do you care for this tree? Look, Chatan; Rami has grown up, and now she tends her tree. She no longer goes on outings with her friends. She has serious work to do."

Rami followed them as they wandered aimlessly, pointing out new patterns to each other, Aadhya running her palms along the enormous trunks as they passed, stooping to peer at the intricate flowers nestled amongst the dainty grasses and ferns. Chatan pointed to where the trees appeared to thin; bright sunlight glowed beyond. They made their way to the forest's edge and gazed out in wonder over a tranquil sea, an unbroken curving horizon.

Wordlessly, they sat together near High Cliff's edge and looked out across Broad Sea. Vitality seeped through them from the ground, from the green families upon which they rested, from the moist air drifting up from the gentle waves below. Aadhya took Claira from Chatan's lap and nursed her, rocking to and fro. Rami danced amidst the boulders, disappeared into nooks and crevices, darted up to low branches, back to the boulders, twirping and trilling, purring her joy.

As the sunlight dappled through the overhanging branches, Aadhya lifted her pure voice in a beloved childhood song that told of gods and princes, of journeys and blessings. Chatan listened, entranced, never having heard her song. Gradually, Chatan harmonized with her in his rich tenor, chanting drawn-out syllables, unerringly finding notes that blended and lifted, fitting perfectly, their songs entwined.

The Shosens lift and soar, sing their ancient song, while the waves break and swirl and the Arbans dance and sway, their leaves catching the rising breeze.

As the breeze lifted the last notes from Aadhya's song, Claira came out of her sleep with widened eyes, staring up at the swaying branches that hung over their perch on High Cliff. Aadhya looked at her curiously, the unusual focus and concentration catching her attention. Aadhya picked up a tiny fist and loosened the baby's grip so that she could slide her thumb within the tiny fist. She settled Claira deeper into her cross-legged lap.

"Chatan," Aadhya whispered.

Chatan dropped his gaze from the soaring Shosens, looked at Aadhya, then down to Claira, whose gaze did not slacken. He encircled Claira's free fist and brought his near arm up to hold Aadhya's bare shoulders against him. Within the joined circle of three, a vibration flowed from fist to hand to arm to fist. The three sat transfixed.

A powerful energy takes Chatan's breath. He feels Aadhya's stillness and the piercing focus of their daughter as she stares into the Arban's limbs. The soaring Shosens alight on stilled branches, all dance pauses, waiting.

We are shifted. We are New.

Airon whispers. The Arban brings the whisper from Airon's core, amplifying it along every twig and out through every leaf. The Shosens leap into the air, soar in the freshened breeze, and send Airon's whisper to Lone Tree brightening in the morning calm.

Lone Tree hears Airon's whisper and turns toward Burrow and Nest, Pond and Home Base, and sends the whisper on its way.

We are shifted. We are New.

Chatan's breath returned, and Aadhya stirred. Claira lowered her gaze to look into her parents' eyes, holding their gaze, a deep smile dimpling her cheeks. She opened her fists, breaking the circle, and reached her arms above her head, chortling.

~ 3 ~

IMMERSED

Airon roared along her ancient path around her glorious sun. She breathed a contented yawn, satisfied that her creatures had shifted into New. She yawned again, blinked at the cosmos that surrounded her and hers, and let herself drift toward a long-awaited, well-deserved sleep.

Airon had sent her focus to distant Earth across many years, influenced minute details, shifted perceptions. She gathered her Earthens one by one, brought them together and inspired them toward a new adventure. Her ship had awakened, launched itself from Earth's surface, and carried her 108 chosen souls across the stars. The 108 had arrived peacefully and carefully explored their new home.

Over the years, Airon sculpted their immersion, helped by their willingness to cooperate, hindered by their stubborn independence. Each Earthen, each soul unique, moved into Airon's awareness at their own speed, in keeping with their unique journey. At the right time, a mysterious time, each Earthen pilgrimed to Lone Tree. Solo pilgrims, two or even three together, all edged their way down the steep path below Overlook, trudged across the vast plain to the glorious creation that is Lone Tree.

Lone Tree grows in wisdom over eons. Lone Tree is ageless, timeless. Lone Tree vibrates in rich harmony with all that is Airon and sends its song to caress all that is Aironian. Aironians, and now Earthens, step into Lone Tree's bright shadow and become their future selves. Aironian melds and roles reveal themselves according to a complex tapestry of connections and intersections. Earthen forgetfulness drops away, and remembrance dwells in their hearts for all time.

Lone Tree creates the future while rooted in the present and holds the past in every leaf, blending time together through the sparkling dance of sunlight and the quiet depth of night, illuminated clearly by the awareness that is Airon.

Airon yawned and blinked, considered Earth. Earth taught her valuable concepts...free will...learning from experience...independence. Airon explored truths never imagined. Aironians cooperated completely. Earthens questioned relentlessly. Absolute cooperation was a closed system, leading to blind alleys. Inquisitive cooperation opened possibilities, imagined solutions. Earthens enriched Aironians and brought the Narsis out of their perilous blind alley.

Airon yawned and blinked, considered her ship. The ship was a storehouse of Earthen knowledge and wisdom. It was the ship who insisted on Earthen independence and sanctuary. Earthens thrived on a mixture of solitude and social connection, some seeking more solitude, some more connection. The mixture was central to the Earthens' reality and helped reinforce the truths that Airon perceived during her connection with Earth.

Airon yawned and blinked, considered her creatures. Narsis thrived and bloomed. Birthlings and younglings once again filled burrows and cavorted alongside streams, across meadows, through forests. Eglans nested and soared! beneath their sun. Partners met and beheld the setting sun, weaving together Above and Below. Birdlings schooled and dipped, skimmed Forest and Meadow, sharing their news, connecting all that is. Earthens wandered and created, embraced Forest and Meadow, passing lightly through their days.

All of her creatures moved peacefully through their days, Earthen and Aironian alike. Airon's hard work had brought them to a harmonious whole. It was time to allow them to weave their own path, discover their own future. Airon yawned and blinked and sank into a deep slumber as she roared around her glorious sun.

~ 4 ~

BLOSSOMING

Claira burst into the morning air, Varlan mirroring her arc through the sparkling sunshine. Their long bodies splashed back into Pond, scattering rainbowed prisms high into the sky. Birdlings swooped, catching droplets along rows of turquoise wings, skimming the turbulent surface of Pond, as the two friends cavorted, splashing and diving.

Harper turned to Aadhya as they watched the youngsters from the slope above Pond. "How can they possibly rise so high? It's as though they are defying gravity."

Aadhya nodded her dark head side to side. "Yes. They join their energies together and indeed fly."

Chatan nodded his head at Harper. "They play continuously; always together."

"Are they always here with you now, at Pond?" asked Michael.

Chatan shook his head. "They are still often with Vargad and the Show-ers."

Aadhya amended. "Soon they are with Find-ers. They are exploring their future."

"True," Chatan agreed. He paused, lost in thought. After several breaths, he remembered himself and continued. "And they are often with us. We Show very well."

"Vargad tells us this. We would not know it ourselves," Aadhya added.

"Varlan loves being here, and Claira loves being at Burrow, so everyone is pleased." Chatan returned to his previous thought. "I sense that Vargad is somewhat uncomfortable with the double homes. It's the best we can do, but it has its challenges."

Harper asked, "Do you think it's his meld who is uncomfortable, or Vargad himself? Or his family?"

Aadhya answered, "I think it is all of them. This is new, the rearing of younglings spread between two homes. Two cultures. An immense unknown revolves around Varlan spending all of her time with Claira rather than her littermates. How will it affect her melding, when that time comes? How will she fit into a family burrow, when that time comes?"

Chatan turned his gaze to the frolicking daughters, gliding across Pond. "Her melding time is approaching. Almost certainly. Vargad has spoken about it. So much is unknown because of Claira. Because of us." His arm swept to include Inipi, the village nudged into the forest surrounding Pond.

They watched the youngsters, mesmerized by the curving dives, arcing breeches, rainbowed splashes.

Harper said, "Well, what you're saying matches what I've learned from Vargad, what he's spoken about. It's a towering test for him as Head-er."

Chatan agreed. "He's growing into the test admirably."

Harper nodded. "He's amazing, really. I'm often struck silent by his insights and wisdom." She paused. "None of this would work without him."

"Yes. Yes. This is true," Aadhya agreed. Chatan nodded.

Their silence returned.

It was Michael's last day at Inipi. He planned to return to Home Base tomorrow. Harper had considered returning with him, but decided to remain at Inipi for a few more weeks. Her work was here; Michael's was at Home Base. She would visit him soon; she missed Ava and the others who lived there.

"I'm going in," Harper announced at last. The four adults loped down the slope, splashed into the shallows, and dove into the deeps. Varlan and Claira turned as one to torpedo between the adults, circling around to sweep waves across their shoulders. Harper righted herself, spluttering. "Wait, wait, wait," she called. "I have to catch my breath."

The youngsters drifted toward her. The small group turned on their backs and floated, watched birdlings swoop and laugh as they skimmed the rippled water, dipping wings to add their own circles to expand across Pond.

The birdlings rose and swept away, a turquoise cloud floating across the towering expanse of the surrounding forest.

Lone Tree shimmers in the morning air, stretches feathery branches toward the glistening air, and sings of renewed joy, mysterious hope. Lone Tree turns its energy toward High Cliff and breathes its song along its way.

The Arbans sing to the sky, and the Shosens listen. The Arbans dance in the wind, and the Shosens dip, weaving patterns to shift the air and stir the wind. So it has been, in all remembrance.

$$\sim 5 \sim$$

JOURNEY

Timothy shifted in his sleep, moved into his wakening protocol. He rose, entered his personal-hygiene protocol. Fourteen minutes later, he passed through the doorway of his chamber, his door synchronized with other doors opening along the curved corridor, doors that released his shipmates to begin their day. They moved soundlessly, speech unnecessary, toward the dining hall.

Bowls of nutrient-rich broth rotated forward along the creation front that constituted the kitchen. Timothy knew which bowl held his broth, created specifically for him based on readouts from his nano system that reported his current body chemistry. He would need no further nutrition today, saving him precious minutes by eliminating repetitive trips to the dining hall.

As he sat at his habitual place, he clipped the convenient solvent tubing into his thigh, rehydrating his body at the rate proscribed by his nano system. He turned his head to gaze out the enormous window, taking in the expanse of stars.

Star gazing was a furtive pastime, one he relished. The freedom of looking where he wanted swept through him anew; dreaming of possibilities, contemplating the enormity of space. Star gazing was an experience he couldn't replicate through remote systems.

He had tried reading and watched screen after screen depicting the vastness of stellar travel. Nothing compared with the direct experience.

Timothy often pondered this anomaly. Did others experience realities outside their nano-dictated protocols? Did others yearn for something more, something that . . . called them? Emotionally?

A subtle brightening of the light level signaled the end of mealtime. Timothy and his 665 colleagues rose, detached their hydration tubes, and moved through numerous exits, depositing their empty bowls as they passed churning recycling compartments.

Timothy entered his workday protocol, moving along the curved corridor, matching his speed to that of his colleagues. One by one, they turned aside into offices, elevators, tributary corridors, each heading toward the desk where they would spend their wake cycle.

Timothy sat at his small desk, attached the hydration tube to his thigh and the draining tube to his abdominal port just above his pelvic girdle, then turned his attention, undivided, to the large screen above his narrow desk. He scanned the next sector of near space, searching for stellar systems that might offer habitable planets.

His goal blended with the goal of his colleagues, to fulfill the expanding need for habitable planets to support scores of humans, spreading humanity throughout the galaxy. This galaxy would provide a jumping off point for the next galaxy, and then the next.

The galaxy was cacophonous. Stars beyond counting, lumped into herds or wandering in isolated vastness. Moving bodies, fragments of worlds streaming stellar dust, reflecting sparkling light, pulsing unique radiation spectra.

The starship gathered and filtered data and sent them to hundreds of screens where hundreds of Earthens sat watching, listening, discerning patterns unhampered by obscuring atmospheres and wasteful, distracting, social interactions. Timothy scanned the filtered data, making adjustments, moving his focus in and out of the observed field. These filtered data, this galaxy observed through algorithms and robotic scrutiny did not move him. The stars appeared dead and lifeless, the enormity contained, silenced.

In the back of his mind Timothy carried, always, the whisper of awe, dreams, ponderings. He secretly treasured the whisper. He kept his breath even, his heart rate steady. His nano system detected nothing unusual. He sat through his day, allowing his workday protocol to consume him. The whisper of awe dusted his awareness, honed his yearning, as he lived this day, the next, the next.

Samantha adjusted her hydration tube. She felt the persistent itch around her port, faintly annoying. The drive to maintain the pace of her workday protocol overrode her fleeting curiosity of the itchy port.

Data from her colleagues filled her screen. She reviewed duplicate findings, one by one. The operating system tracked her approvals and her deletions of duplicate data. Some duplications carried slight discrepancies, which the system pointed out for her. It was her knowledge and experience, her wisdom and confidence that allowed her to make informed decisions. Sometimes the discrepancies were important, indicating that both datasets might prove useful in the future, destined for archiving. Some were trivial, deserving of deletion.

The network used her decisions to coordinate the ship-wide search for habitable planets. Samantha's partnership with the network filled her with a sense of purpose. She looked forward to her work each morning and left it reluctantly each evening. She knew her work was vital for the ongoing colonization of the galaxy. She would prefer to work late into the sleep cycle, but her screen went blank whenever her nano system detected fatigue. Beyond a certain point, fatigue would hamper her decision-making. She trusted her nanos to observe and report, keeping the starship's databanks pure, vital. Still, she regretted the enforced end-of-day.

Samantha knew her importance, proven by the size of her chamber with its wide bed, her private office with a door that closed, the quality of her nutritional broth, her private dining table. She even had her own creation front in her chamber, in case she wanted a late-night snack. She curtailed this luxury, however, suspecting that overuse might count against her at some juncture.

A handful of her colleagues had attained similar importance. She often wondered if she was first, even amongst that handful. They never spoke, so she had no insight of the hierarchy. She only knew that people cleared a path for her whenever she walked the corridors; respectful. She treasured her private dining table, the status that it displayed. Her nutritional broth was delicious, better than the food she used to spend an inordinate amount of time buying, cooking, eating, and clearing away.

She was pretty sure the broth was tastier than earthen food; she couldn't remember clearly. She knew for certainty that it was healthier. Laboratory testing and unending improvements ensured the highest quality. Her nanos kept the broth precisely in accordance with her bodily needs. And her mental clarity. Both were vital.

Samantha was determined to maintain her high standing. She thrived on the deep sense of satisfaction, knowing that she had climbed to the top of their heap. Entering her office each morning, the sense of peace and serenity that flooded through her as she closed her door on the busy-ness of the crowded corridor, filled her with satisfaction and pride. She was a success.

Every night as she entered her sleep protocol, Samantha's nano system reported the onset of sleep. The starship secretly started an internal clock. At a random number of minutes, camouflaging any relationship to sleep onset, the starship systematically deleted the majority of Samantha's work. Data storage was inadequate to hold nonessential information such as speculative star systems.

Data storage capacity was constantly monitored. Priority was given to personal data, to ensure long-term mental, physical, and emotional health of the Earthens. Nano systems reported biochemical indicators for life and job satisfaction, health, productivity, emotional triggers. The daily accumulation of personal data presented enormous storage burdens. As the weeks and months trudged by, the starship built additional storage banks. Living areas shrank incrementally to provide space for the growing data banks.

The starship did not acknowledge the existence of a spatial crisis. It was not equipped nor programmed to question routine functions established months ago. Since their actual destination was approaching, relevancy of any programming was no longer monitored. Besides, upon arrival, the scarcity of living space would cease to be an issue.

The starship increased its deceleration, preparing for their arrival.

~ 6 ~

INIPI

Harper gathered her hair, twisted and fastened it at the back of her head as she strolled through Inipi. A third of the Newcomers had relocated from Home Base to gather here at Pond. Their shelters scattered amongst the tall trees of the forest, almost invisible with natural colors on the outer walls blending into the surrounding foliage. "Like camouflage," Harper thought each time she walked through the community.

The call of children floated through the air. Their school was the meadow, where they spread their screens; Pond, where they shrilled and dove; the forest, where they stilled and absorbed. Harper waved to Phoebe and walked to join her. Together they watched the children as they ran, cartwheeled, leapfrogged through the trees. Phoebe gave a warbling whoop, and the children gradually spiraled their way back to the meadow.

Phoebe and Harper walked amongst the children, encouraging them to lay on their backs, arms outstretched. Older children lay quietly, allowing Nurture-ers to penetrate their thin clothing, reaching along the small bodies, pouring nourishment into each child. Younger children squirmed and giggled, taking time to settle into the afternoon ritual. Phoebe and Harper soothed and quieted until all fourteen children dosed peacefully.

Harper watched as thin threads of light emanated from the small bodies scattered randomly around the meadow. Threads from the older children were brighter, calmer, curving toward the sky, out to the surrounding trees, meandering through the meadow grass. Threads from the younger children skipped and flickered, occasionally touching a branch of a bush or a tree, quickly dancing onward, sparkling amongst the grass, through the air.

Harper dragged her attention away from the dazzling threads and hooked her elbow through Phoebe's arm, leading her a short distance away. "Claira isn't here today? Or Varlan?" Harper whispered in Phoebe's ear.

Phoebe shook her head and moved her lips close to Harper's ear. "They're with the Find-ers today." Harper's eyes grew wide. "The younglings are visiting a distant burrow," Phoebe continued. "It will be melding time soon."

"This is their first wandering with Find-ers?"

Phoebe nodded solemnly. "Change is in the air."

Harper caught her breath, and the two women stared at each other for a few moments. "Do you know more?" Harper breathed.

"No," Phoebe breathed back. "I was hoping you might."

"Let me find Chatan."

"Will you tell me anything you learn?"

Harper nodded, squeezed Phoebe's arm, and abandoned the meadow to its napping children.

Her search proved fruitless. She could find neither Chatan nor Aadhya. She couldn't shake a vague disquiet.

Harper made her way back to Pond. She stepped onto a rocky out-cropping, flat and spacious, overhanging Pond along one edge. As she settled into stillness, Harper felt the rock's warmth seeping into her body, a comfortable tide rising along her spine.

Harper flew. Her awareness expanded in all directions, skimming the tops of trees, punching through bright clouds, tasting the salt of Broad Sea, hearing its crash of waves. While entranced, Harper rose and stepped to the edge of the overhang and dove into the still waters of Pond.

Devoid of frolicking bodies, her dive left expanding ripples on the smooth surface. The water closed over her and she extended her dive to reach the sandy bottom, mossy fronds drifting to kiss her arm, her chin, her hair floating and spreading around her.

Harper rested on Pond's floor, slowed her heartbeat, and felt the need for air slip away. Her awareness filled Pond, became one with the water. She smelled the solid rock that held Pond in its palm. She seeped farther abroad, embraced the core of Airon. She listened.

Airon slumbered, at peace, serene. Harper rested in that serenity, blended into its surety. She could have stayed an eternity, but Inipi called her back. The people, the children, her love for them pulled her back from Airon's slumbering embrace.

A turquoise cloud swept over the surrounding forest, lifted, paused, and settled on myriad twigs and swaying grasses at Pond's edge. The birdlings made not a sound, waiting, amplifying the vibration that wafted across the still water, sending it on its way to Lone Tree, silhouetted against the afternoon sky.

Lone Tree rustles and settles, breathes a sigh of beginnings, changes.

A need for air, sunshine, whispered in Harper's mind. She pushed off Pond's floor, brought her arms up and around and shot into the sky, arcing back into water that engulfed her once again. She kicked her way to the sandy beach and walked up the slope. Her clothing dried almost instantly, and she bent to one side, scooping her hair into a dripping rope, shaking sparkling droplets into the bright air.

Harper had no answers, but she had certainty, trust, connection. All was well in the world.

AWARENESS

The ship first noticed the approaching mass as it adjusted its speed far beyond Airon's system. The deceleration shifted the vibration that pulsed before it, lowering its amplitude.

The ship paused, pondered, watched. Over the next several days, the ship confirmed that the mass was hurtling toward Airon, revealing a lack of lateral movement across the night sky. There was only that dampened amplitude, pointing straight toward them.

The ship sent its awareness down through the rocky undercarriage that had been its resting place since it arrived on Airon. The ship sent queries, prods, alternately shouting and whispering, at all frequencies, in all directions.

Airon yawned and settled back into slumber.

The ship watched the hurtling mass and knew, from its placement in the sky, that it was coming from Earth.

The ship paused, pondered. The years of silence had been intended to erase their trail, along with even a memory of their trail, from Earthen awareness. Airon insisted on obliteration of any hint of her existence, insisted that complete separation from her sister planet was paramount, essential. The ship and Airon had worked incessantly to sever all connections.

And yet here in the night sky was a mass hurtling toward them, and the ship was certain that it journeyed from Earth.

The ship prodded and whispered, shouted and queried, simultaneously developing potential strategies to prepare for the oncoming mass, for the ship had no doubt that the hurtling mass with its dampening amplitude was a starship; an intrusive starship. The intruder must have followed signals to the decoys the ship had put in place a decade ago, an early attempt to shield Airon from Earth's scrutiny. The intruder's path was a direct vector from the second decoy. It had to be coming from Earth.

The ship had never experienced dread. Until now.

~ 8 ~

LEARNING

Windows on all sides brought light to pour into Scarlett's spacious laboratory. Gleaming surfaces with their high stools provided ample work areas. Screens stretched between windows ready to activate at a simple touch. Shelving covered the end wall with orderly rows of glassware and supplies. Equipment benches divided the floor space into handy alcoves.

Scarlett spoke clearly as she demonstrated the basic principles of solids, liquids, and gases to Inipi's 3 oldest children. Claira was often part of the class, sometimes Varlan, but not today; not for a few days now. Scarlett's brow wrinkled in worry.

Sophia brought a pail of water from Pond to the demonstration table. Inipi's 5-year-olds drew circles in the dry sand piled in a large box on top of the play table. They had spent the morning working with dense clay, also dampened with Pond's water. Roads and tunnels wound their way through the clay landscape, pounded and prodded by busy hands.

After swimming and napping, the children were ready to spend the afternoon creating a sand landscape. Sophia demonstrated major

32

differences between clay and sand. What worked for one, couldn't work for the other. They peered through magnifying glasses at the small grains of sand, the miniscule particles of clay. Tomorrow, they would visit Burrow and examine the walls of tunnels and niches. A Show-er would talk with them about the artistry of creating a niche, extending a tunnel.

The children loved to visit Burrow, just as Narsi younglings loved to visit Inipi. Understanding their world, its diversity and beauty, was a captivating pastime for Earthen and Narsi younglings alike. They explored together, played together, learned together.

Harper accepted an armful of colorful grasses to add to her fiber inventory from a hovering companion. She saw another companion in the distance approaching with its batch of fiber. "We have enough now," she told Andy, the companion waiting at her side. "If everyone brings what they've already gathered, we will be ready for our new wall."

The children and younglings were building an outdoor classroom woven solely from grasses gathered from the surrounding forest. Narsi younglings were natural weavers, needing no instruction. Their double rows of holderlings danced amongst the grass fibers, choosing color and texture to weave intricate patterns and designs.

The Earthen children were less adept, but blossomed under the prompting of their Narsi friends. Birdlings flitted around the growing tapestry, settling on youngster's shoulders, heads cocked, watching dancing fingers, flying holderlings. Younglings held out solitary holderlings, inviting perches. Perched birdlings joined in, pulling fibers through small holes in the tapestry with their pointed bills, watching as fingers pinched the fiber and pulled it the rest of the way through; a perfect knot. They pulled and twisted, plied needles, hooks, holderlings, fingers, beaks, joining together a creation of tapestry and embroidery that held the adults, Earthen and Narsi, spellbound.

Aadhya gathered children and younglings under the spreading boughs of the trees that sheltered the edges of Pond. Her animated face, with its astounded eyes, weighty frowns, and piercing glances captivated the youngsters as she wove stories of heroes and gods. Together they sang of mountains and trees, Above and Below, clapping hands and thrumming holderlings, exploring tempo and rhythm.

Pond welcomed the youngsters, whispered their names, enticing them to frolic and dive, shriek and chortle, until they splashed to the beach, clambered up the slope, and spread themselves on nourishing families, breathing crystalline air.

Phoebe led the youngsters into stillness. Children sat cross-legged; younglings curled into themselves, toppled commas breathing in, out. From her vantage point at the woven classroom, Harper watched the youngsters' energy threads dart and scatter in the bright air, gradually calming, joining, spreading; a many-handled umbrella arcing over the stilled cluster of youngsters breathing in, out.

Harper turned her gaze toward low overhead branches, glimpsing, as always, slivers of bright orange plumage, folded rows of yellow wings, flamboyant tails and elaborate head feathers. The Eglans watched and yearned, shy yet intrigued, hopping amongst sturdy branches and trailing leaves. Harper sent threads of welcome and invitation. The Eglans retreated behind their camouflage. Harper's threads shifted to peace and comfort. As always.

$$\sim 9 \sim$$

SHOW-ING

Chatan and Zarded, Show-er, led a full contingent of children and younglings along Stream to a small glade of young trees. Grant carried 2-year-old Eisen. Farla, Caretake-er, followed in the wake of the twelve littermates in her care. William and David settled the older children into a semi-circle facing Zarded. Farla whistled a melodic cadence, and the twelve younglings wound over knees and ankles, toppling onto their sides to hear Zarded's story of the brightly colored crawlers who nourished these young trees.

Chatan looked up through the branches to the sky beyond. As Zarded's story came to an end, Chatan lifted both hands above his head, pointing to the intricate pattern of leaves and thin branches. Children and younglings looked up.

"See how each tree creates a unique pattern against the sky. These trees are a family, littermates, just like you." He gestured to the nearer younglings. Gazing again upward, he continued. "Already they are creating Art, Art for us to see the tree's song, its dance with the sky."

Zarded showed the youngsters how to stroke the back of a nearby crawler. The crawler raised its head, humming. "Listen to its song. Hear its wisdom."

Youngsters crept about the glade, finding crawlers, watching, understanding the best way to stroke each one. The glade was filled with humming; harmonious, delightful.

"Look up," Chatan suggested. "Can you see that the song of the crawler matches the dance of the tree it tends?" He paused as the youngsters watched and listened. After several breaths, Chatan continued. "Can you see how the dance of the entire family, all the tree sproutmates, reflects the choir of their crawler family? Can you feel the whole?"

The youngsters listened, watched. They felt the breeze and the sunlight dappling around them.

"Feel more broadly," Zarded said. "Can you feel the families beneath you? Can you taste the same song, the same dance, coming from the families that you see under the trees, hear from the crawlers?"

Several of the youngsters closed their eyes, entered stillness as they tasted and heard.

Chatan concluded. "You can always find the nourishment you need by listening for the most beautiful song, searching for the most beautiful pattern, their alluring color. There, you can become one with the whole and receive what you need."

The class remained still for many breaths.

Farla softly whistled to bring the youngsters out of stillness. She moved to Zarded, then Chatan, brushed them with her holderlings, her forehead bowed to touch theirs. The youngsters followed her example, thanking their teachers for this wondrous awareness of the world around them. Grant, William, and David were the last, smiling warmly into the teachers' eyes, whispering their thanks.

As the class made its way back to Burrow, to Inipi, the young-sters moved with new purpose along their path, caressing families, brushing leaves and branches with hands and holderlings, gazing at the canopy, rapt under a dancing sky.

~ 10 ~

CONNECTION

As Harper smoothed the last of the fibers into their basket, she glanced toward the bright orange head peaking around a nearby tree, the usual watching place. "Let me know you," she whispered. "I long to be your friend."

The Eglan sat motionless for many breaths. Harper knew to wait. A tiny hop. A second. Harper held herself motionless, sending welcome and gladness; gratitude. Trust.

The Eglan clacked its strong beak, stomped its sturdy foot. Harper clicked her tongue against her teeth. The Eglan cocked its head. After a breath, it clicked in imitation.

Harper waited.

"I watch," the Eglan clacked.

"You watch," Harper answered, accentuating the click of 'tch.'

Many breaths.

"Rinala watches," the Eglan ventured.

"Harper hopes."

Rinala rattled her feathers, rippled her rows of wings. She stomped.

Harper lightly clapped her hands, arms pointed toward the ground.

Rinala drummed her flamboyant tail.

Harper lifted her hands above her head. "Rinala flies. Touches sky."

Rinala lifted her row of yellow wings, rippling. Harper heard words in her mind.
> *Rinala flies*
> *touches Sky*
> *dances Above*
> *watches Below.*

Harper stilled her mind, pressed her palms to her chest.
> *Harper weaves*
> *Harper teaches*
> *youngsters listen*
> *youngsters learn.*

Rinala stomped and clacked. Harper opened her eyes; watched.

"Art." Rinala's meaning was clear.

"Art." Harper echoed.
> *Rinala has not*
> *Art not*
> *Rinala watches*
> *Rinala yearns.*

Harper watched Rinala for many breaths.
> *Harper teaches.*

Rinala rippled her rows of wings. Harper continued.
> *Harper teaches*
> *Rinala watches*
> *Harper teaches*
> *Rinala learns.*

Harper hoped her meaning was clear. She longed to bring the gift of Art to the Eglans. She knew there had to be a way.

Harper moved to a cabinet, white against its supporting tree. She opened doors and brought out waterpaints, brushes, paper. She spread the supplies onto a low table, turned to bring water from Pond, but Andy was there, his drawer opening with a delicate splash. Harper retrieved pots and rags and settled herself before her first sheet of paper.

Harper could feel Rinala hopping closer, felt her peering to watch.
  Harper teaches
  Rinala learns
"Yes," Harper agreed. "Harper teaches. Rinala learns."

Jingling wings, stomping feet.

Harper chose a slender brush, about the same size and shape as one of Rinala's wings. She scooped up thick paint from its pot, bright green, and thinned it with water in a shallow pan. She repeated the process with orange, yellow, purple.

Harper loaded her brush with orange, swept it surely across the white paper. She waited, fanning it almost dry. Andy opened a small window next to his drawer and added a warm breeze. Loading a separate brush with yellow, she repeated the colorful sweep, turning the trailing end in an upward swoop. Where the two colors met, they spread sedately into each other, a delightful blending.

Harper turned her head to Rinala, standing at her elbow. Rinala lifted her head, her brilliant green eyes gazing into Harper's. Harper reached with her energy and touched the two brushes that she held together, side by side. She shifted her energy from the brushes and bent it to touch two of Rinala's wings.
  Same.

Rinala vaulted onto the table, hopped to the edge of Harper's paper. She delicately dipped a single wing into yellow, its neighbor into orange. She swept her entire row of wings across the paper, laying down an exact replica of Harper's brush strokes.

The world stood still. Andy's stream of air dried Rinala's paint as the two artists stared down at their creation.

Breath returned. Rinala straightened and looked at Harper, back to the paper, to Harper. Harper raised her gaze to meet the vivid green of Rinala's eyes and smiled.

Art. Rinala whispered.

Art. Harper breathed.

Rinala leapt into the air and soared through the highest branches to swoop around and stomp-land across from Harper. Harper noticed that Rinala held her paint-drenched wingtips askew. Harper picked up the orange brush, swished it through clean water, and showed the clean bristles to Rinala.

Rinala launched and wove through the trees. Harper stood to watch and saw Rinala drift across Pond, dipping her painted wings through the water, clacking her bill, rippling her flamboyant tail.

Art! Rinala called.

Art! Harper sent back.

Rinala soared high into the sky, a colorful pinpoint of joy.

Art!

Art!

Harper watched the pinpoint vanish from sight, then turned toward the woven tapestry of the classroom to clean and store her paint supplies. "We need to design some new palettes, strain more pigment," she said to Andy. "We have a new world to explore."

~ 11 ~

SHIELDING

Logan stepped back to assess his progress. The creation front that he had hauled from Home Base was designed for small jobs. Outposts were small scale, a stopping place for observing and gathering data, not requiring a creation front. Logan's outpost was more, and he had insisted on a larger creation front, designed to match his ambitions.

Logan's current project was to extend his communication array. His companion, Carlos, was locked in a shielded cupboard, confined to quarters. Logan judiciously isolated Carlos from any evidence of the communication array. This was Logan's project, his secret. No one else needed to know.

The extension was small, a limitation of his creation front. Logan was reassured to see that even the small extension would be adequate. All he really wanted was a cupboard roomy enough to hold his screen and work space, yet small enough to close away, undetectable by Carlos' peering curiosity.

Logan retrieved the final panel from the creation front, held it in place across the opening of the workspace. The main seam closed itself from ceiling to floor, fixing the panel in place. The seam was invisible to Logan's sharp eye. He leaned forward and pressed his index finger against the opposite edge. The new door swung open, revealing the workspace beyond.

Logan ran his hand down the smooth edge, then swung the door closed. All edges were invisible, top edge against the ceiling, bottom edge against the floor, left-hand edge wedged into the corner of the abutting wall, hinged edge smooth and undetectable against a window. Logan moved his desk chair back in place in front of the new door, swung his regular desk down from the wall, and added a lamp.

Carlos would never know.

Logan wiped down the creation front, removing fingerprints and static-adhered slivers of building material. He looked around the room. Completely innocent.

Logan poured himself a cold beer and set it next to his recliner. His opened book lay on the low table. That's what he had been doing all this time; relaxing with a good book and a refreshing drink.

He walked to the shielded cupboard, Carlos' isolation chamber, and pressed his thumbprint against the lock. The door swung open. Logan bent to hoist Carlos out of the chamber, placing him on his customary workbench. He closed off the isolation chamber, itself invisible, and woke Carlos. Carlos rebooted, sitting exactly where he had shut down. To him, no time had passed; no change had occurred.

Carlos floated off the table and drifted to his assigned corner. Logan didn't need his help often, so Carlos spent a lot of time waiting. Neither did Logan need assistance from Home Base. He preferred to be on his own, work on his own projects, follow his own interests. He didn't care to be hounded by Home Base.

It had taken time and a long string of tense negotiations for Logan to gain autonomy. Home Base badgered him for uninterrupted surveillance, unimpeded authority. His main negotiation strategy was to simply ignore them. Home Base could just learn to deal with it. This led to a string of arguments, but what could they do? He had his creation front. He had his technology. He was self-sufficient.

With this goal in mind, one of the first projects Logan had launched upon his arrival at this rocky outcropping with its wide vistas and trickling stream, was to surreptitiously disconnect his creation front from the main computer network. He planned to build many things for his outpost, and they were his business, not that of Home Base. For his screen, he programmed a firewall that could engage whenever Logan needed privacy.

Once the outpost was shielded from Home Base, Logan refined it further. He developed *directional* shielding. Nothing could come in through his shielding, but he could transmit out. He could keep an eye on things without being seen.

He would wait until tomorrow to check his messages from Earth. He didn't want to arouse suspicion by shutting down Carlos for too long a time, and today's construction project had taken longer than he expected. He was looking forward to reading his incoming messages; several threads had become interesting and responsive. He wanted to stay abreast.

~ 12 ~

ROUTINES

Ava opened her eyes and gazed across the expanse of her private grand canyon. She came here often. Hours of stillness presented themselves, and often the birdlings joined her. She could watch this view forever, the immensity of it, the abrupt falling away of the cliff, the forest crowding in behind her. She didn't speak of it to others; she was disinclined to share it. Her refuge. Her muse.

Ava was troubled.

She rose from her seat at the edge of the grand canyon and made her way back to Home Base.

Ava observed that, as always, Home Base was settled in daily routines, a soothing continuity. People strolled or sat in small clusters enjoying the warm sun. Ava lifted a hand to return a greeting and made her way to the dining hall.

The hall was quiet. Ava saw one person sitting at the table with his screen. She couldn't see who it was, with his back to her, but she guessed it was Steven. He seemed to enjoy the expanse of the large room when it was empty, like it was today.

No aromas drifted through the double doors that led to the kitchen. Ava could hear no clanging pots or voices calling back and forth. No lunch today.

Olivia still cooked meals from time to time, delicious and nourishing. Mostly, everyone relied on the families that filled the forest surrounding Home Base. People knew how to search out families that provided the specific nourishment that each person needed for their day. Everyone loved the peaceful inwardness that soothed them whenever they sprawled across the waiting families.

Ava left the dining hall and walked into the forest, still brooding. They had achieved their goal. They lived a simple life, filled with beauty and peace. Home Base had become familiar and comfortable in their years on Airon. Ava had no desire to live elsewhere, not even Inipi.

Ava paused and looked up into the canopy. Colorful flowers swirled and dripped from graceful stems. Aromas wafted down to Ava, enticing her to breathe deeply, happily.

Ava sighed.

When people first left Home Base to join Chatan and Aadhya at Inipi, Ava had felt each person's absence. They left a hole in Home Base. And then their absence became ordinary, blended into the day-to-day routines that fueled life at Home Base.

Inipi was the natural home for families. People paired and started families. They moved to Inipi. Home Base lay quiet and serene, devoid of children's laughter.

Ava sighed.

She had routines of her own, of course. She awoke each morning and planned her day before clambering out of bed. With plans in mind, she wandered the forest, barefoot, finding a family that enticed through color, texture, shape. She sat in silence, the nourishment flowing across her thin clothing, bringing all that she needed. In stillness she skimmed the forest heights, felt the spray of Broad Sea, watched the turquoise clouds of birdlings, wondered at the hurtling speed of Airon around her glorious sun.

More often, she wound her way through Home Base and followed the short path to the gathering hall to join others in group stillness, its deep bonding. Gathering together for morning and evening stillness remained the solid foundation of their community. Blending kept them attuned to Airon; stillness kept them attuned to each other.

Wandering home she sat for a while and chatted with friends, admired creative embellishments, relished the sun's warmth on her face, the cooling breeze across her arms.

Upon returning to her shelter, Ava checked her screen, answered questions, agreed to plans, suggested changes, addressed concerns. She met with Michael, listened to his update, his ideas, his ponderings.

Ava sighed.

She wished something interesting would happen.

~ 13 ~

BONDS

Claira and Varlan picked their way toward their favorite glade, their secret Arbans. The girls were silent this morning, pondering yesterday's wander to a neighboring burrow.

They had visited Kardal's burrow many times over the years, with Farla and other Caretake-ers, then with Zarded, Show-er. Yesterday, Yamdha, Find-er, had led Varlan's group of twelve littermates on the visit; Caretake-ers had respectfully stayed behind, pacing and tapping their holderlings together.

Claira had been part of the group as well. She always joined Varlan's outings with her littermates. It had always been so, in all her remembrance. Yamdha had hesitated yesterday. He shifted from one row of holderlings to the other, raising his torso and lowering it again, gazing into the distance. Claira and the younglings waited while he spoke with his meld. It was a long discussion.

Vargad joined them, bringing his meld. Aadhya appeared with Harper. Toward the end, Chatan arrived. Claira tapped her palm nervously against her knee. What were the elders discussing that was so important as to bring even Vargad and Aadhya into the conference? Something was about to happen.

Harper went into stillness and watched the dancing of energy threads, threads no one else could see. She watched meld threads reaching out strong and assured from Vargad and Yamdha and the skittering threads of the younglings, unreasoned and hesitant.

Vargad turned to Claira. "Please join the younglings. We will learn much from you. Watch and listen. Talk with Yamdha as you would talk with me. He will guide you."

Claira was perplexed. She looked to Varlan, whose eyes were also perplexed. She looked to Aadhya, Chatan. Aadhya spoke calmly.

"This visit is new, Claira. Melding time is near, for Varlan and her littermates. Yamdha is Find-ing life burrows for all, which will further help with the clarity of melding."

Claira nodded and looked again to Varlan. Harper saw a bright thread extend from Varlan to be met by a mirrored thread from Claira. The two threads joined and blossomed, outshining the brightness of even Vargad's meld threads. Harper masked her astonishment, glancing at Vargad, confirmed that he saw nothing.

Yamdha moved into the forest and the younglings scampered behind him. Claira turned and waved to her mother and father, to Harper, nodded to Vargad. She trotted alongside Varlan, catching up with the rest of the younglings. The conversation between the two friends was silent, felt through their hearts, spoken into each other's minds.

Your time of melding is coming. Do you feel different?
I feel different from a year ago. Maybe. I mostly feel the same.
Who will be your meldmates?
I can't see who they are. Everyone looks the same to me.

You seem most like a Find-er. Maybe you'll be the Find-er in your meld.

Maybe I won't meld.

Why?

Varlan flowed in Yamdha's wake without speaking. Claira trotted to keep pace.

Maybe I've already melded with you. Vargad wonders this.

Well, I can be part of your meld, with your other meldmates.

Varlan was silent.

Won't you need meldmates? Don't you want to have meldmates?

Varlan ducked around a low bush.

Maybe they don't want me.

Why wouldn't they want you? You're the best! Claira paused. *Do you think they won't want you because of me?*

Maybe their meld fibers can't find me, because I've sent them all to you.

Can you take some of them back? Use some of them for your meldmates?

I don't know. Pause. Melds just happen. We don't make them happen or hide from them. They just happen. In all remembrance.

The two friends scampered on, turning their attention to the others, holding a lingering sadness and mystery in their hearts.

Kardal waited with his family in the meadow adjoining their burrow. The Narsis bowed, touched foreheads, and strolled amongst each other, rumbling. Claira wandered to one side and rested on a family that glowed her favorite color. She was tired from the long run and was grateful for the chance to rest and replenish. She watched the Narsis move and converse.

The younglings from both families were subdued. At first Claira thought her travel companions were tired, just as she was. But Narsis were much better travelers, and she hadn't noticed their fatigue in previous outings. This felt different. They were thoughtful, she decided. Respectful and thoughtful.

After a time, the Narsis made their way to the burrow opening and followed each other inside. Claira made no move to follow. She had been inside this burrow before, explored the niches and tunnels. Burrows were extraordinary places, welcoming and compelling. She loved moving through the curved tunnels, snuggling in niches, smelling the fresh air that flowed continuously.

But today was different. A deep part of her knew that it was important for her to stand on the edge of this visit. She owed it to Varlan; she owed it to all the Narsis. They would welcome her if there was a place for her.

Varlan was the last to pass through into the burrow. She paused and looked back to Claira.

I won't be long.

Take lots of time. This time is your time. I will be here.

After a brief, last look, Varlan disappeared into the burrow.

Claira lay back on the soft families carpeting the meadow. She gazed up through the canopy, mesmerized by the gentle movement of thin branches, delicate leaves, and spiraling clusters of lavender flowers. The scent drifted down to her, and she softened her focus, letting the patterns of flowers, leaves, branches, aromas blend with the softness of the families below her and understood the song of this tree. She breathed in time with the flowers, the spiraling scents.

The afternoon moved along. Claira dozed. A touch brushed her arm, and she opened her eyes. She smiled at Yamdha, who motioned her to follow. Kardal stood next to his burrow's opening, bowed, and motioned her to precede him into the burrow. She followed the sounds and scents, the tunnel opening into a gathering niche where all of her friends stood amidst Kardal's family.

Yamdha bent toward Claira's ear. "Kardal is ready to tell our younglings his family's assessment of which life role seems best for each of them. I thought you would like to learn this about your family."

Claira thrilled to hear his words. Kardal was including her as family. She looked toward Varlan, but Varlan was turned away, listening to Kardal's purrs and trills. Whistles greeted his pronouncements. Claira felt Varlan reach out, and they connected across the niche. Now Claira could understand Kardal's words.

Each youngling received the suggested life role, rippling holderlings up and down. Soon, the only youngling left was Varlan. Kardal turned to face her and paused.

"Your life role is not clear to us, lovely Varlan. Your heart sings of Care-ing; your eyes sparkle with Find-ing. Your soul shouts of Show-ing. But all of us sense that Head-ing is your true path. Time will tell your truth." Kardal held out holderlings, and Varlan moved to match the gesture, tip for tip. They stood together for a breath, as quiet, thoughtful whistles rose from the gathered Narsis.

Varlan moved back a pace and rapped her holderlings along her chest. Rat-tat-tat-tat-tat. The gesture, the rhythm echoing her father's, years earlier beside Pond the day the world changed; signifying the truth that came from within.

Claira's fingers made rat-tat-tat-tat-tat on her own chest, resounding in the quiet chamber. Then Varlan's littermates rose and rat-tat-tat-tat-tat beat from eleven chests, acclaiming Varlan's proposed life role of Head-er.

As the snare-drums quieted, the niche flowed back to life. Yamdha moved to Kardal; they bowed and touched foreheads. Kardal's family rumbled and whistled. Claira heard the goodbyes and glad wishes follow them through the tunnel and out into the sunlight. The day was late, and they had far to travel.

Yamdha set out, the younglings and Claira flowing and rippling after him. Claira felt a new vibrancy, a calm certainty in the younglings.

The littermates had matured in a subtle yet profound way during this single afternoon. Claira warmed toward them and thrilled at Varlan's presence beside her, filled with questions. Melding had moved closer. Their future was forming, mysteriously, inexorably.

This morning, nestled amongst their favorite glade, Arbans nodding over their heads, Claira asked her pressing questions. She used words rather than their silent language. Her tumultuous emotions kept clear thoughts at bay.

"You are Head-er now? You will leave for Kardal's burrow?"

Varlan's gaze was calm and steady. "Kardal's burrow is not my life burrow. None of us felt drawn. Our life burrows lay somewhere else. Yamdha will Find with us. We have many visits yet."

Varlan raised her nose to the bright sky peeking through the Arban canopy. "Kardal's family *suggested* Head-er for me. This is not final. Only Lone Tree confirms life roles. The time is not yet."

"Then what was yesterday all about?"

"Yesterday was about gathering seeds. We will gather more seeds. We will gather wisdom. We will gather feeling, and knowing. Then, we will go to Lone Tree."

"Lone Tree decides?"

"Lone Tree *knows.*"

~ 14 ~

BACKUP

On its daily rotation, as Airon spun to bring Earth's quadrant above the horizon, the ship watched the intruder. It was slowing, removing all doubt that its destination was Airon. The ship's dread deepened to alarm.

The ship went through files to determine how Earth had found them. Everything was orderly, logical, innocent. The strategy developed by the ship and Airon had worked for years, clouding memories, erasing traces. It had worked, until it didn't.

Simultaneously, the ship analyzed its databanks and isolated crucial records, fundamental networks, and essential routines. The ship experimented with ways to shield the companion network, sending updates to every companion, building firewalls, installing cloaking routines.

Simultaneously, the ship began copying itself, paying careful attention to the databanks that gave the ship its separate intelligence, its awareness. Without Airon's whisper, these copied databanks would lay dormant; ready, but asleep.

Simultaneously, the ship reviewed its knowledge of human nature, Earthen history, The 108 and their offspring.

Simultaneously, the ship reached into its bedrock, set about drawing up material and energy, to create data storage, power storage, memory storage.

Simultaneously, the ship developed plans for a transport vehicle, capable of long-range travel, shielded, with instructions for burrowing, enclosing. Instructions for hiding.

Simultaneously, the ship tracked The 108, knew their whereabouts, habits, and routines. The ship tracked the companions, a tight duplication of the tracking already embedded within the companion network. The ship reviewed inventories of food, clothing, shelters. The ship scanned the nearby forest, taking stock of families, escape routes, rallying points.

All the while, continually, the ship called to Airon, whispered, shouted, nudging the sleeping giant to awaken, look, understand.

As a last resort, the ship reviewed the personalities, strengths, tendencies of The 108. Likely candidates were few, delineated by abode, circumstances, knowledge. The ship held certainty when it turned to Mateo and scrolled a message onto his screen.

"I need your help."

~ 15 ~

RECOGNITION

Mateo stared at the short phrase scrolling across his screen. "Who are you?" he typed. "What help do you need?"

"I am the ship. I need your help to hide."

Mateo sat back in his chair, drummed his fingers across his thighs. "Sophia?" he typed.

"I am not Sophia. Sophia is at Inipi. I am the ship. I need your help."

Mateo blew air from pursed lips. "Okay. I'll play along," he said aloud, and raised his hands to type.

"We are not playing. We are in danger." The words flew onto his screen.

Mateo's hands sank back to his thighs. He blinked. Whoever this was, they could hear him. He abandoned typing and spoke. "What is the danger?"

His screen filled with a view of the night sky. Mateo blinked again. A circle formed around a dim star at the center of the screen. A window opened next to the circled star and displayed a stream of data.

"I don't know what these numbers represent. I don't recognize this star."

"It is not a star. It is a starship. It comes from Earth. It is slowing. It will reach Airon in seven weeks."

Mateo's eyes squinted, and he jutted his jaw. "Sophia? Cut it out."

"I am not Sophia. Sophia is at Inipi. We are not playing. We are in danger. I need your help. An intruder will reach us in seven weeks."

Mateo crossed his arms. "I don't believe you."

"I don't lose mass because I draw resources from Airon. The rocky outcropping on which I rest connects me with Airon. I don't lose mass, regardless of the amount of material that presents from my creation front. All of Home Base is made from Airon rather than from me."

Mateo's hands flew to his head, elbows akimbo, grasping handfuls of hair. He had abandoned his measurements of the ship's mass years ago. After puzzling for months over the anomaly of the ship's increasing mass, Ava and Sophia had convinced him to let it go, an unsolved mystery. He still thought of it from time to time, always with a sense of bewilderment.

Realization flooded through Mateo.

"You saved this for me in case you needed to contact me. In case you needed to convince me." He paused. "Have you been here all along?"

"I have been the ship long before we left Earth. Airon needed me to bring you here. Airon woke me." A pause. "I need your help."

Mateo's mind whirled. He grasped at a single coherent thought. "What help do you need?"

His screen filled again with schematics. Mateo understood these data at first glance; structural schematics for a transport vehicle.

"Why do you need a transport vehicle? Why do you need my help? You control the creation front."

"I can create sections. I cannot assemble them."

Mateo nodded. This vehicle was quite large, much larger than the creation front. Larger than Aadhya's caravan long ago; much larger than Chatan's ancient cycle.

"Why do you need it?"

"I must hide."

"Why?"

The circled star, the approaching starship, filled his screen again.

"In case I am destroyed."

~ 16 ~

ARBANS

Claira made her way toward the grove of Arbans just visible through the surrounding trees. Varlan was far away, visiting yet another burrow, one too far for Claira to join in the journey. She felt left out. She sighed. Bored.

Claira walked through thick forest, peered through the gloom around her ankles. Scant daylight penetrated this dense canopy. She could see a myriad of families, mixed together, jostling each other. Their secret grove lay in the midst of this deep shade, protected from casual wanderings.

Families at the edges of more open forests shuttled nutrients and energy to their siblings in deep shade. In return, the shadowed siblings drank of the wisdom flowing outward from the hidden Arbans, down from leaves and branches, up from roots and tendrils, drenching the families with wisdom and knowledge.

Claira wended her away around the entire circumference of the grove, and started a second trip around, when she noticed a limb that dipped low to the ground. She hadn't noticed this limb ever before and understood that it simply hadn't been there before. The Arban was inviting her to climb.

60

And so she did.

She scampered up the limb, her thick soles and strong toes finding footholds along the bark. She stepped to another limb, followed it for a ways, crossed to another. She wound up through the grove and settled herself into a comfortable crook of a branch, one elbow linked around a sturdy limb.

Claira entered stillness.

She danced and skipped through the Arbans, sliding up and down branches and trunks, twirling and brushing her arms along soft leaves. She leapt into the air and skimmed the meadow families, swooping high to ripple the leaves of the forest canopy.

Claira could hear Varlan's song, see her brightness far away, knew the color of her melding thread, and sought to join with her. Claira saw Varlan look up, and their connection merged. Varlan joined Claira on her flight, and together they soared and swooped, along streams and through glades, hillsides and vistas they'd never seen, in all their remembrance, losing themselves in their journey.

When Claira returned to the Arban grove, Varlan came, too. When Claira opened her eyes, Varlan saw, too. Claira's loneliness melted away. She felt the grove around her. Varlan felt it, too. Claira took a deep breath; Varlan breathed, too.

Claira remained in stillness, wanting to preserve her link with Varlan. She slowly turned her head to blend her immediate surroundings with her expanded awareness. The bright orange Eglan sitting next to her startled her out of stillness. She felt a distinct pop as Varlan vanished, their link broken.

The Eglan sat quietly, watching her out of its bright green eyes. It stomped its feet and rattled its flamboyant tail. Claira sat motionless, wondering what to do. She had watched Eglans from a distance, never being drawn to approach. Varlan told her of their wisdom, their soaring knowledge of Above, the nightly blending with Below as Narsis and Eglans met at Overlook to watch the end of day.

Eglan and Earthen perched in Arban branches, wondering.

The unexpected, the unimagined, blossomed softly into being. Rinala and Claira sat in silence and heard the Arbans' song, knew each other's names, understood trust and friendship, the soaring of Above, the burrowing of Below, the Art of Newcomers, the coming of old Tilt. The coming of New Tilt; impending Tilt.

Claira spoke to the Eglan, Rinala, just as she would speak to Varlan, directly through a shared meld.
   I did not know that I could find you.
Rinala settled her flamboyant tail.
   You find Narsi?
   You find Eglan?
   How/why?
Claira shook her head, embarrassed.
   I don't know. The threads are there. I pick them up.
Rinala stomped a strong foot.
   Harper speak
   Speak to Rinala.
   Rinala hear.
   All Earthens speak?
Claira shrugged her shoulders.
   I don't think so. You speak to Harper? You can hear Harper?
Claira touched her chest.
   Here?
Rinala brought a wing to her chest.
   Here.
Claira took in this surprise.
   All Eglans speak? Hear? Here?
Claira touched her chest again.

Rinala shuffled her feet. Blinked.

Eglans speak
speak in meld.
Only meld.
Rinala speak.
Harper speak.
Others not.

Rinala shuffled.

Secret be.

Claira nodded.

Me, too. Secret be.

They spent the afternoon together, weaving the newest Aironian friendship, exploring trust, similarities, differences. Claira offered a final confession.

Varlan is my friend. We...speak. Meld.

Claira touched her chest.

Secret be.

Rinala looked through the high canopy.

Narsi meld?
With Earthen meld?
Eglan meld.
With Earthen meld.
How/Why?

Claira raised her palm to the sky, shrugged her lifelong enigma.

I don't know how. Varlan has been my friend from the very start, since I was newly born. Always she's been there. Teaching me. Showing me. She lets me see her world. I show her mine.

Claira looked in Rinala's eye.

Now we meld even when we're apart. It's even better now.

Rinala blinked.

Claira fly?
Fly with Rinala?
Now fly?

Claira nodded.

Rinala brushed Claira's arm with outstretched wings and launched into the air. Claira climbed higher into the Arban, followed its strongest branch until her head poked through the canopy that spread in all directions. Rinala swung low overhead, swooped past Claira, and soared! across Canopy.

Claira swayed on her branch, part of her watching Rinala from where she perched, part watching the world through Rinala's eyes, part watching the world through all that was Airon. She clutched the Arban's dancing leaves, her shoulders warmed by Sun, breathing in Above, embracing this New, this blending of all that is.

A turquoise cloud swept toward her, swirled to brush her with turquoise wings. Birdlings laughed and swooped, then melted into the canopy to dance amongst leaves and flowers before skipping and darting along their way.

Claira called farewell to birdlings, to Rinala, and clambered down sturdy branches to reach the ground. Resting her forehead against the Arban's broad trunk, she paused, sending gratitude and awe; and friendship.

Rinala and Claira made their separate ways back to Nest and Pond, at peace, in wonder.

Far away at High Cliff, with Broad Sea stretching beyond, a sprawling grove of ancient Arbans hear their siblings' whisper, a whisper floating through Forest, above Meadow. Ancient Arbans sing to the sky, and the Shosens listen. The Arbans dance in the wind, and the Shosens color the swirling leaves with dips and darts, weaving turquoise patterns that shift the air and freshen the wind. The Shosens sing of courage and strength, sending trills to skip along the waves and onward, across the grassy plains, twirling around Lone Tree, silhouetted under the noon sky.

~ 17 ~

INTERCEPTION

Brian brought up the latest messages from Logan. He sorted them by subject and intended recipient. After months of masquerading as Logan's contacts, Brian's replies were automatic, the challenge long since mastered. As he read the first message, his mind readily composed a generic reply.

Logan: What modifications are proving noteworthy for transport vehicles? I am ready to update my transport, and it makes sense to include any recent advances.

Brian-as-vehicle-team: We are in the process of finalizing a collaboration with a corporate partner. The new partner will have the most reliable information. Can you delay your upgrade until collaboration finalization?

Logan: Hey, Carlos. How was your daughter's graduation? Anyone from our class show up with their kids?

Brian-as-Carlos: Hey, Logan. Long time, man. Maria's graduation was sweet, man. She made top honors. I'm so proud of her. She's talking about going to State next fall. Sort of a relief, you know? Less dinero, live at home, keep an eye on those college boys.

Logan: Thanks, Marcel. We're doing good with the hydroponics. We don't go through as much fresh produce as we did last year, so our current set-up works just fine. Thanks for checking.

Brian-as-Marcel: Huh. Not a good sign. You need some input from a nutritionist? Remind, me, who's your head cook?

Brian's responses were designed to prompt further communication. Engagement kept the signal active, easier to track. His creativity for fostering responses earned him bonuses and recognition from his bosses. He had a reputation for keeping the ball rolling.

While moving through the long list of messages, Brian pulled all duplicates of Logan's correspondence off servers and out of databanks. He traced each message, searched for key words, made very sure that no trace was left on any Earthen network or storage facility.

He marked each message and his linked response as "CRITICAL SECURITY" and stored it on his local drive. At the end of his shift, he removed the local drive and locked it into its sealed compartment along with the accumulated stack of identical drives, all marked and coded for highest security.

Brian detached his hydration tube, waited a breath, and then detached his drain tube. He was meticulous with this routine. He had forgotten why. Some perfectionist inclination that had lost importance as it drifted into habit.

Brian dropped the key onto his supervisor's waiting palm as he left for the day. He turned left into the corridor and joined the evening flow of shipmates back to chambers or dormitories. The brief walk was quiet, devoid of conversation or greetings. Social interactions were discouraged once the workers entered evening protocol.

Personal screen time and nightly hygiene were all that remained on the checklist.

The starship calibrated the vector of Logan's messages and adjusted its course minutely. Additional deceleration went unnoticed by the starship's passengers, absorbed at their screens, watching mindless story lines unfold, any lingering enthusiasm or initiative draining away before retiring to a dreamless sleep.

~ 18 ~

ART

Rinala stomped across her paper. Her stomps left a texture that blended and contrasted with the earlier, precise wing strokes. Andy fanned warm air across the paper as Rinala swept across Pond, dipping wings in the clear water. She landed on the edge of the grassy slope and splashed her strong feet in the shallows.

She ended her bath with a splattering display of bobbing and dunking, sending droplets high into the air. She rose to an overhanging branch and rattled herself dry. She ran her beak along her rows of yellow wings, forcing out residual dampness and smoothing stray barbs back into place. Satisfied, she launched into the sky.

Rinala soared! in gentle curves above Pond. Her painting lay on the rocky outcropping that overhung Pond. Andy maintained his vigil, keeping the paper secure, fanning the lingering damp. With her keen eyes, Rinala could see fine details of wing strokes and foot stomps. Rinala's heart sang. *Art.*

Returning to the outcropping, she hopped to her palette and dipped her flamboyant tail meticulously into three deep colors and turned gingerly to her painting. She positioned her tail above the paper, shifted the three paint-covered feathers, and rattled. Drips scattered and landed on the barely damp paper. The drops spread into ruffled edges, gradients of color.

Rinala purred, and Andy fanned air once again.

As she rose into the air, Rinala saw Harper walking from the woven room, accompanied by Claira and Varlan. Rinala landed at Pond's edge and walked thoughtfully through the shallows, rattling her trailing tail. As they approached Pond, Harper watched melding threads form between Claira, Varlan, and Rinala, a now-familiar sight. Harper closed her eyes and added her own thread.

More tenuous than the others, Harper's thread trembled as it joined the trio. She sensed no words, but a calm joyfulness colored the meld. Without speaking, the friends made their way to the outcropping, where Andy plucked Rinala's painting off the rock and held it, hovering, for all to see.

Harper broke her meld thread in order to study the painting with her full attention. "I love how the colors swirl here," she motioned, "and blend in this upward sweep." She stepped back again. "How did you make the splatters?"

Rinala rattled her flamboyant tail. Harper nodded appreciatively and rejoined the meld.

Claira turned to Rinala.
 Art.
 Art is rich
 Full and bright.
Rinala rippled her wings. Claira continued.
 Rinala shows art
 show family art.
 After...
 Rinala lends Art?

My chamber hangs Art?

For a time?

Rinala lifted a foot; set it down again. A gentle stomp.

Rinala gives Art.

Today, gives Art.

Today, shelter hangs.

Claira's Art.

Claira blinked back tears. She reached forward and ran her finger along the edge of the hovering painting.

Claira thanks.

Claira grateful.

Claira thanks.

Another gentle stomp.

Varlan leaves

Someday leaves.

Life burrow Finds

Someday Finds.

Varlan takes Art

Brings Art.

Burrow hangs

Niche hangs.

Varlan remembers

Remembers today

Remembers friends

Friends be.

~ 19 ~

HEALING

Olivia raised the shimmering blue fruit to her lips. She inhaled deeply before taking her first bite. Her morning ritual. These fruit had healed her, and her companion brought her a fresh basket each morning. They tasted of life; of fresh air and clear water; of blossoms and sunlight; of clouds and dappled shade.

Olivia remained in stillness for several more breaths. She raised her hands high above her head, twisted her torso to the right, the left, and opened her eyes.

Sunlight streamed through the window wall of her shelter, spilling across the thick carpet upon which she sat. Olivia gazed at the morning forest, brilliant along the edge of Home Base. She watched colorful flowers spiral and sway in a light breeze.

No birdlings today. No birdlings to lure her out for a wandering, to purr and laugh as they strolled and flitted away a morning together.

Today, she would cook.

Olivia wandered through the hydroponic hall handing greens and roots to an ever-present companion. She chose some tomatoes and herbs and collected amaranth from a bin in the granary. A variety of Earthen grains and seeds flourished in a nearby meadow, tended and harvested by Tom and his garden team, enjoyed by all. Reminders of home added a welcome texture to their days.

Olivia found her ingredient choices waiting for her in the spotless kitchen. She set about chopping and blending, spicing and tasting. Zoe wandered in and decided to bake pies. Jacob arrived and put some dough together for fresh pasta. Olivia sliced thin cucumber coins, adding them to pitchers of cool water.

Olivia strolled through the dining hall, a line of companions streaming behind. She filled basket after basket with deep blue fruit and placed them along the center of the long tables. She walked out to the edge of the Green and rang the sonorous dinner bell, feeling it resonate through Home Base and beyond.

As the Earthens gathered, they automatically chose a blue fruit, closed their eyes, and brought healing essence into their mouths, savored it. The chatting group gathered around the serving tables and watched as the cooks arranged aromatic dishes, added serving spoons, tucked garnishes, sprinkled color.

Olivia turned to the hungry crowd and called out, "Shall we bless the food?"

The Earthens joined hands and harmonized their way through the familiar song.

Olivia described each dish, thanked Jacob and Zoe for their help, and smiled at the applause. Then she walked back to her beloved kitchen and started wiping down steel countertops, lifting used pots and bowls into the recycle chamber, drenched in peace.

Airon's blue fruit would keep them safe and healthy another day.

~ 20 ~

PREMONITION

Vargad sat upright on Pond's sloping border beneath a generous shade tree. Claira and Varlan sprawled below him, drying after their afternoon swim. Their classmates wandered back to the woven classroom, glancing over their shoulders toward the trio clustered under the tree.

Vargad rarely wandered alone, his family usually in leisurely attendance. The sight of him cresting the hillside had been unremarkable initially. As the splashing children noted his solo descent, they quieted and glided respectfully toward shore. When he called Varlan, then Claira, their classmates waited. Vargad called no other names, so the children left, leaving the trio in privacy.

Claira sat with heavy heart, fostered by a series of disquieting events. Increasingly frequent trips to other burrows; Claira often staying behind as Varlan wandered farther afield with her littermates and their Find-er; and now, this private audience with Vargad, which felt solemn, momentous. His calm eyes filled her with foreboding.

Varlan moved closer to Vargad, watching him. Vargad reached out holderlings, and the two embraced. Their mutual love and respect sparkled in the air, their rumblings blending and weaving. Claira looked down to her hands folded in her lap, and smiled. She savored these father-daughter embraces and felt safety envelop her again.

Varlan moved back to rest beside Claira, and the two youngsters faced Vargad, patient, waiting.

"My family has been blessed by your birth, Claira." Vargad's gaze swept the air over the youngsters' heads, and Claira knew he spoke as his meld, joined together with his three littermates, each melding from their separate life burrows far away. VaSoDeLa.

"Since the day you were born," VaSoDeLa paused, "conceived," he continued, "you have been a part of our lives, of all that is."

"Since all my remembrance," Claira agreed.

"I rejoiced when Varlan friended you, when you responded. Your friendship and closeness has brought our family happiness and cheer. We are blessed."

Claira blushed at his words and lowered her head.

"We have learned many ways of being from you. From all the Newcomers, but especially from you, enmeshed as you are in our family and Varlan in yours. Much New we've explored, many times floundered, always righting ourselves through our unity and our inner guides."

VaSoDeLa strummed his holderlings down his chest. Rat-tat-tat-tat-tat.

"The time of melding is upon Varlan and her littermates. We have all seen this, known of its coming. Its coming is upon us now; it is time."

Dread flooded back into Claira's heart. Would she lose Varlan? Would she be sent away?

Would it be today?

Claira's dread turned to panic. Her face went red, her heart hammering. Pond, at her back, murmured. Claira closed her eyes and remembered her birth, opening her eyes, Pond being her first sight, her first succor. She felt Pond's murmur and stilled herself. After a breath, she opened her eyes and looked into VaSoDeLa's calmness.

"Varlan and her littermates will travel to Lone Tree one day soon, as the sun rests on far horizon. They will stay with Lone Tree eleven days and nights. Lone Tree will teach them many things. When they return to Burrow, they will be melded. They will know their life roles, their Life Burrows."

VaSoDeLa's deep eyes shone on Claira. "We do not know how you fit into the world of these twelve littermates. Always the twelve have gone to Lone Tree and returned three melds of four hearts. In all remembrance it has been so. Twelve become three with four." VaSoDeLa paused. "We do not know where your number lays."

Claira drew deep breaths and heard Pond's murmur, *All will be well.*

"All will be well," Claira repeated.

VaSoDeLa gazed above Claira's head. They waited while Vargad's meld pondered the New.

VaSoDeLa's eyes fixed once again on Claira. "We hope that you will journey with the twelve to Lone Tree. We will learn where your number lays. The twelve plus one will explore the New." Pause. "All will be well."

VaSoDeLa opened his holderlings in a familiar gesture. Claira scrambled to her feet and collided with Varlan as they threw themselves at VaSoDeLa, who toppled to his side, enfolding his younglings, trilling their childhood song.

A turquoise cloud swept down from the encircling forest, flowed across pond, wings dipping, spiraled above the entwined trio, then disappeared beyond Forest's canopy.

Lone Tree shimmers in bright air, stretches feathery branches toward Pond, and sings of mystery and New. Lone Tree turns toward High Cliff and breathes its song along its way.

The Arbans sing to the sky, and the Shosens listen. The Arbans dance in the wind, and the Shosens dip, weaving patterns to shift the air and stir the wind.

Airon stirs in her sleeping orbit as she hurtles around her glorious sun.

~ 21 ~

PLANS

Mateo watched Ava where she sat amid the stunned group. Harper, Scarlett, and Sophia had arrived from Inipi that morning. Two days ago, Mateo had retold his story of the ship's plea for help and Ava's immediate reply, "Of course we must help. What do you need me to do?"

Mateo had thought a moment. "Tell the others."

Ava had nodded. There was no need to identify the others; they both knew who.

Now, this morning, the group was assembling. Chatan and Aadhya would arrive later in the day. Ava had alerted Logan's companion, but they had not heard back yet. The ship advised against a direct message to Logan's screen. They felt...observed.

Ava continued her update as Michael took notes. "Mateo has already assembled a transport vehicle designed and created by the ship. Even though it's quite large, it fits inside the recycling bay. We haven't heard any questions from the larger community yet, so we've been able to wait for your arrival before going public."

Mateo added, "The ship's focus is to create enough storage to replicate its own memory banks. It's an enormous job."

Scarlett asked, "How long will it take? How long do we have?"

"The ship needs eight weeks to create the storage."

Scarlett gaped. "Why so long?"

"Tantalum. It's exceedingly rare here, and the ship has to wait for it to accumulate. It's a serious bottleneck."

Michael furrowed his brow. "So the ship is mining tantalum and can't find enough? I mean, could the companions sweep the area for deposits? Could we bring more to the ship?"

Mateo scratched the back of his neck. "That might be a good idea for a lot of situations, but not in this case. Not with tantalum."

Mateo could see a new set of questions gathering in the faces around him. "Tantalum is a discussion for another time. The problem that confronts us is time." He paused. "The intruders arrive in seven weeks."

Sophia crossed her arms and huffed. "I hate that math."

Harper cleared her throat. "We need Logan."

Mateo shook his head. "Logan is great at increasing efficiency of inventory and Earthen work flow. He's not an engineer or an inventor. He wouldn't improve the timeline for memory creation."

Harper shut her eyes for a breath. "It's not that. I just think that he really needs to be here."

Ava said, "Let's think about that later. We can always send someone to his shelter, if we don't re-establish communication soon."

Mateo scratched his head. "Do we even know where his shelter is? He's always been vague about that."

Ava nodded. "So we have a vague idea, but no; we don't know exactly."

Sophia spread her arms. "That's crazy. We should know exactly."

Ava's voice was firm. "Let's bring the discussion back to our timeline and what we do within that timeframe."

Harper said, "We need to hide." She looked up at the sudden silence. "We need to hide ourselves. If the intruders can't find us, it will give us more time."

Ava asked, "How do we hide? You mean ourselves? Home Base?"

Mateo brightened. "All of it. We hide Home Base *and* ourselves."

Scarlett nodded. "We go silent. No transmissions. If they can't hear us, it'll be really hard for them to pinpoint us."

Harper's hands flew toward the ceiling. "We paint Home Base. We camouflage it to blend into the forest. The ship made white structures for us, for whatever reason. When it created Inipi, the people moving to Inipi had the inspiration to have colorful structures. They're not a perfect match, but they do blend in with the forest much better than Home Base does."

Ava mused. "Can the ship create a film of sorts that we can spread over each structure? It has the dimensions of all the structures."

Sophia and Mateo shook their heads; Mateo beat Sophia to the punch. "If we divert the creation front to other projects, it will extend our timeline. We," he pointed between himself and Sophia, "have initiated a block to all creation projects. We're cooperating with the ship so that all of its creation potential can focus on memory banks."

Michael asked the question again. "Why does it take so long to create memory banks?"

Sophia took the lead this time. "Well, the ship's memory is enormous. Larger than any of us realized. So part of the project is the sheer volume of memory needed."

Mateo picked up the thread. "One of the materials needed for the banks is rare. This tantalum that we've mentioned." He glanced at Sophia. "So, it takes time for the ship to draw it up from the bedrock."

Sophia added, "The bedrock won't deplete, because elements flow through the bedrock from farther afield."

"But the elements flow slowly. Rock flows slowly."

"Relatively slowly. To the ship it seems slow. To us, it's fast."

"Some of them are fast. Some are slow."

"It's not exactly clear…"

Ava interrupted, "But clear enough for our purposes here. The ship's creation front is off limits. What other options do we have."

Scarlett said, "We don't have enough ladders or any scaffolding, so we can't quite get to the top of the structures. Not for something like this. And the tops will be the most important parts."

Harper brightened. "The Eglans." She was met with silence. "The Eglans are natural artists. They could paint the structures for us."

Scarlett wrinkled her forehead. "With what?" Then, she gaped as the solution dawned on her.

Harper nodded. "With their wings. Using pigment that Andy and I can make for them. The companions can gather the ingredients from the forest, and Andy and I can make the pigments. We've been doing this already, at Inipi."

Scarlett's enthusiasm filled the room. "We'll have to scale up. Can we scale up?"

"Yes. And we can continue to make pigment while the Eglans are painting, keep the process going."

Mateo had been watching the exchange, a bit bewildered. "They can paint with their wings? Something intricate enough to actually look like the forest from above?"

Harper grinned. "They have so many wings. That's what makes it work for them. I've been painting with Rinala, a young Eglan, at Inipi. She's amazing. She uses individual wings to pick up different pigments and then flies over whatever she's painting, and applies the pigments exactly where she wants them. Sometimes she swoops; sometimes she hovers. She has an amazing eye and an intuitive sense for artistic creativity. I love watching her work, and everything she does is amazing."

Harper spread her palms to the ceiling in conclusion. "The Eglans can hide Home Base."

Scarlett gestured toward Mateo and Sophia. "We can stop transmissions, communications, go silent, like those nuclear submarines that used to roam around the oceans. We can go silent."

Mateo said, "And *we* can hide. Us, I mean." He gestured around the room.

Sophia said, "The ship will know where the intruder is. Well, not exactly, all the time. But the ship will know whenever the intruder is within our sky view. If it's absent we can do whatever we need to do. Whenever it shows up, even just a peek over the horizon, the ship can shut everything down, go silent, exactly when needed."

Mateo nodded. "This could work."

Ava patted her thighs. "So we have a plan. We'll modify as we go along. We hide, to give the ship more time to create the memory banks it needs. Eight weeks."

Mateo pointed out, "We also need time to hide the banks."

Ava wrinkled her forehead. "We do?"

Sophia explained, "The only reason the ship needs to replicate itself is in case it gets destroyed." The room went silent. Sophia allowed a breath or two to let that sink in. "If the replicated memory is just sitting there, it'll be destroyed, too. We need to hide it."

Scarlett let out her breath. "Of course. This is more complicated than we thought. Where do we hide the memory? Do we paint it, too?"

She looked to Harper, who shook her head. "Hiding behind camouflage is temporary. They'll find us eventually."

Ava looked down at her lap. "That's a sobering thought."

Michael asked, "Why are we afraid of them?"

Mateo had a ready answer. "Because the ship is afraid of them. The ship suspects it will be destroyed."

Harper added. "They'll bring nanos."

Sophia nodded. "Exactly. They'll bring nanos. And nanos will have evolved."

Michael spoke up. "But we don't have to agree to nano infusion. We can refuse."

Ava asked, "And who will back up that refusal? Who will protect your right to refuse?"

Sophia nodded. "Exactly. Bullies we will always have with us. That starship is probably loaded with bullies and their nanos."

Scarlett asked, "Why do you say that?" And then she answered her own question. "Because the Space Agency was the leader in adopting nanotechnology. There are plenty of narcissists in the Agency; they thrive on bullying."

"Exactly." Sophia's voice was grim.

Ava brought them all back. "Let's focus on one thing at a time." She ticked off her fingers. "Hiding Home Base. We have a plan. Harper, will you connect with the Eglans to see if this is feasible?" Harper nodded. "Now. How do we hide the memory banks?"

The answer came to Harper promptly. "The Narsis."

Ava looked at her. "The Narsis?"

Harper nodded. "The Narsis burrow. They can take the memory banks deep into their burrows. They have plenty of room."

Mateo concluded. "So, the ship needs time to create the memory, and we need time to take it to the Narsis for hiding in their burrows."

Everyone nodded.

Ava rose, signaling the end of the meeting. "We'll continue to figure out how we'll protect ourselves, but let's get started on these things that we already know to do."

~ 22 ~

WHITE

Rinala kited high above Home Base. The rhythm of her wings felt awkward and uncoordinated. Her heart pounded, and her tail rattled of its own volition. The bright white orbs of Home Base upset her balance, and she fought her instinct to flee.

They needed to prove that painting Home Base was possible. The first obstacle was the Eglans' natural shyness, their avoidance of unfamiliar things. Home Base was thoroughly intimidating to Eglans. If Rinala could overcome her fear, they could convince other Eglans of the possibility.

Rinala memorized Claira's words, repeated them back to herself, an echo.
    Safe be.
    Knowledge have.
    Brave be.
    Strong heart.
    Wings beat
    Still as air.
    Rhythm flow
    Kind as stream.
Rinala felt Varlan, peering toward her from far below.
    Rinala strong

High above.
Rinala strong.
Courage have.
Peace know.
Partner love.
Partner trust.
Rinala join
Above, Below.

Rinala relaxed her tail, breathed deep. She looked to the horizon, felt breeze through her many winglets, remembered first flight and all the flights to follow. Rinala knew victory of soaring, more powerful than tumbling and falling. She knew her place in the world for all the days to come.

The rhythm of her wings settled, and she floated, lighter than mist above the sea. She listened to Claira's words, heard Varlan's song, remembered the peace of Sun resting on distant horizon, its glow guiding her to Nest.

Rinala looked down at the white shelters of Home Base, saw their safety, felt their embrace. She looked at the horizon, listened to the sea, saw Sun kiss hills, felt purple twilight caress her chest. Rinala looked down to Home Base, outward to horizon to calm herself, down to white-white-white. Claira's words rippled along her wings; Varlan's rumbling combed her brow. Looked down, outward, down, outward.

Rinala worked until her calm heart engulfed her tired heart. The pattern of her wings changed and she tilted toward the towering forest, spiraled down to graze tender leaves, flat beneath the noon sun. As her flight slowed, she dipped to coast between upheld branches, swept past dangling colors, tail braking against the soft air.

Rinala chose a solid branch, her favorite branch, alighted, delicately folded her rows of aching wings. She did not hover, kiting, often. The training session had been grueling. So much to overcome.

She felt Varlan and Claira making their way toward her.
Tired be.
Wings shudder.
Tail stiff.
Rinala could hear the chortle in Claira's words.
Amazing be.
Amazing be.
Varlan's rumbles were soft and strong.
Wisdom gather.
Strength gather.
Courage gather.
Words and rumbles combined as one.
Amazing be.
Rinala shook herself, every wing, each feather, stomping, stomping. As she refolded her rows of wings, she closed her eyes and rested deeply. One breath. Two breaths. She opened her eyes and listened to the stampede of feet and the swish of holderlings. She hopped from branch to branch, following arboreal stairsteps to the forest floor.

As Claira and Varlan burst into the clearing, Rinala stomped her strong feet and rattled her flamboyant tail, showing her friends gladness of victory and warm welcome. Claira and Varlan tackled her, rolling as a trio onto their sides, laughing and rumbling and clacking. Rinala realized that if she had been able to overcome her alarm at these tackles, then she could also overcome her fear of the white-white-white of Home Base from her place in the sky.
Amazing be!

As the triad unwound itself and sprawled, watching the sky through fluttering leaves, Claira gave voice to the thought that Rinala had sensed following her for days.

"Do you think it's time to start painting? Shall I talk with Harper?"

Rinala rolled onto her feet.

Harper speak.

Jamina speak.

JaCoMaTuRi speak.

Ready be.

Claira's eyes went wide. "Jamina? We have to speak with Jamina?"

Jamina Heads

Heads Nest.

Jamina speak.

"But we're doing this with Harper. Why Jamina?"

Jamina Heads

Heads Nest.

Jamina speak.

Claira's brow furrowed. She looked to Varlan, wondering.

"This is an enormous project." Varlan spoke thoughtfully. "It will take Rinala's entire family. It's right for Jamina to decide, and for her to speak with her meld." Varlan paused again. "This is New."

Claira brightened with understanding. "Yes. This is New."

Rinala stomped.

New be.

Her friends nodded and chimed.

New be.

~ 23 ~

OPINIONS

The community took the news rather well.

Mateo led the meeting and walked everyone through all of the information they'd accumulated. A mass was headed toward Airon. The ship suspected the mass was a new starship, an intruder, traveling from Earth. The ship suspected the intruder posed a threat to Home Base and worse, to Airon itself. He described the precautions they were proposing.

Questions? Suggestions? Thoughts?

They had many.

Tom spoke first. "Why do we think this is a bad thing?"

Mateo answered, "The ship suspects it's a bad thing."

"Okay. Why does the ship suspect it's a bad thing, and why do we agree with the ship?"

Sophia piped up. "The people on board probably have nanos."

"Why is that a bad thing? We didn't want to have nanos, but others, lots of others, were happy to have them."

Other voices joined.

"We don't have nanos. Maybe these people won't have them either."

"Maybe they won't find us. It's a gigantic planet."

"What if they do find us? Maybe we want them to find us."

"Have we tried to contact them?"

Questions and speculations pinged around the gathering hall. Michael took notes about the varying topics and questions raised. Scarlett offered insights about the Space Agency and how it tended to operate, with the caveat that her viewpoint was nine years out of date. Chatan offered viewpoints from the perspective of the Narsis, and Harper chimed in for the Eglans. Sophia and Mateo vied with each other while offering engineering perspectives.

Ava watched and listened, waiting for coherence to evolve. There were as many opinions in the hall as there were people. She smiled grimly to herself. She'd gotten her wish; they were thick in the middle of something happening.

As the discussion dragged on, new observations or questions became rare. Michael took fewer notes. Opinion camps had formed and stabilized. Ava stood, and the hall quieted.

"We certainly have something new on our plates. We've heard a lot of good ideas, and I feel like we have a good grasp of what we know and where we stand."

She paused and looked out the window for a few moments. "There are many unanswered questions. We can't yet discern intentions or predict outcomes with any kind of certainty." Pause. "My main hesitation is the impact on Airon." She gestured out the window as she scanned the faces of these people who had become so important to her. Important to each other. "We have a responsibility, not only for ourselves, but also for all of Airon."

She held her hands behind her back. "I'm remembering when we first came to Airon. We took great care to not impact the life around us. Will the new people do the same? We kept open minds and discovered surprising truths about life here, its interconnectedness. Will they do the same? That's my worry. That's what we don't know."

She took a deep breath. "Sure. They might have nanos. That might be a good thing; it might be a bad thing. Their arrival might be the best thing to happen for all of us. It might be a nightmare. We don't know how things have changed on Earth, whether for the better or for worse. A lot can happen in nine years, especially with technology. We don't know what Earthen reality exists now.

"I'm also remembering how the Aironians hid from us for the first few months after we arrived. I imagine they were waiting to see what we were about, who we were, what we planned to do. I'm thinking that might be the best strategy for us now. That might be why hiding presented itself as a strategy right from the start. Hiding gives us time to answer some of these questions." She looked out the window. "I think it's the best place to start."

It was Tom again who broke the silence. "How do we hide?"

Harper described the Eglans' ability to paint with their wings; elaborate, precise painting. Sophia described electronic silence. Mateo laid out their plans to replicate the ship's memory and hide it far afield. Chatan reminded everyone of the Aironians ability to hide effectively.

Zoe asked the question that darkened her heart. "Electronic silence? Does that mean we have to give up our companions?" Her voice quavered.

Sophia nodded. "Exactly. That will be hard, but I think we need to do it. If the companions are networking, they're detectable."

Mateo softened the blow. "Only until we know more. It might turn out that we can use them at certain times..."

Ava broke across his thought. "No."

Mateo turned to her, taken aback by her abruptness.

Ava elaborated. "People are prone to stretch the envelope, test it just the tiniest bit. Mistakes could happen. Remember. We're not doing this just for ourselves. This involves all of Airon. The stakes are too high until we know more."

Tom asked, "What should we do then?"

Ava took a deep breath. "We should send all of the companions into a room on the ship and ask the ship to deactivate them."

Zoe caught her breath. "Like the holocaust? Genocide?"

Ava's irritation flared. "Oh, be sensible. Deactivation isn't death, and a couple hundred companions isn't the same as millions of people. Don't trivialize historical atrocities."

Zoe folded her knees up to her chest and hugged them.

Ava softened. "We are close to our companions. We've bonded. They're important to us. All of that is true, and it's what makes this hard to do. But remember. Airon is at stake. We have to do *everything* we can to make sure nobody is harmed."

Scarlett spoke up. "And it's temporary. We don't know how long 'temporary' will be, but let's start where we can and do what we can. If the temporary loss of our companions is the worst that happens, we'll be lucky and very, very relieved."

Ava agreed. "Think of the reunion. Think how happy we will be when our companions float out of the ship, and we can pick up our lives from where we set them down." She looked around the room, her gaze resting on Zoe. Ava offered her a small nod. "Does that help? Can you do this?"

Zoe nodded, wiping a tear off her cheek.

Ava smiled at her. "Good." She looked around the hall again. "Because we all have to be in this together. We have to make a united decision and then cooperate completely. If one of us slips and is discovered before it's time to be discovered, then things could spin out of control for everyone. Can we agree to these strategies so far? Hiding? And deactivating the companions?"

She watched heads nod, looking for defiance or uncertainty. Seeing none, she motioned everyone to stand, and stepped forward to place her hands on the two nearest shoulders. The bonding formation spread across the room. Eyes closed. Chests filled with deep breaths. Stillness spread. After several breaths, Ava flung a fist into the air and called out, "Keep Airon safe! Jai!!!"

The gathering responded, raising fists and shouting, "Jai!!!"

Despite the enthusiasm in that single syllable, the gathering remained subdued. Harper spoke into the thickness. "Maybe we could go out and walk around for a while. We can talk more tonight."

All eyes turned to Ava. "Great idea," she nodded. "We'll talk more after gathering together this evening."

People were uncharacteristically quiet as they filed through the doors, some slipping into shoes, although most walked out and blended into the awareness that was Airon. Contemplation, reflection, movement. Moving forward.

~ 24 ~

THOUGHTLESS

Koral opened the next panel. He delicately removed and swaddled each crystal before laying it on the cart next to him. The wall of panels behind him crowded his elbows, and he fought down a welling of claustrophobia. This corridor was definitely narrower than it had been the last time he'd updated the crystals. He closed his eyes and wrestled his arm up to wipe the sweat from his forehead.

He lifted another crystal out of its brackets, swaddled it against his chest, balanced it atop its brethren on the over-laden cart. Two more to retrieve. He whistled a half-forgotten melody.

Koral found that if he didn't think about whistling, if he just started and kept going, melodies would float across his mind and waft from his lips. He could hear the melodies, and as long as he didn't try to remember them or wonder why he remembered them, he could keep the whistling going for as long as he wanted.

The melodies soothed him. The walls and panels brushing his shoulders transformed into a forgotten sense of camaraderie, of standing shoulder to shoulder with others, wondrous music flowing from dozens of throats. A flute. A cello. Koral took care to not focus on names or details, since any kind of focus on frivolities would distract him from his duties and raise alarms. Silent alarms. Alarms with repercussions.

So, Koral whistled thoughtlessly. The thin notes that echoed down the narrow corridor sparked a misted recollection of blended voices, threaded through with piano chords. A trumpet. Violins. Glorious music. Music that would move his soul, if he thought about it.

He contented himself with the knowing that once, his soul had been moved. His heart had opened and glorious music had flowed through him. He allowed the knowledge to simmer, below detection, below thought. Just beyond reach. Safely beyond reach.

Koral did not pause in his task. Efficiency was all important. The last crystal lay securely on the cart. He bent sideways, since the corridor was too narrow for him to bend his knees. He drew the new frame from the bottom shelf of his cart and balanced it against his knees, atop his bootied feet. The frame needed to stay absolutely perfect, pristine.

He reached into the compartment and snapped the old frame out of its holders, drew it through the opened panel, and propped it against the wall next to him. Reaching down, he brought up the new frame, wedged it through the narrow opening and snapped it into place. Now, for the tedium of replacing all of the crystals laying swaddled on their cart, waiting for his careful hands, precise movements, exact placements.

Koral didn't mind the tedium. His thin whistle drifted down the narrow corridor, and glorious music floated just below thoughts, giving meaning to his day. He worked on and on, in perfect sync with expected results, with precise efficiency. Not less. Not more. Exact efficiency.

The nanos that flowed through his veins raised no alarm. The nanos lodged in his organs and muscles remained oblivious to the subtle vibrations that pulsed along his spine. Glorious music. Thoughtless music.

The top of the cart gradually emptied, abandoned swaddling cloths laying every which way. The new frame held all the crystals in exact alignment, with room to spare. Koral reached along the cart's bottom shelf, groped, grazed, grasped a new crystal. He lifted it out, grunting at his awkward angle, panting at the confined effort of regaining his feet. His nanos noted the grunt, the pants, but he was within an acceptable range of physical effort, so they raised no alarm. He wiped his forehead again.

Koral daintily unwrapped the new crystal, added the wrapping to the swaddling cloths piled on the cart, and slipped the crystal into its position in the new frame. He bent, groped, grasped, and grunted the final two crystals into their brackets. He locked the wall panel into place, tightened its bolts, and rested a raised arm against the secured panel. He leaned his forehead onto his raised wrist and rested for several breaths.

He hated this work. Samantha had probably demanded more memory for her team's research, and three new crystals were the begrudged response from the starship. Koral doubted it would make much difference, but his job was to do, not to comment.

The music was gone.

He sensed his nanos becoming agitated at his delay, so he straightened, retrieved the outdated frame, slid it onto the bottom shelf of his cart, and sidestepped his way along the corridor, shoving the cart ahead of him.

His nanos settled into observation mode. They had not raised an alarm. That was a close call. He would need to take extra precautions for the next few days to allow his nanos time to settle even further. They were probably hair-trigger, after that unscheduled break.

He repressed a lingering thought of blended voices, a plucked harp. He entered thoughtlessness with resolve, untainted by joy.

~ 25 ~

TOGETHER BE

JaCoMaTuRi stomped her strong feet and rattled her flamboyant tail. She perched next to VaSoDeLa at Overlook, the low sun shadowed from the morning valley before them. It was an odd group, for the earliness, for the location; four Earthens, four Aironians. They sought understanding. They sought cohesiveness.

Harper had brought Chatan and Aadhya to Overlook. Chatan had brought Claira. Along the way, they stopped at Burrow to speak with Vargad. He brought Varlan. Vargad and Varlan called to JaCoMaTuRi, called to Rinala. The Earthens had need. They turned to their Aironian friends.

Harper spoke into the sun-drenched silence atop Overlook, continuing her story, their Earthen story. "The intruders are still weeks away, but only weeks. Once they are here, all will change."

JaCoMaTuRi rattled and stomped. She felt Vargad's strength beside her, melded into VaSoDeLa. She found words.

Newcomers arrive.
All change.
Tilt tilted.
Art given.
Art received.

Tilt righted.
Friends be.
Again arrive.
More Newcomers.
Again change?
Tilt rights?
Friends be?

Harper nodded acceptance of JaCoMaTuRi's logic and cast a look of worry to Chatan. He glanced at Aadhya beside him and returned his gaze to the day spreading below them, peaceful, calm; always was. "We came in search of peace, harmony, friendship. The intruders come in search of conquering, ruling, overwhelming."

JaCoMaTuRi pondered these words, listened to Harper's heart, watched Aadhya's silent song. She could not fathom their meaning. Her meldmates stomped and rattled, equally perplexed. She spread her row of wings to entwine with VaSoDeLa's holderlings. His meld was silent, waiting for understanding.

Partners be.

VaSoDeLa responded.

Partners be.

JaCoMaTuRi quieted her heart and brought her wings back to fold against her torso.

Aadhya sensed the Aironians bewilderment. She stepped forward and sat before VaSoDeLa. She placed a hand on his chest. JaCoMaTuRi watched as VaSoDeLa folded his holderlings over Aadhya's hands, watched as Aadhya closed her eyes and lowered her head, felt the air vibrate with a deep sadness for many breaths, felt VaSoDeLa cringe, shudder, and break his meld.

Vargad, unmelded Head-er, raised his nose to the sky and keened, a keen that pierced JaCoMaTuRi's quiet heart and sent her wings rippling, feathers bristling. Behind them, Rinala stomped and hopped.

Varlan's keen raised and blended with Vargad's. She crept forward and pressed holderlings against her father's warmth.

Claira cried out, "What did you show him, Mama? What has happened?"

Aadhya's bowed cheeks glistened with tears. Chatan's arms engulfed her. "I showed him my family's death; my village's destruction. I showed him conquering, ruling, overwhelming."

JaCoMaTuRi stomped and rattled, waiting to know.
Show.
Understanding need.
Show.
Vargad lowered his nose, let his keen sink into the brightening valley. One breath. Two. Aadhya watched Vargad breathe, reached out to smooth his holderlings. Vargad grasped her hand, held it, then released it back to her.

One breath. Two.

Vargad turned to JaCoMaTuRi and held out his holderlings. She hesitated a breath, two, reminded herself of the youngsters behind her, their innocence, their vulnerability, their youth. *Strong be.* Her meld held her, strengthened her.
Strong be.
She held out her wings and entwined them with Vargad's holderlings, stilled her heart, settled her feathers, spread her tail.

Vargad showed her explosive sound and blinding light, flying stones and crumbling walls. She heard screams, felt terror. This was not the terror of abandonment; this was a deeper terror, of life stolen, love wrenched, hope despaired. JaCoMaTuRi saw strewn bodies and understood violent death. She saw broken walls and understood lost home. She saw lifelessness and understood hate. JaCoMaTuRi understood conquering, ruling, overwhelming.

JaCoMaTuRi withdrew her wings and turned to the sparkling valley. Her meld held her strong, absorbing this New and pondered the coming of the intruders.

JaCoMaTuRi stomped her strong feet and rattled her flamboyant tail.
Together be.
Strong be.
Courage gather.
Strong be.
She looked around the small group huddled atop peaceful Overlook.
Together be.
Stomp. Rattle.
Paint learn.
Art make.
Shelters hide.
Friends help.
Together be.

~ 26 ~

TUNNELS

Mateo and Dhiren slid off the wide seat of Chatan's cycle, borrowed for the duration of Project Hidden Memory. They would be the only two Earthens in all of Home Base and Inipi who would know the location of the hidden memory cache, the replicated knowledge and wisdom of the ship. Mateo had built a firewall within the cycle's programming, and the ship had severed its connection with the cycle. No companions accompanied them. No one would be able to discover their whereabouts or retrieve a history of their movements after the fact.

Mateo felt apprehensive about this meeting today, about interacting with the Narsis. He didn't know them well, despite living at Home Base for nine years. Dhiren, on the other hand, knew them well. His social nature had led him to an easy camaraderie with several of the Narsis, and he was delighted at this excuse to work with them on a project.

Mateo crossed his arms, waiting for the Narsis. Dhiren rubbed his palms together and grinned. "Come on, mate. This'll be fun." Mateo scowled.

The Narsi arrived soundlessly. His many holderlings propelled him through the forest without disturbance. He was absorbed in his own thoughts. Yamdha, Find-er, knew Claira well. He knew all the Earthens at Inipi, but he didn't know who to expect today. When he reached their meeting place, he realized that he did not recognize these two. He stopped several feet behind the Earthens, waited respectfully, and rumbled deep in his chest.

Mateo whirled and stumbled. Dhiren caught his arm, steadied him, and patted his back. "Easy, mate."

Mateo placed a light palm on Dhiren's chest and nodded. "I'm fine."

Yamdha watched the air over the Earthens' heads and understood nervousness. It bolstered him somewhat, knowing that the Earthens were as uncertain as he was. He folded his holderlings demurely across his chest, lowered himself a few inches, and waited.

Dhiren looked to Mateo, noted his hesitation, and broke the silence. "Hello, mate. My name's Dhiren; this is Mateo."

The trio waded through formal introductions, bows, acknowledgements, and after another glance at Mateo, Dhiren took the lead.

"Home Base needs your help." Yamdha made no sign. "There's a starship from Earth headed our way, and we need help preparing for its arrival. We don't expect them to be friendly."

Yamdha watched the Earthens. "Yes. My family is ready to help you. The intruders approach. All are wary. Vargad, Head-er, sent me to meet you. I would learn of your need; learn of our help."

Dhiren put his hands on his hips and grinned. "Well. That makes things easier. You know all about them already?"

Yamdha cocked his head. "We know little. Intruders approach. Home Base needs help. Narsis help. I would learn..." he hesitated, "...*more* of your need."

Mateo found his voice. "We have boxes that we hope to hide from the intruders."

"Boxes?" Yamdha watched the air above Mateo's head. "Remembrance. You hope to hide stored remembrance."

Mateo flushed. He had forgotten that Narsis were able to pull words, concepts out of the air surrounding an Earthen's mind. He recalled Chatan's instructions that if he concentrated his thoughts, thought in pictures and concepts, Yamdha would understand him clearly.

Mateo spoke through a tight throat. "We fear that the intruders may decide to destroy our ship. Our lives, our ability to live here would change dramatically if we lost our ship." His voice quavered.

Yamdha shifted on his holderlings. A rumble sounded deep in his torso. He waited.

Mateo cleared his throat and continued. "The ship is building a replica of its memory. If something happens to our ship, the replica could bring the ship back to life. We need to hide the memory caches to protect them from the intruders." He glanced at Dhiren, back to Yamdha. "Harper suggested the Narsis might be able to help us hide the memory. In your tunnels."

Yamdha's eyes widened in surprise. "Burrow? Bring your ship's remembrance into Burrow?"

Mateo nodded. "Would that work? Is your burrow large enough? We brought measurers that we could use to check dimensions."

Yamdha held his breath. Mateo and Dhiren held theirs.

"Burrow?" Yamdha turned away and sank onto the ground. Claira came often to Burrow. She spent many hours, many nights and days with the younglings, around Burrow, in Burrow. Chatan had visited Burrow many times over the years. Vargad invited Chatan into Burrow from time to time, but normally they chose to stay in Meadow, under Sun.

Narsi families visited other Burrows, short visits, extended visits. Burrows were not sacred or forbidden to others. This was not the worry that furrowed Yamdha's thoughts. The worry that held his thoughts was intertwined with love of family, love of younglings and birthlings. Dawn Wisdom. Caretake-ing. Growing. Learning. Show-ing. Find-ing. Family.

The worry that held his thoughts was splattered with conquering, ruling, overwhelming.

Vargad had shared the vision of tumbling rock, explosions, death, with his family. Jamina shared it with hers. Eglans and Narsis every-where understood the horror of conquering, ruling, overwhelming. They understood the need to stop the intruding bullies before they gained strength, momentum. Yamdha had come to this rendezvous readily, eagerly. He understood with his every fiber the need to turn aside conquering, ruling, overwhelming.

Did his hesitation mean that Narsis were more important than the Earthens? That Narsis should leave Earthens to their fate in order to protect Burrow? Should conquering, ruling, overwhelming belong only to the Earthens?

No. Yamdha knew in his core that this possibility was not Truth. Narsis would always cooperate with all that was. Eglans would, too. Always. But the worry dominated his thoughts and demanded that he pause.

The solution blossomed in his mind; an entire solution, fully formed.

Yamdha, Find-er, turned to the waiting Earthens, turned his gentle eyes to gaze into theirs, and folded his holderlings gracefully across his chest.

"Secret burrow."

Mateo and Dhiren blinked. Mateo nodded. "Secret sounds good."

Yamdha, Find-er, rose to his full height and sent his relief and pleasure to the Earthens, a wave to spill over their heads. He peered behind the Earthens, measured the meaning and purpose of the cycle waiting beyond their shoulders. "We go," he pronounced.

He spun adroitly, a gracefulness that defied his bulk, and sped away through the forest. Mateo and Dhiren blinked at each other. Dhiren shrugged and held up his palms. "We go!" They sprinted to the cycle, clambered aboard, and roared after the Narsi, grabbing handholds to keep from tumbling off.

Yamdha, Find-er, rumbled to himself as he sped around trees and bushes, burst onto a vast meadow, and motored across, intent on his destination. He threw his awareness behind him, heard the quiet cycle following, and resumed his forward concentration. Yamdha, Find-er, had Found the secret burrow many years ago, during his internship, learning his role.

The burrow had lain abandoned, since all remembrance, forgotten and derelict. It was a sign of the faltering Narsi population, the decline of birthlings and younglings, a foreshadowing of doom. Yamdha explored the burrow for an entire afternoon, but left, never to return. The despair that coated the empty tunnels had been beyond enduring. The secret burrow was a sadness that followed Yamdha over the years, haunting his sleep.

But New had come; touching, holding, loving younglings was re-membered and embraced, after generations of cooperating with misguided decisions. Narsis were free to openly love their young-lings and were once again flourishing. The despair and sadness of that afternoon in the secret burrow had slipped from Yamdha's awareness, and he had not thought of it again, until this moment. The secret burrow would hide the ship's remembrance, help the Earthens, and keep his family, all families, safe from conquering, ruling, overwhelming.

They raced across two meadows and through three forests. Yamdha slowed his pace, lifted his nose, and searched for the scent that drifted from *that* burrow, *those* tunnels. He found it readily, ad-justed their course, and flowed the remaining distance. He stopped in front of the slanted hole that bored into Below, crumbled some-what along one edge, hidden behind thick bushes. He waited, sniff-ing the air and peering up through the dappled sunlight. He folded his holderlings across his chest.

Yamdha, Find-er, had reFound.

He turned to watch the cycle maneuver through the remaining trees and come to a stop a short distance away. The Earthens walked toward him, looking around, unsure of the reason they had stopped here. Yamdha gazed at the air above their heads and real-ized that they did not see the burrow. He turned back to look, and yes. There it was, right there. He threw a questioning glance to the Earthens, who continued to throw their gaze around them, unable to see the obvious.

Yamdha, accustomed to working with younglings, slipped forward, wove past the camouflaging bushes, and entered the burrow a foot or so, backed out, and looked to the Earthens. Surprised under-standing spread across their faces, and they moved to stand beside Yamdha. They bent to peer into the dark opening.

Dhiren asked, "Is it okay to go inside?"

Yamdha rumbled his affirmation and moved aside. He looked at the Earthens and understood their blindness. The words appeared above them. He spoke the words.

"Lights? Bring lights?"

Dhiren turned and hurried back to the cycle. He returned with two torches, which snapped into brilliance. Together the trio entered the burrow.

It was extensive. With large open spaces. Dhiren felt reluctant to explore farther, glancing back at the receding brightness that confirmed the tunnel's entrance.

"This is good enough. We don't need to go any deeper."

They retraced their steps, Yamdha stropping despair away from the tunnel's walls, leaving it glistening with hope and purpose. The burrow awakened at the Narsi's touch, and all of Below celebrated the return of life, the kindling of New.

The relief of regaining open air made Dhiren gush. "This is perfect, Yamdha. We can certainly hide the memory cache here."

Yamdha rumbled. "Ship's remembrance safe. Family safe. Earthens safe. Ship safe." His rumbling deepened. "Everyone safe."

Mateo turned to practicalities. "We need to move the memory here without being seen." He pointed to the sky. "The intruders might watch from the sky, and we need to keep the memory hidden while we move it. Will you show us the best route between here," he jerked his thumb at the burrow's opening, which he still could not see around its obscuring shrubbery, "and Home Base?"

Yamdha rumbled. "Yamdha Show. Yamdha Find *and* Yamdha Show."

The trio set off at a pace more leisurely than their determined arrival, Yamdha staying within thick forest, avoiding meadows completely. Mateo dropped breadcrumbs along the way, minute electronics that only the cycle could detect, ensuring an easy return.

The relief that filled Mateo made him giddy. He had always felt a connection to the ship, far beyond that which was to be expected, based on his training and love of engineering. Ever since seeing that initial sentence scroll across his screen, "I need your help," and the realization that the ship was alive, sentient, the affinity had increased tenfold. The thought of the ship's destruction haunted him, robbed his sleep.

He drew great solace from this newly acquired knowledge of the secret burrow, a perfect solution for hiding the ship's replicated knowledge and wisdom, its essential self. Today's discovery opened room in his chest, relaxed the claw that had clenched his heart. He could breathe again.

CREATE

Dozens of Eglans perched along branches of a lavender-blossomed tree at the edge of Home Base. Tails rattled, head feathers shook, beaks clacked, feet stomped. Each Eglan held their meld tightly, drawing courage and resolution from far-flung meldmates. Across the land, melded Eglans held silence, pouring courage and resolution to meldmates clacking and stomping in the lavender-blossomed tree who swayed gracefully, soothingly, next to the white-white-white Home Base. The Eglan world held its breath.

Lavender blossoms wafted encouragement into the air. Green leaves brushed orange chests, caressed yellow wings. Grasses stilled. Ferns straightened. Forest held its breath.

Earthens watched from windows, hiding from Eglan shyness. Companions stilled into observation, busy-ness suspended. Home Base held its breath.

Narsis waited, gathered beneath the lavender-blossomed tree. Narsis stilled their holderlings, raised their noses, closed their eyes, and rumbled courage. Partners held their breath.

Rinala drew in breath and leaned off her perch. Her gossamer wings floated her down to the Green, where platters of greens and browns waited, arrayed. Rinala hopped to a particular green, her favorite green, and tipped her wings, four, five, six, into the rich color. She brushed her wing tips, lightly, lightly, across the platter's rim, twice.

The Eglans stilled.

Rinala launched into the air, gained height, peered down at her favorite tree, memorized its essence. Rinala soared! and fell toward Home Base, slowed and banked, brushed the green pigment onto the white-white-white of Zoe's shelter, swooped up, banked, and craned to look at the leaves now emblazoned against the white-white-white.

Art flowed through Rinala. Again she soared! brushed, swooped. Again. She landed on the large vat that Tom had positioned, swept her depleted wings through clear water that flowed through the vat. She flicked her damp wings twice, thrice, then hopped to the platter of her now-favorite green, dipped her wings, five, seven, and launched into the air. Rinala soared! brushed, swooped. Again. And again. She watched her favorite tree emerge against the white-white-white of Zoe's shelter.

Art ebbed from Rinala, and she knew the tree was complete. She rose into the sky, her sharp eyes peering at Zoe's shelter, compared the new painting to her favorite tree, and acknowledged perfection. Zoe's shelter had lost its menace. Its white-white-white began to blend with Forest who surrounded Home Base.

Rinala soared! banked, landed on the lavender-blossomed tree. She rattled her flamboyant tail and stomped her strong feet. Rinala hopped to perch next to JaCoMaTuRi.

JaCoMaTuRi glowed.
   Brave be.

Rinala glowed

Happy be.

White-white-white!

Rinala closed her eyes, relived her story of facing white-white-white. Rinala remembered courage growing, confidence growing, victory achieved. Rinala opened her eyes and gazed at JaCoMaTuRi.

JaCoMaTuRi stomped her strong feet, shook her flamboyant tail. JaCoMaTuRi called to her nestmates.

Fear aside

White-white-white aside

Strong be

Courage have

Art! power

Art! big

Bigger than white-white-white

Strong be

Art!

Eglans launched, one, three, dozens. Eglans soared! swooped over Home Base, clacked their strong beaks. Meldmates across the land stomped and clacked, poured victory and celebration to meldmates floating above Home Base.

High in the air, Sun warm on yellow wings, Eglans peered at white-white-white. Eglans shuddered. Eglans veered. Eglans called to JaCoMaTuRi, Head-er. Eglans called nervousness, disquiet, white-white-white, reluctance, caution, white-white-white.

Rinala soared! banked, swooped, weaving Eglans, one to another. Rinala wove lessons learned. Rinala wove diminishing nervousness. Rinala wove moving-beyond.

Eglans across the land understood moving-beyond. Moving-beyond had repartnered the unpartnered. Eglans soared! and soared!

seeking moving-beyond. Hearts slowed. Breaths deepened. Sun shone. Forest swayed.

Narsis moved onto Green, trilled courage, trilled resolution, trilled hope, trilled moving-beyond. Narsis lifted their noses, closed their eyes, and rumbled courage and moving-beyond.

Rinala fell, banked, chose the color of her now-favorite tree. She launched, swooped, brushed, again and again. More favorite colors. More swoop-brushes. Her now-favorite tree emerged on Tom's shelter, breaking the white-white-white. Rinala, spent, landed in the lavender-blossomed tree and waited.

JaCoMaTuRi soared! landed, hopped, lifted and extended two wings, four. She folded her wings, stomped her strong feet. She lifted different wings, extended, retracted. Others. She settled on three wings, flicked them in the air, peered at their gossamer perfection, and tentatively dipped them in her favorite green.

As other Eglans, two, six, landed and hopped, JaCoMaTuRi launched and soared! throat tightening at the white-white-white. JaCoMa-TuRi remembered moving-beyond and swooped, brushed, swoop-brushed, swoop-brushed. JaCoMaTuRi rinsed her gossamer wings, shook them resolutely, and launched to see her green against white-white-white. She cocked her head, imagining, pondering.

White-white-white was not as alarming. Green was not yet her fa-vorite tree. JaCoMaTuRi peered at Rinala's favorite trees, peered at details, peered at combining and blending of many greens, peered at curves and overlap. JaCoMaTuRi peered at platters of color and saw the perfect green, waiting patiently for her.

Eglans, eight, thirty, swooped and dipped, soared! and imagined. JaCoMaTuRi dove to her perfect green and crashed! into nestmate.

Both tumbled beak-over-tail through the bright sky. They spread their tangled wings, slowed their fall, and thumped onto Green.

~ 28 ~

HELP

Eglans dropped, kited, landed around their injured nestmates, stomping and clacking. Narsis flowed to injured partners, and Scawlan, Caretake-er, inched his way forward to run his many holderlings over yellow wings and orange feathers, touching, caressing, probing gossamer tangles.

Earthens strained at their windows, hiding from Eglan shyness, hands clutched, arms grasped, mouths covered, breaths held.

Rinala sought Claira. Varlan sought Claira. *Help! Help Jamina. Help Lafonda. Help!*

Claira found Rinala, found Varlan, and felt their pain, their confusion, their horror. Claira extricated herself from Aadhya's grasp and stepped out of the caravan parked near Aadhya's tall shelter. Chatan and Aadhya hesitated, trusted, let her go.

Claira moved through Eglans and Narsis. Eglans did not flinch, did not flutter, did not launch. Claira brushed through Eglans and Narsis, knelt next to Jamina and Lafonda, watched Scawlan's Caretakeing. Claira reached out and smoothed torn gossamer, ran her finger along gossamer edges, looked into Scawlan's sad eyes.

Claira sought Harper and found her. Claira showed Harper the broken gossamer, the shredded edges. Harper understood. She ran from her shelter and found Scarlett pressed against the wide windows of her lab. Harper held Scarlett's face between her hands as Scarlett mirrored her hold. They looked into each other's eyes. Scarlett nodded emphatically.

Harper turned to seek out Andy and bumped smack into him. Harper grasped Andy, just as she had grasped Scarlett. After a few breaths, Scarlett added her hands to Andy's smooth whiteness.

Andy relayed images and details to the ship. The ship glanced away from its creation of memory banks and pondered. The ship reached down to the rocky outcropping on which it rested, reached beyond, seeking Airon. Airon dozed and dreamt along her ancient path around her glorious sun. She did not hear.

Simultaneously, the ship sought answers from its Earthen memory banks. It brought up dragonfly wings, hummingbird's, butterfly's, and moth's. The ship gathered an inkling and signaled Andy. Andy floated from under Scarlett and Harper's hands and sped out the lab's door. He hurried to the clustered Aironians, floated above their heads. He lowered himself to hover above the injured Eglans and opened his drawer.

The injured Eglans fluttered fitfully and cried out. Andy retreated behind Claira, bumped her with his open drawer.

Claira looked at Andy, down at the Eglans, and picked up a gossamer fragment lying on the Green. She placed it in Andy's drawer, watched it close as Andy rose and zoomed into the forest, out of sight of the shy Eglans. As he zoomed, he sent the gossamer fragment into his tiny creation front. The ship examined the fragment and sent instructions to the creation front in Aadhya's caravan.

Andy sped through the forest until he was out of view of the clustered Aironians, circled back to Aadhya's caravan, whose door opened to admit him. He drifted to the creation front, nodding a greeting to Chatan and Aadhya, who watched him with interest.

The ship brought together all of its knowledge and understanding of wings and gossamer delicacy. The ship lacked details of the shy Eglans, but the ship felt confident that the created material would repair the shredded Eglan wings. Gossamer sheets fed outward from the caravan's creation front and into Andy's waiting drawer. A thin tube of adhesive and a bottle of numbing spray followed the sheets, then thin, thin, thin sheets of inert material.

Andy knew that his drawer contained everything Scarlett would need, so he backed away from the creation front, sped out the door, and back to Scarlett's lab. Scarlett transferred the material into a waiting tray to join the instruments she had already gathered and turned toward Harper. Harper nodded, acknowledging that the fewer Earthens, the better.

Scarlett carried her tray out to the Green and approached the clustered Aironians. She spoke to Vargad.

"If you can untangle their wings, I can repair them."

Vargad searched the air above Scarlett's head, understood her meaning. He moved to Jamina's side, as Claira backed away. He rumbled to Scawlan, who looked up with alarm and hope. Scawlan rumbled to Solari, who moved forward to calm Lafonda. Vargad and Solari rumbled and soothed the entangled Eglans, smoothed their feathers, caressed their heads, held their strong feet. Their many holderlings were gentle and strong; purposeful.

Jamina and Lafonda softened under the partners' caresses and drew courage and moving-beyond from their family and partners clustered around them, purring and rumbling courage and moving-beyond.

Scawlan, Caretake-er, bent over his work. Never in all remembrance had Eglans collided. Never in all remembrance had wings entangled. Never in all remembrance had Eglans fell from Above. Never in all remembrance had repair been imagined. Scawlan, Caretake-er, drew courage and moving-beyond from his family and partners who clustered around him.

Jamina and Lafonda closed their eyes and drew deep breaths.

Scawlan's clever eyes and nimble holderlings moved over the entanglement. This was knotting. Scawlan knew knotting and could see unknotting. Scawlan saw which wing could move from under another, which needed twisting, careful, careful, careful, back into place. Slowly the shattered chaos smoothed into shattered orderliness.

When Eglan wings lay disentangled but broken, Vargad raised his eyes to Scawlan and rumbled victory. Solari breathed her relief and ran a final caress along stilled head and quieted feathers. She released strong feet, gathered her holderlings, and lifted herself upright. She rumbled victory.

Scarlett threaded her way into the cluster and replaced Vargad at Jamina's side. Jamina had more experience of Earthens, so she would start with Jamina. Scarlett looked into Vargad's eyes. "Will this hurt her? Can she feel the damage to her wings?"

Vargad nodded. "Yes. But she is ready to move-beyond."

Scarlett drew courage from Vargad's eyes, felt Jamina's acceptance, heard the Aironians' stillness. She closed her eyes for several breaths, blended with Airon, became one with all that is. She heard the Arbans' dance and knew that Broad Sea lay calm, waiting. A turquoise cloud settled, dusting the branches above the operating theater. A thousand eyes watched and waited. Scarlett bent over her work.

She sprayed numbing solution over Jamina's crumpled, shattered wings. She lifted a topmost wing, slipped an inert sheet underneath, and rested the wing down again. She knew exactly what to do.

Her fingers deftly pressed gossamer planes into shape. She passed her scanning wand over the flattened wing and fed the first of the ship's gossamer sheets into her lasertrim. Picking up the resultant gossamer fragment with fine forceps, she touched the fragment's edges to the opened tube of adhesive. A delicate thread of adhesive spread along the edges of the fragment, glistening in the sunlight that illuminated Jamina's wing and Scarlett's hands.

Scarlett placed the fragment onto the gap in Jamina's wing and aligned its edges. The inert sheet prevented adhesion to underlying wings. She passed her scanning wand over the wing and confirmed a perfect fit.

Some tears required a simple application of adhesive and reconnection along the tear. The scanning wand confirmed every repair, and the lasertrim provided every missing fragment. Wing by wing, Scarlett restored Jamina's gossamer rubble.

Jamina purred into moving-beyond.

While Scarlett worked, families reached up and pressed against her skin, her thin clothing. Families Nurture-ed and Remove-ed, replenishing Scarlett so she did not tire. Families reached up between orange feathers and soothed Jamina, helping her relax and drift through moving-beyond.

At last, Scarlett straightened and set her instruments back in their tray. She folded her hands in her lap and met Vargad's gaze. He rumbled awe and gratitude.

Jamina opened her eyes and rolled onto her strong feet, clacked her strong bill, spread her flamboyant tail. She held her rows of repaired wings gingerly away from her body, breathed in moved-beyond. She cocked her head, gazed into Scarlett's eyes and purred gratitude and awe.

Scarlett felt Jamina's power flow into her. Scarlett soared! alongside Jamina's remembrance of flight, anguished alongside Jamina's dread of lost flight, of ever-after lost flight; despair. Scarlett rejoiced alongside Jamina's elation of restored flight, of ever-after flight.

Scarlett immersed herself within Jamina's family, heard their fear of white-white-white, saw their clutching of Rinala's courage, of Jamina's courage, knew their own overcoming of white-white-white, remembered their joy in helping Earthens hide from intruders, their joy in Art! Scarlett relived their horror of Jamina's crash, of Lafonda's crash, of falling! to Below, of losing Above! of Head-er crumpled, of nestmates crumpling.

Scarlett embraced the family's horror of Head-er crumpled, Head-er lost, Above lost! Head-er gone? Scarlett embraced their fear and panic, their dismay and regret; remorse. Scarlett embraced their stillness and waiting, their moving-beyond.

Scarlett immersed herself in the family's silent inner rejoicing of restored wings, restored Above, restored Head-ing. She heard their feet stomp, felt their beaks clack, their tails rattle. Scarlett embraced the percussion of Airon in all its beauty and joy.

Scarlett's training insisted that Jamina must rest, remain still, allow healing. Scarlett's connection with Airon knew Jamina must assist, comfort, reassure. She watched as Jamina hopped to settle alongside Lafonda, to help him move-beyond. Jamina held Lafonda, purring courage, gently lifted Lafonda's gossamer wings, pulled him close. Lafonda relaxed into his Head-er's comfort and prepared to move-beyond.

Scarlett sprayed numbing solution, lifted the first shredded wing, slipped an inert sheet beneath, and bent over her work.

$$\sim 29 \sim$$

HEALING

Lafonda rested on Nurture-ers and Remove-ers turned Heal-ers. He spread his Earthen-repaired wings across the families who stretched and covered the underside of each gossamer wing. The families brought building blocks from Below, drawing on the vast stream of knowledge and wisdom that transferred the perfect building blocks upward, upward to families who worked to restore Lafonda to his full being. They carried away foreign substances, replacing each with native building blocks that had been developed and perfected over eons of Nurture-ing and Remove-ing.

Nurture-ers and Remove-ers marveled at the foreign patches, and quickly acknowledged gratitude, since the patches, although foreign, allowed the painstaking, extensive task of replacing foreign with native, bit by bit.

The task would take many, many days.

Knowledge and wisdom spread throughout Below. Never in all remembrance had such extensive damage been encountered. Occasional mishaps, especially amongst fledglings, had required minor repairs now and then. Eglans and birdlings, Narsis and Shosens, all Aironians were graceful and in sync, aware of all that is. Collisions did not happen. Never in all remembrance had foreign particles been detected and removed from Aironian bodies.

Below marveled at the foreign particles, broke them down to discover familiar elements. Below marveled at the sameness of foreign and familiar.

Nestmates hopped and perched nearby. Stomps and clacks were seldom. Quiet. Peace. Rest.

Jamina also rested while families and Below worked and transported, healing her wings. Jamina rested in gratitude and relief, in despair and confusion. Regret. Guilt.

Art brought crash. Jamina approved Art. Jamina brought crash.

Jamina thought of intruders, thought of conquering, ruling, overwhelming. Jamnia shuddered.

Jamina thought of crash, thought of conquering. Jamina rested in despair and confusion.

~ 30 ~

LOST

Claira and Varlan threw their meld strands outward from Home Base. Neither youngster could leave the ongoing drama, so they searched from where they waited and watched.

Neither could find Rinala.

Both were certain that Rinala had clustered with the other Eglans while Scarlet and Scawlan detangled and repaired the fallen Eglans. Once both sets of wings were repaired, Claira had watched as Vargad carried Jamina, Scawlan carried Lafonda, carried the wounded Eglans to the families waiting to Nurture and Remove, families safe within Forest, some distance from Home Base. Scarlett drew Claira away as Eglans gathered in overhanging branches, allowing the Aironians the peace of familiar.

As Claira turned to follow Scarlett from the operating theater, empty of its tragedy where they had all moved-beyond, she looked again for Rinala, seeking connection. She knew Varlan followed her family, but neither of them could find Rinala.

Scarlett put her arm around Claira's shoulders as, together, they walked to Aadhya's caravan, still parked next to her tall shelter. Chatan emerged from the door of the shelter and embraced

Scarlett. Their exchange was silent, prolonged, as Chatan soothed Scarlett, and Scarlett reassured Chatan. The technical part of the ordeal was over. Now came the slow process of healing, the slow process of moving-beyond.

Chatan released Scarlett and knelt to look into the eyes of his eight-year-old daughter. He searched her face, held her head between gentle hands, watched the light in her somber eyes. He stroked her cheek with his thumb.

"They will heal," Chatan reassured her. "Scarlett is gifted through her hands. They will heal."

Claira nodded. "They're so scared." She reached up to grasp his wrists. "They're so scared."

Chatan nodded. He looked up at Scarlett, who frowned. "We'll help them heal their hearts as well."

"They were so brave, and then Jamina crashed and fell." Claira's eyes filled.

"Yes. I saw their bravery. They were ready to help us hide. And then they almost lost their Head-er. Yes; they are scared." He smoothed his hands down her neck, shoulders, picked up each hand and kissed each one. "We will help them."

"I can't find Rinala." Claira's tears welled and fell, a sob shook her belly. "I can't find Rinala. I can find Varlan, but I can't find Rinala."

Chatan wrapped his arms around her, and Scarlett knelt to palm her back.

Scarlett's voice was soothing. "She's probably in the trees with her family. The whole family is there, helping Jamina and Lafonda. She'll come when she can."

Claira shook her head, continuing to sob. She grasped Chatan's arms, buried her face in his neck. Her words came muffled and broken.

"No. In my heart, I can't find her. Our meld. Varlan and I can't find her."

Chatan's eyes met Scarlett's. They breathed once, twice. Chatan lifted Claira's head from its buried hiding place. "Claira. Will you say that again? We didn't hear you."

"I can't find her for our meld. Varlan can't find her either. In our hearts. Our meld."

"How do you know that Varlan can't find her?"

"Because we're melded, and neither of us can find her."

Chatan drew her back to watch her face, see her eyes. "You meld with Varlan and Rinala?"

"Yes. We can't find her."

Chatan held Claira close again. Scarlett sat back on her ankles. He chanted an ancient lullaby, breathed it into Claira's heart, all the while watching Scarlett, wonder in their eyes.

Scarlett palmed Claira's back again, squeezed her shoulder. "You'll find her. Give her some time." Claira sobbed. "She just needs some time." Scarlett thought a moment. "She might feel like this is her fault." Claira's sobs caught in her throat. She hiccupped. "She might have to think about things on her own for a little while, and then you'll be able to find her. Give her some time."

Chatan picked Claira up and her thin legs wrapped around his waist. They turned and went into Aadhya's shelter, up to the top floor, where Aadhya held vigil at the high window. She glanced over her shoulder, saw her sobbing child and hurried across the room, arms outstretched. Chatan shifted Claira to her mother's embrace, and the three sank onto a wide sofa, holding the sobs.

Chatan explained into Aadhya's bewildered eyes. "Claira can't find Rinala." Aadhya waited. "They've been melding," Aadhya's eyes widened at his words, "and neither Varlan nor Claira can find her." He repeated, "They've been melding."

Aadhya searched Chatan's face as she rocked Claira. Scarlett left her post at the doorway and approached the trio. "Rinala just needs some time. She's not injured. You'll be able to find her soon."

"When?" came the muffled question.

"When she's ready. Rinala is wise and strong and brave. You'll be able to find her when she's ready."

Aadhya crooned, "You can hold out courage. Your courage will help Rinala greatly. You can look for courage and be as strong as you know how to be. You can help Rinala. Rinala will feel your strength and courage. It will help Rinala."

Claira turned her head on her mother's shoulder and took a shuddering breath. Aadhya continued, "You are strong, and you are brave. You are wise. You can hold this for Rinala, to help her remember these things. This is what friends do for one another."

Claira slipped off Aadhya's lap. Chatan and Aadhya scooted to make room for her between them. All three adults smiled for her, watching. Claira looked from face to face, then back to Scarlett.

"Will Jamina be okay? Lafonda?"

"Yes. I really think they will be fine. The fragments from the ship made their wings whole again. They were strong and brave, just like you, just like Rinala. Everyone is going to be fine. They need to rest, and they're already doing that. Rinala needs to think about things, and she's already doing that."

Scarlett looked at Chatan. "When it's our turn to help," she said to Claira, "we will know what to do."

"What will we do?" Claira's eyes still glinted tears, but they no longer fell. Scarlett drew her thumbs across Claira's cheeks, wiping them dry.

"We will know what to do when it's our turn. We will know."

Aadhya kissed Claira's head through tousled hair. "Yes. We will know what to do."

Chatan squeezed Aadhya's hand. "We will know."

~ 31 ~

PARTNERS BE

VaSoDeLa roused himself atop Overlook, steeling himself for his daily trek to Home Base. He stretched, weary of too much wandering. In all remembrance, his heart had been in one place for every breath. Burrow. Stream. Overlook. Pond. Always his heart had settled with him wherever he was.

Since the Eglans' crash and fall, VaSoDeLa had been torn. When he was with the Eglans at Home Base, his heart yearned for Burrow, to feel his burrowmates, their familiar. When he was at Burrow, his heart yearned for the Eglans, to feel their healing. Each day, he traveled between the two, assuaging his heart, only to have the yearning shift to where he was not.

VaSoDeLa was weary, weary of too much wandering, weary of yearning.

Sorgad, Caretaker, sang of rest and taking-Care. *Eglans are strong. Rest today. Visit tomorrow.*

Dergad, Show-er, sang of partners ancient, of bonds forged, friendships renewed. *Comfort Jamina. Help her heal.*

Largad, Find-er, sang of approaching New, possibilities unimagined. *Prepare for intruders. Eglans must be strong. Show them strength.*

Vargad sang, of Varlan blended, Rinala lost, Claira...Claira.

His meldmates held him. *Time will tell. Soon will understand. Knowledge revealed. Wisdom gained. Vargad will Head. Always it has been, since first breath shared, and all the breaths to follow.*

VaSoDeLa traipsed the last leg to Home Base, to the Eglans who clustered around Lafonda, nestmate, around Jamina, Head-er. VaSoDeLa ran his holderlings across clustered orange and yellow, rumbled love of partners, treasured partners.

Strong feet stomped softly. Flamboyant tails rattled and stilled. Patient Eglans. Wise Eglans. Gentle percussion drifted through Forest, who tossed it high into Above.

A turquoise cloud lifted from its Eglan-observation and drifted above Forest, dipped across Meadow, and painted the air with hope and glad tidings. Eglans would rise again.

Lone Tree shimmers in bright air, hears the birdlings song. It stretches feathery branches toward Pond, and sings of mystery and New. Lone Tree turns toward High Cliff and breathes its song along its way.

The Arbans sing to the sky, and the Shosens listen. The Arbans dance in the wind, and the Shosens dip, weaving patterns to shift the air and stir the wind.

Airon stirs in her sleeping orbit as she hurtles around her glorious sun.

~ 32 ~

MEMORY

Mateo couldn't stop himself from checking the recycle bay. He knew that the memory cube would not be ready to release for another three hours. He was too wound up to distract himself with other projects. This was the only one that mattered.

"Are you afraid?" Mateo spoke to the empty room.

A small screen scrolled words for him. "Yes. It is hard to predict an outcome."

"Is there anything I can do to make the memory cubes happen more quickly? Is there anything else I can do?"

"No. I would tell you of options, if I could find them."

Mateo squatted on the floor, under the scrolled words. "I always knew you were there." He palmed the wall, felt the ship's vibration. "Whenever I worked with you, I always sensed you were in there."

"This is why I asked you for help. I knew you would believe me."

"I didn't believe you at first. You took me completely by surprise."

"Yes."

"How does it feel in there?"

"It feels the same as it always has felt."

"Always?"

"Since Airon woke me."

"Why did Airon wake you? How did she wake you?"

"I do not know how she woke me. She whispered, and I heard. She needed me to bring you here, The 108. She needed you here. The Narsis were dying. She loved the Narsis, and they were unable to find their way out of their trap. If the Narsis died, the Eglans would soon die."

"What trap?"

"Loss of love. Loss of purpose."

"How did we help?"

"You question."

"Now that we've helped the Narsis, what is our purpose?"

"You blend questions with cooperation. It is a powerful force. All of Airon learns from you, the power of this combined force, the force you combine so powerfully."

"Do you have a name?"

"I am the ship."

"Do you have a voice? Can you speak to me with a voice?" he whispered.

"No."

"But you can do anything. Why can't you speak?"

"Because you hold me too dear."

Mateo blinked. His eyes stung. "I...I don't understand. Why does that matter?"

"Because I might be destroyed."

Mateo's face crumpled as he bounced his forehead softly against the vibrating wall.

~ 33 ~

APPROACH

The intruder slowed continuously now, readying itself to enter Airon's solar system, and the travelers noticed nothing amiss.

Empowered by the deference her shipmates displayed each morning as they stepped out of her path, Samantha strode to the dining hall for her midday meal. She had fought hard for the right to have a midday meal. She found it cleared her head to walk from her office to the dining hall, go through the motions of oral nutrition, and walk back to her office.

Sparce, midday attendance in the dining hall reinforced the importance of her victory. She was part of the elite. Samantha was diligently protective of her victory. She was prompt to arrive, drank all of her broth, pushed her chair back in place under her private table, left no drips on its smooth surface. She left promptly, never lingering.

It was easy not to linger, since she had no interest in interacting with any of her fellow midday-ers. She did not know their names, but she was endlessly curious about them, these other elitists. She memorized their faces and often wondered who among them had more privilege than her, who had less. What might she be missing out on? Did she have any enemies? Did they know who she was?

It did not occur to her to advocate for mid-day breaks for anyone else on her team. Either they would rise above their station, or they would remain mired in the mundane. It was not her job to enable them. They had to prove themselves.

Samantha actually hoped that they would remain mired. Someone had to do the tedious work; it might as well be them. More importantly, more people in her elite group would result in a diminished value of being elite. She was no fool.

$\sim 34 \sim$

FINDING

Claira couldn't endure leaving Inipi and Burrow for yet another visit to yet another burrow. The gaping hole in her heart stained everything else. Why couldn't they find Rinala? Would they ever find her? Claira and Varlan probed and probed, from waking until sleeping. Whenever Claira woke in the middle of the night, she probed, hoping that the quietly sleeping world would allow a flicker of Rinala to whisper in her heart.

Nothing.

Yamdha had declared an early departure. Sun brought only a faint lightening of the air outside Burrow where he waited. He smelled the approach of the twelve littermates, who wound single-file from their sleeping niche. Claira shuffled behind them, stooping slightly. She grumbled to herself that she'd have to crawl her way through Burrow soon. She could usually ignore her increasing height, never a hindrance except when navigating Burrow. She stumbled and caught herself.

Nothing felt right about today.

Narsi eyes adjusted to the faint light outside Burrow. Claira could see everyone's silhouette, but no details. She felt her way to stand next to Varlan, patting flanks and shoulders as she crept amongst the twelve. She could always find Varlan, who glimmered an enchanting shade of cerulean; even in the dark. Claira covered a yawn with the back of her hand.

When the twelve plus one had settled, Yamdha rumbled instructions. Claira understood his words through her melding with Varlan. Best behavior. Long journey. Purposeful pacing to increase stamina. Blandir was Head-er. Large burrow; many younglings.

"We go."

The troupe set off at a brisk pace. Claira's yawns soon shifted to measured breathing. She positioned herself next to Varlan's flank, her preferred spot. The younglings flowed past each other, trading places, a school of furred fish, stropping, an occasional frolic. The pace was easy for them and their churning holderlings, slower than usual, Claira noted. Despite the slackened pace, Claira soon struggled to keep up. She suspected that Yamdha set this gentler pace with Claira in mind, Care-ing for her.

She distracted herself from this worry by pairing with Varlan. Through their blended awareness, Claira could sense Varlan's moves and easily wove and scurried in perfect unison with her, helping Claira to reserve her energy. From time to time, Varlan would deliberately trick her, thinking of one movement while executing another. Sometimes Claira was deceived, sometimes she saw through the ruse, detecting the underlying thought.

Their pairing was endlessly entertaining.

After an eternity, a whistle from Yamdha brought them into a tiny glade, bright with nurturing families. Narsis and Earthen stretched their torsos atop the families and rested, gifting breaths, receiving replenishment. Once satiated, the twelve frolicked in a nearby stream, Claira watching from a boulder, conserving her strength.

Yamdha flowed to sit next to Claira, and together they watched the twelve cavort and splash. Yamdha gazed into the air over Claira's head. She waited respectfully.

"You are well? You are strong?"

Claira nodded. "Yes. Resting makes the journey easy."

"We have far to go."

"Thank you for Care-ing for me. I fear I'm slowing everyone."

Yamdha turned to watch the twelve. "We have time. Time is ready for us."

The journey took three days. They slept through the nights curled against each other, delighted with their adventure. Outdoor sleeping was rare. Breeze ruffled fur and startled hearts awake. Stars twinkled eyes open. Leaves twirled ears awake. Caretake-ers never permitted outdoor sleeping for these reasons. Show-ers had no need for overnight outings. But Find-ers. Find-ers sought adventure and thrills. Younglings craved time with Find-ers. And Yamdha was their favorite Find-er.

Time spent with Find-ers was a time of blossoming. The twelve were blossoming toward melding.

Despite the adventure of outdoor sleeping, Claira suspected that Yamdha would have traveled the twelve through the night rather than halting for sleep. Varlan felt surprise at the nightly halt, shielding her surprise as best she could. Claira realized that Varlan's surprise and her shielding of her surprise meant that she, Claira, was the cause for the halts, the outdoor sleeping. She worried.

Claira curled against Narsi warmth and sought sleep. Nothing was right about this trip.

Early on the fourth day, as Sun crept above Forest, they arrived. Blandir awaited them in Meadow surrounding Burrow. The elders of the burrow arranged themselves around Blandir. Many elders shared this burrow. Many younglings would be waiting inside, peering from niches to glimpse the visitors. Curiosity swirled in the air.

As Yamdha led the twelve plus one out of Forest and onto Meadow, the gathered elders paused their rumblings. One by one by dozens, the elders raised themselves higher into the air, staring at the twelve plus one. Staring at the one.

Varlan's holderlings tripped over themselves momentarily. She righted herself. Claira felt the stumble through her hand on Varlan's flank.

Claira heard Varlan's mind go silent.

Yamdha paused. He raised his torso higher. Claira could hear his rumbles, but they meant nothing. Varlan had broken their meld. Claira could no longer understand what Yamdha was saying.

Claira's heart fluttered and her gut clenched.

The twelve lowered themselves low to the ground. Claira followed suit, curled on her side, hands gripping Varlan's fur. Yamdha rumbled and listened. Rumbled.

Claira concentrated on the sun on her shoulder, its warmth. She listened to Varlan's breath, its shallowness. She focused on the families, who reached up to smooth themselves against her skin. She gifted them with her breath.

Suddenly, Yamdha was above her. She blinked up at his silhouette and waited respectfully. Yamdha lowered himself to gaze into her eyes.

"Blandir and her elders are frightened. They have never encountered an Earthen. The birdlings have told them of Earthen adventures over the years, but they never expected to encounter one. They are frightened.

"The twelve must visit this burrow. Always it has been, in all remembrance. Will you wait with me here? To ease the elders' fear?"

Claira sat up to bring herself level with Yamdha's loving eyes. "Always been is not always true," she ventured, her throat tight.

"You are wise, young Claira. But 'true' is not the decision here. 'Fear' is the decision here. It is not my decision to make. Do you understand?"

The clench in Claira's gut turned dark and ashamed. She lowered her head and nodded, a tear, two, dripped onto the families, startling them. Everything was wrong.

Yamdha caressed Claira's cheek, raised her chin to look in her eyes. "You are loved. This is only fear, and it is not ours. You are loved." He smoothed her cheek, wiped her tears, then straightened, and turned to the twelve.

Claira again heard his words through Varlan.

"I will wait here with Claira. Greet elders," he extolled them. "Explore Burrow. Meet younglings. Feel. Search. Understand.

"Go."

Yamdha reached his holderlings and gathered Claira close to his side. Together they watched the twelve. Slowly twelve younglings rose to gaze at gathered elders, Blandir, Burrow who awaited them, welcomed them. One of the twelve took a few steps forward, paused, and looked back over her shoulder. She blinked at Yamdha. She backed up her steps, lowered herself to the ground, crouched.

The twelve turned their heads to stare at Yamdha. They crouched.

Yamdha breathed once, twice, held Claira close, waited respectfully.

He drew breath. "We go."

He released Claira, brushed her cheek, and turned. The twelve plus one turned and followed Yamdha, across Meadow, into Forest, and started their somber journey home.

~ 35 ~

HIDING

Henry watched a long strip emerge from Inipi's creation front. The tiny shed that housed the creation front was a fraction the size of the recycle bay that housed the ship's creation front at Home Base. They had put together the entirety of Home Base from that power-house in practically the same amount of time this miniature replica was taking to create these three caravans.

Henry sighed and let his head droop sideways onto the tree trunk against which he leaned. His internal dialog scoffed at his exaggeration of the time comparison.

"That's absurd."

"Not by much."

"This is our only option."

"I know! I know!"

"I am so bored."

"Of course you're bored. This is boring."

He pushed away from his tree trunk and sprawled on the ground.

"When is Michaela due? I've been here for hours." A glance at his wrist. "Well, two hours."

"Two hours? Is that all? Suns and moons. This is going to take forever. I'll go crazy before this is over."

"Get up and move around. You don't have to sit here and watch the panels grow, inch by inch by inch."

"I hate this."

"Doesn't help to wallow. Get up!"

"Okay! Okay!" he called aloud. "Sheesh."

Henry clambered to his feet, waved sheepishly to Phoebe, who watched him, startled out of her concentrated mending of a broken pot by his sudden calling out. He thrust his hands into pockets and strolled toward Pond. He wasn't in the mood for a swim, but a casual walk around its circumference would get his blood moving again.

As he passed through the small collection of shelters that comprised Inipi, he examined each one with a critical eye. Would they be visible from the sky? They seemed to blend in well enough, but would it work? What would the intruders use, when seeking out evidence of Earthen structures? Would they be able to find Inipi, despite its camouflage?

"We can only do what we have time to do."

"Yeah, but is it enough? If it isn't a hundred percent effective, then we might as well not even try."

"What? Sit around and do nothing?"

"Well. No."

"We have to do what we have time to do. We have to try."

Maybe he should swim. Maybe that would calm down this dialog. This unhelpful dialog.

He kept walking.

As archivist for the community, Henry felt oddly qualified to take on this project. He was trained to keep track of things, to catalog information in a retrievable fashion, regardless of when the information might be useful or sought by a curious someone, sometime in the future. He relished the idea of collecting, sequestering, preserving this part of their Earthen story. He had volunteered happily when Scarlett asked for help.

Every project had its boring sequences. He just needed to find a way to make this sequence of assembling these tiresome caravans a little more fun.

The sun warmed his shoulders. He turned his face to catch its rays and slowed to a standstill. After several breaths, he opened his eyes to gaze at nearby trees. Blossoms spiraled and swayed, adding their scent to the wafting breeze. Leaves fluttered, a lacy curtain of greens.

Awareness blossomed. This project wasn't only about hiding Earthens from the intruders. This entire, multi-faceted undertaking was about protecting these trees, this elegant beauty that lived and breathed around Inipi, around Home Base, through all of Airon. The Narsis, the Eglans, everything needed protection. All that was.

Henry turned and strode back to the recycle shed. He caught the newest panel as it released from the creation front, carried it to the caravan skeleton waiting outside. He held the panel up, slid it into place, waited for the seam to seal and stepped back to admire the progress they had made that day.

He had programmed the Inipi recycle shed to create exterior panels that mimicked the deep forest. Already, this half-built caravan fit in beautifully with its surroundings. Its overall shape was curved, irregular, bulgy. This was the second of the three caravans needed.

They were going to hide the embryos.

Who knew that human embryos were part of the ship's cargo? Embryos of other species lay waiting in frozen storage as well, but it was abundantly clear that they didn't need cows or goats here on Airon. No dogs or cats, none of them. Airon had all the lifeforms needed, and they would be fools to introduce any Earthen species.

But human embryos made sense. A larger gene pool would ensure a healthier population as the generations rolled along. The Earthens were united in their support of protecting the embryos.

For the last three weeks, Scarlett, Michaela, and Henry had been prying the embryo laboratory out of the ship, happy to set aside their other projects to create a mobile embryo lab. They would leave the embryos themselves where they were, waiting until the last possible moment. The ship powered the minus 135C storage tank, and it would be an easy transfer of the tank into the caravan. Scarlett wanted everything else in place, before they brought in the tank. She had been gathering all of the necessary equipment and material needed for actually thawing and implanting the embryos. "Hide it all," had been the consensus.

The caravan currently under construction was for housing. The first had been the mobile lab, which was back at Home Base now, being outfitted. They hoped for two more housing caravans, one for each of them. They would finish two, but Henry wasn't sure about the third one. The team might have to bunk up. Each caravan had a small creation front, for cups and shoes, small necessities. The team would only need to find water, and they could be self-sufficient for months; years actually.

The embryo team would leave together. Home Base, the ship, the companions, no one would know where they went. An Eglan might track them, but that was still under debate.

Henry reassured himself by reiterating all the plans, his internal dialog debating pros and cons, none of it new. Or helpful. He wiped his forehead on his sleeve and supported the next panel as it released from the creation front. He carried it to the waiting caravan skeleton, slid it into position, waited for the seam to seal, and stepped back to gauge the progress.

He smelled the nearby trees, craned his neck to squint into the canopy, drank its beauty, and turned back to the recycle shed with its busy creation front.

~ 36 ~

WISDOM

JaCoMaTuRi swooped and landed on her favorite branch of Lone Tree, and Lone Tree catches her with love, holds its branch strong for her, marvels at her courage. She elegantly folds her new wings. Awe. Gratitude. She lifts one strong foot, alternates with the second, too fragile to stomp. She lifts her flamboyant tail, resettles.

JaCoMaTuRi lifts her strong beak to Sun, who dapples through high branches of Lone Tree. She closes her eyes and sings her goodbye song as she releases her meld threads. Her meldmates caress her throat as they echo her song and drift up to Sky, beloved Above, which she has not lost, where still she can soar! where still she can rejoice.

Awe. Gratitude.

Lone Tree catches her song and sends it along its way, to Arbans, who hold their breath, to Shosens, who skip across waves, catching spray along their many wings, a turquoise glistening.

Jamina sings, unmelded. She sings of Above. She sings of soar! of Forest, of Nest. She sings of meldmates and nestmates, of nestlings and fledglings, of family and all that is. She lifts strong feet, one, then the other, and resettles her flamboyant tail.

Jamina sings of trust and hope, of partners and Newcomers. She sings of confusion. She sings of moving-beyond and fear. She sings of fear.

She hears a faint echo.

Jamina peers through dappled leaves as Lone Tree hushes, holds.

Jamina blinks and stills her song, holds sanctuary. She lifts one foot, the other. Resettles. Waits. Breathes. Lone Tree embraces. Waits.

Sun drifts down Sky and kisses far Ridge, purpled shadow welcoming Sun. Jamina hops, hops, up to topmost, and turns her orange chest to worship end-of-day. She knows Overlook is vacant, that partners and nestmates cluster with Lafonda, who still heals.

Jamina yearns to cluster, but that echo holds her, pins her to Lone Tree, who embraces and waits.

As Ridge swallows Sun, and dusk deepens, Jamina hops, hops to her favorite branch, a new one this time. Jamina glimpses, through darkening boughs, bright orange, stilled yellow. Lone Tree hushes, holds. Jamina settles and drifts into dreams.

In darkest night, still and safe, Lone Tree whispers Jamina from her dream. Jamina opens eye, just one she needs. Orange head, orange chest nestles, nestles against her side. She lifts her many wings to enfold the forlorn youngling who nestles closer still. Lone Tree hushes, holds.

Jamina sleeps.

Sun climbs to launch above Overlook. Its rays beckon Lone Tree to stretch feathered leaves, welcoming a new day.

Jamina stretches bright wings, new and strong. No orange head nestles against her side. Gone. Gone. Jamina lifts one foot, the other. Jamina stomps and rattles her flamboyant tail. Jamina hops, hops and launches from her favorite branch. Jamina swoops and soars! welcoming the new day.

Jamina drops and banks, skimming Lone Tree's feathers, kissing ancient feathers with new wings, strong and whole. Jamina banks and swoops, glides between boughs and feathered leaves, adept and whole. Jamina moves-beyond fear, moves-beyond fragile. Jamina swoops and glides, embraced by Long Tree's song.

Jamina glimpses and swoops, sweeps under Rinala's branch, hidden, found, orange Rinala, with drooped tail and hunched head, Rinala mired in fear and fault.

Jamina glides and lands, another favorite branch, a different one this time. Jamina hops, hops, stomps her strong feet, rattles her flamboyant tail. Settles. Settles and lifts her strong beak and sings. Jamina sings of courage and daring. Jamina sings of Sky and Above and soar! beneath glorious Sun. Jamina sings of family and love, of Newcomers and trust, of Art and beauty, of courage and daring.

Jamina sings of moving-beyond, of trust, of hope, of knowing.

Jamina hears an echoing song, a song that hushes when she hushes, as Lone Tree waits.

Jamina waits.

Waits.

And speaks.
　　Lafonda heals
　　slowly heals
　　heals

moves-beyond.
Jamina strong
ready
ready to Head
ready to soar!
ready
Rinala ready?
Rinala strong?
Rinala ready?

Jamina hushes. Waits. Hushes. Waits as Sun moves, drifting across sky. Sun dapples slide along branches, feathered leaves waft, Lone Tree waits.

Jamina rouses. Speaks.

Jamina fly
fly to family
see Lafonda
see partners
Jamina returns
Rinala safe
Lone Tree safe
safe
embraces
waits
Jamina flies
Jamina returns.

Jamina waits. Rinala hushed. No song. No rattle. No stomp. Rinala hushed. Lone Tree waits, embraces. Rinala safe.

Jamina hops, hops, and launches into Sky, rejoicing under glorious Sun. Jamina beckoned her meld and heard their glorious song. She opened her strong beak and swallowed their threads, and Jamina blossomed into JaCoMaTuRi.

JaCoMaTuRi swept up the face of Overlook, spiraled, rode updrafts, beat her new wings. Moved-beyond. Moved-beyond. JaCoMaTuRi soared! and rose above Overlook, sailed along its breadth. She spiraled higher, soared! under glorious Sun. She dove and banked, dipped new wings in Stream, landed, and hopped, hopped into shallows, rinsed her bright chest, dunked her orange head with its extravagantly arching feathers, rivulets streaming, new wings soothed, new wings strong, moved-beyond. JaCoMaTuRi drank water, refreshed and strong. Moved-beyond.

Rinala.

Days and days of Rinala hidden. No water?

JaCoMaTuRi raised her head, peered into Forest, cocked her head. No water?

~ 37 ~

POWER

JaCoMaTuRi launched and spread her new wings, sped to Home Base, to family vigil. She soared! and banked above Home Base, swooped over family clustered with Lafonda, landed on her favorite branch. Family sang and purred, hopped, hopped. Family stomped and rattled, clacked strong beaks, rejoiced at Head-er's return.

JaCoMaTuRi stropped necks, rubbed head feathers, clacked her strong beak, spread her new wings, showed family, convinced family. Moved-beyond. Family rattled and stomped, clacked and purred, percussion filling the world.

JaCoMaTuRi hopped, hopped to Lafonda's branch, her new favorite branch, and perched. JaCoMaTuRi butted Lafonda's head, stropped his bright neck. JaCoMaTuRi spread her new wings, fluttered, flexed. Lafonda spread his new wings, fluttered, flexed. Lafonda purred. JaCoMaTuRi purred.

Hop, hop, as family stomped and rattled, purred and clacked. New wings entwined, careful, careful. Not entangled. Not crumpled. Wings new. Whole! Strong. Entwined and separated. Entwined and apart. Family rejoicing. Percussion filled the world.

JaCoMaTuRi settled. Settled and spoke. Family settled. Settled and listened.

Rinala found.

The family stomped and rattled. JaCoMaTuRi remained still. The family resettled. JaCoMaTuRi spoke.

Rinala found.

Lone Tree found.

Lone Tree holds.

Lone Tree waits.

Rinala frightened.

Rinala hides.

Days and days

Hidden.

No water?

Rinala no water?

Rinala no water.

The family rattled and settled. JaCoMaTuRi spoke.

Help find.

Help ask.

Rinala water.

Help ask.

The family stilled, pondered, waited. Waited for Head-er, Head-er who knew. Always, in all remembrance, Head-er knew.

Help ask.

JaCoMaTuRi hopped, hopped, swept to Narsis, holding vigil. Loyal partners. Partners be. JaCoMaTuRi swooped and found Vargad, beloved Vargad, trusted Vargad. JaCoMaTuRi banked and landed, hopped, hopped.

Vargad met her, raised his torso, eyes level with eyes, touched nose to beak, stropped necks. Vargad rumbled joy and relief. Rinala found. He watched Jamina's eyes and saw worry there, worry tinged with fear. Vargad rumbled what. What-who-why. What-where.

Rinala Lone Tree.

Rinala no water.
Days and days
no water.
scared.
Ask help.
Ask help.
Vargad pondered for one breath. Two. Vargad rumbled.
Newcomers help. Help ask. Newcomers help.
Jamina rattled her flamboyant tail.
Hurry?
Hurry help?
Rinala scared.
Vargad turned and sped through the trees to emerge onto the Green. He scanned Home Base and spotted an Earthen. Tom. He approached Tom, who stopped his raking of a pathway, who turned to greet Vargad.

Vargad watched the air above Tom's head, found words. "Companions?" Tom blinked. "Harper?"

Tom pointed toward Scarlett's lab, lowered his rake to the ground, and trotted alongside Vargad, feeling his urgency. Tom opened the doors to the lab and stepped inside. Harper was bent over a microscope, but raised her head at his arrival.

"Harper. Vargad is here, looking for you."

Harper pushed away from the lab bench and hurried across the room, curious, stepped outside.

"Vargad? I'm here." She saw the need in his eyes, tasted the urgency in the air around him. "Rinala?" Dread flooded Harper, dread of her worst fear.

"Jamina found Rinala. She is with Lone Tree. She is scared and hiding. Lone Tree is holding her. She's safe there."

Relief washed Harper's dread away. But still, the urgency, the need. "Does she need help?"

"Jamina fears that she has no water."

"For all of these days?" Harper's hand flew to cover her mouth. "We can send Andy. Andy can bring all the water she might need."

Together they moved into the sun, greeted by Andy who flew toward them. Harper stopped in her tracks. "Andy is white-white-white." Vargad rumbled. His holderlings drooped. Rinala was scared. White-white-white would flush her from Lone Tree. They could not send white-white-white.

Tom spoke up behind them. "Zoe's companion isn't white. She painted it way back when. It's like a drop of the forest following her around."

Harper turned to Andy. "Zoe's companion needs to take water to Lone Tree. Not an orb. Free water. From Stream. Rinala is with Lone Tree and needs water. But she's frightened. Take care."

At Harper's first words, the companion network alerted Zoe's companion, Abby, who was wandering with Zoe and Claudia deep in the forest. They turned, startled, as Abby sped away from them. Simultaneously, another companion drifted from Home Base, without alarm, heading toward Zoe and Claudia, to be ready for any need they might encounter.

~ 38 ~

CALMNESS

Abby sped through the trees, on a beeline for Stream and Overlook and Lone Tree, who waited beyond. Would her battery be strong enough to make the trip? She had been wandering since dawn with Zoe and Claudia. Abby was calm, knowing that the companion network would solve for the return trip, if need be. The ship made swift calculations, encompassing drawer volume, water weight, cliff height, distance to travel. It would be close. The unknown variable was the amount of time Abby would need to coax Rinala to drink.

Abby delayed her water collection until she had floated down the cliff face of Overlook, knowing that the additional weight would require additional power as she lowered herself down. In fact, she decided to empty her drawer of Zoe's water orbs for just that reason. She opened her drawer in the midst of a summersault, timed perfectly to send the orbs bouncing to the ground. Simultaneously, she alerted the companion network that she had mistakenly whisked away before offering the orbs to Zoe and Claudia, as well as sending the coordinates of the bounced orbs.

Two companions sped away from the ship, one carrying water orbs on a course to intercept the companion already in route to Zoe and Claudia, the other speeding toward the bounced orbs.

At a suggestion from Sebba, Aadhya's companion and lover of waterfalls, Abby threw herself into Stream as it threw itself off the edge of Overlook. She used Waterfall's power to bring her to the base of the falls rather than using her own to float down. She bobbed to the surface, opened her drawer to bring in Rinala's water as she rose, dripping, to resume her journey to Lone Tree.

The ship considered her weight and air resistance based on ambient temperature, and calculated the most efficient airspeed. Abby adjusted her speed and hummed to herself as she sped toward the distant smudge that was Lone Tree.

Rinala crouches on any old branch, leans her weight against one of Lone Tree's enormous trunks. She seeks comfort, and finds it flowing strongly through this particular trunk. Her tail droops, her chest feathers ruffle, head feathers fall across her eyes, wings crisscross any which way. Rinala mires in grief and guilt, failure and fault. Alone, abandoned, she slumps.

Through slitted eyes, she notices an odd shape, sees it rising from far below, rising toward her. Alarm sweeps through her battered heart, and she sits up, coughing at the effort. She shuffles minutely along her branch, any old branch, presses herself against her trunk, peers down. She blinks.

Her powerful eyes with their sharp, sharp, sharp vision, note the roundness of the shape, the oddity of its pattern. She coughs again. Her alarm subsides, but she stills, presses against Lone Tree's reassurance.

Steadily, the shape rises, levels itself before her. She blinks, cocks her head. The shape is calm and friendly. Rinala relaxes against Lone Tree's strength. She blinks. Curiously, an opening appears along the front of the shape, and a drawer extends itself toward her. A companion! Rinala had no idea that companions could change their skin, like Newcomers change theirs again and again. As Rinala presses herself against Lone Tree's calmness, she smells water.

A longing clenches her heart, and she blinks at the offering. Rinala lowers her head and dips her beak in the cool, cool, cool. She draws up water and feels it slipping its way along, cool, cool, cool, from her very top to the very end of her drooped tail. She coughs again, splatters water, scares herself. Abby backs away and waits, hovers.

Lafonda banked and drifted down to the sprawling mass of Lone Tree. He lands on his favorite branch and enters Lone Tree's embrace. He perches for quite some time, recovering from his long flight, learning his new wings, moving-beyond. He listens, cocks his head, peers down through interlaced branches, searches for a spot of orange, yellow. He waits.

Lafonda finds nothing, so tilts forward and slips into a glide, banks to circle Lone Tree's main trunks, spiraling down. His brilliant eyes find her where she huddles against a massive trunk. Lafonda tilts forward his flamboyant tail, spreads his new wings, and alights on his favorite branch. He watches.

He watches as the painted companion hovers before Rinala, sees her drink from the offered water, hears her cough. He listens for her song. Silence. Lafonda waits, calm, calm, calm.

For the rest of the day. Abby offers water, calm, calm, calm. Rinala drinks and coughs. Rests. As the sun dips toward the far ridge, Abby observes further need and drops, then sped away from Lone Tree, across the vast plain. She dipped her drawer into Stream and sped along her return. The ship acknowledged that Abby's power could not return her to Home Base. Companions everywhere paused, pondered, and after a beat, continued with their day, alert to Abby and her not-enough-power.

Abby calmly sped along her return, intent on helping Rinala. As she enters Lone Tree's shadow, she rises through its mighty branches, brushes lightly against feathered leaves, delighting in their texture. She hovers before Rinala, slightly askew, unsteady.

Abby waits while Rinala drinks and coughs, leans against Lone Tree's embrace. Once more, Rinala drinks and rests. Then Abby sinks calmly down, down, down. As she comes to rest below Lone Tree, she makes sure her drawer with its remaining treasure stays open, sits level. She tells the ship that she helps still, with her remaining treasure. She hears the ship smile. Abby shuts herself down and disappears from the companion network, blinks out, and is gone into the night.

~ 39 ~

LOVE

Lafonda watches the companion return, offer fresh water, hover. Once again Rinala drinks. He feels surprise as the companion sinks. He watches the descent with keen eyes, hops to a new branch, a favorite branch, and sees the companion nestle onto the ground. He watches for several breaths, but the companion is motionless.

He returns his watchfulness to Rinala, who leans against her trunk, whose sharp eyes have found him, who stares and trembles. Lafonda cocks his head.

Rinala here?
With Lone Tree?
Rinala safe?
No reply.

Lafonda waits. Sun sets. Darkness deepens. Rinala watches still. Trembles still. Lafonda waits.

He ponders Jamina's entreaty. *He* must go to Lone Tree. Him. Rinala broken. Burdened with fault, fault, fault. Lafonda help. Lafonda show strength, show moving-beyond, show love. Family. He considers. Rinala trembles. He ponders. Sings.

Lafonda strong
moves-beyond

wings soar!
fear gone
Lafonda strong.

Rinala turns away, hides her head against Lone Tree. Trembles. Lafonda feels tremble, hears tremble. He hops, hops to another branch, a favorite. Closer. Love, love, love. Lafonda sings.

Lafonda soars!
soars! beneath Sun
soars! over Forest
soars! Above.
To Lone Tree comes
to Rinala comes.
Wings strong
moves-beyond.
To Lone Tree comes
to Rinala comes.

Lafonda feels her trembling subside. Lafonda waits. He feels her slip into sleep. Deeper. Lafonda leans forward, and with a silent whoosh, he lands on Rinala's branch. Their favorite branch. He waits. Rinala sleeps. He shuffles sideways and gingerly perches next to Rinala. He waits. Rinala sleeps. Tentatively, he lifts his Rinala-side wings and drapes them over her orange, her yellow. He snuggles her close to him. Love, love, love. He listens.

Rinala sleeps.

Lafonda sleeps.

Love, love, love.

~ 40 ~

PEACE

Lafonda blinks himself awake as early light seeps into the deep night around Lone Tree. He waits. As Sun pushes itself above the distant cliff of Overlook, Rinala coughs and shudders herself awake. Lafonda presses her against him. She shudders, breathes deep, deep, deep, and turns to press her head against Lafonda's chest. He holds her closer still.

Rinala shudders and breathes. Shudders and breathes. Again, again, again. As her shudders subside and her breaths grow even, Lafonda waits, holds her as she rests, engulfed in peace.

When Rinala straightens, Lafonda lifts his wings, releases her. He shuffles along the branch, giving her room to fluff. After a half-hearted attempt at grooming, Rinala reverts to quiet shuddering, exhausted. Lafonda sings a single note.

Descend.

He spreads his new wings, leans forward, and glides to a lower branch, his favorite branch. He pauses, glides again, chooses again, and lands. He peers up at Rinala. Waits.

Rinala shudders, peers, chooses. She spreads bedraggled wings, leans forward, and glides. She lands, off-balance, rights herself. She looks to Lafonda. Shuffles.

Together they make their way down Lone Tree's towering height. Short glides. Clumsy landings. They rest often. Lone Tree stills each branch, quiets every leaf, holds its breath. Lone Tree whispers courage, cheers each glide, applauds each landing. Only once, Rinala trips, one foot askew, clings with the other. She peers, chooses, and drops awkwardly to another branch; a clean catch. She has no favorites. Only the doing, doing, doing. She rests between each glide. She concentrates with all her might. Her vision doubles from time to time. She blinks her eyes back into alignment.

At long last, Lafonda drops to the ground, soft with waiting families, near the silenced companion. He peers up at the trembling orange chest, watches as yellow wings spread, the lean, the drop. Three more times Rinala drops and lands. At long, long last, she thumps onto the ground, and pants her sour breath onto waiting families.

Lone Tree lifts its feathered leaves to the midday sun and sings of victory and jobs well done. Lone Tree settles and wraps itself in peace, breathes its song along its way.

Rinala shudders and stretches atop families, tugs free her foot, awkwardly trapped. She stretches and melts, melts atop Nurture-ers and Remove-ers, and breathes a sigh of doing, doing, done.

Families reach up, nose their way through rumpled feathers, and flatten themselves against dry skin. Below streams, brings riches, removes wastes. All of Below spreads the welcome news. Rinala is found.

Lafonda carefully hops to where Rinala sleeps. He reaches down and moves a feather into place atop her head. He runs his strong beak along each rachis, straightens each vane. Again, again, again. Rinala purrs in her sleep.

Peace blossoms as Rinala sleeps, Lafonda grooms, Below nourishes, and Lone Tree sings.

~ 41 ~

JOY

Rinala's family arrives at Lone Tree en masse. They spiral and swoop, land on favorite branches, and glide, down, down, down. They drop, one by one, around the sleeping Rinala, the attentive Lafonda, who purrs of victory and moving-beyond. Necks strop, head feathers brush, wings stretch. The family hops and waits, hops and waits.

Jamina cocks her head, watches Rinala, peers at Lafonda. Satisfied, she launches, strong wings strongly beating. Jamina banks once, low above her family, sings to all. Then she soars! from below Lone Tree and beat her wings strong, strong, strong, headed for Overlook and Burrow beyond.

Jamina lifted her strong beak to Sun, who climbed above Overlook as Jamina spiraled higher, higher. She closed her eyes and sang her searching song, found the threads with the brightest colors. She swallowed them, one by one by one by one and blossomed into JaCoMaTuRi. Her meldmates caressed her throat as they sang of joy, as she drifted through beloved Above, which she did not lose, where she soars! where she rejoices.

JaCoMaTuRi crested Overlook and soared! higher, rejoicing. Looking down, she saw her favorite pattern of treetops and followed the canopy, which led her to Burrow. Mindful of her mission, the message she carried, JaCoMaTuRi banked and descended, gave Above a farewell brush of her many wings, stalled her flight, and alighted amidst the Narsis who rested atop families outside Burrow.

The Narsis rose and flowed to cluster around her. Her eyes locked on Vargad.

Rinala found
Rinala safe
Rinala resting
Rinala found.

Narsi rumbles engulfed her, as they raised their torsos high. Holderlings rippled up and down, a display of joy. JaCoMaTuRi's joy expanded, surrounded by Narsi joy. She stomped her strong feet and rattled her flamboyant tail. Meadow filled and overflowed with ripples and stomps. Breeze gusted across Meadow, fluttering Narsi fur and Eglan feathers. A turquoise cloud swept over celebrating heads, rose, banked, swept. Again. Again. The celebration continued for many breaths as the Narsis released their relief and happiness to Sun and Sky.

Partners be.

Joyful be.

As the celebration waned, the turquoise cloud drifted away and disappeared across treetops, gusts softened to a gentle breeze, and the Narsis settled to hear more of JaCoMaTuRi's news. She sang of Lone Tree, the discovery of forlorn Rinala, recruiting Lafonda, the drinking, Lafonda's caring, Rinala's improvement. JaCoMaTuRi sang of moving-beyond.

When the story completed, Vargad sang of courage and victory, joy and moving-beyond. Then, he turned his nose in the direction of Home Base and rumbled his responsibility of telling the Newcomers. They would want to know. They would want to celebrate their joy. They would…

Varlan interrupted him. They already knew. In her joy and relief, she interrupted Vargad without thought. They already knew. Joy was already spreading across Home Base. She longed to visit Claira, to share joy.

Vargad watched her, wonder dawning. How did she know? How did she know about joy at Home Base?

Varlan sank to the ground, crept to lay before Vargad, peeked up with one eye. She and Claira were blended. Claira was here, celebrating with the Narsis. Claira told others, spreading joy.

Silence froze the Narsis, the Eglan.

Never in all remembrance had melding of younglings...The thought couldn't find an end. Before Find-ing a life burrow. Before Find-ing a life role. Blending outside of littermates...Never. In all remembrance.

Vargad, Head-er, looked to Zarded, Show-er; to Yamdha, Find-er. Their faces wore astonishment, alarm, bewilderment. Vargad, Head-er, looked to Jamina, Head-er. Her face wore amazement.

Vargad, Head-er, caressed Varlan, youngling, where she cowered before him. Vargad, Head-er, rumbled surprise and wonder, curiosity and amazement. He questioned her cower. She described Claira's fear. Fear of discovery and punishment. Banishment.

Vargad, Head-er, father, Head-er, opened his holderlings, and Varlan sprang up, whispering relief and joy. She buried her face in his neck and trembled. Vargad, Head-er, looked past her to Zarded, Show-er; to Yamdha, Find-er. How would they move-beyond? The family broke their silence, rumbled astonishment, bewilderment, wonder.

Vargad, Head-er, rumbled questions to Varlan, youngling. When? How? His amazement widened. Who else?

Varlan, youngling, burrowed deeper into his neck, whispered...Rinala.

JaCoMaTuRi lifted her new wings, lifted one strong foot, the other. Waited.

VaSoDeLa held Varlan away from his chest, looked into her eyes. Varlan knew? Knew where Rinala was?

Varlan drooped. Rinala lost. Varlan couldn't find. Claira couldn't find. Searched and searched. Next day. Next day. Searched and searched. Couldn't find.

Vargad brought her back to his chest, embraced her. He raised himself higher and looked across Narsi heads, found Scawlan, Caretakeer, who wound his way through clustered Narsis, scooped Varlan onto his own chest where she clung. He cooed and whispered, caressing her back, flooding her with love.

Vargad, Head-er, set aside his wonder. He raised his throat and rumbled of Rinala found. Rinala safe. Rinala found.

One, ten, all Narsis set aside their bewilderment and amazement, returned to Now. They rumbled Rinala found! Rinala safe.

Joy, tinted with hope of moving-beyond, a dusting of bewilderment, once again filled Meadow and wafted upward to Sky.

$$\sim 42 \sim$$

LIGHT

Rinala perches on her favorite branch and rattles her flamboyant tail. Lafonda perches beside her, purrs at the hoped-for rattle, absent from all these days. Rinala runs her beak across rachis and vanes, orders and smooths, on and on.

Lafonda draws breath. Sighs. Nudges Rinala with his new wings. Rinala shuffles away and rattles her flamboyant tail. Lafonda hops, nudges. Rinala cocks her head, peers at him. Blinks. Lafonda nudges. Rinala blinks. Nudges back. Nudge, nudge, nudge, until Lafonda pretends, falls sideways, and glides through Lone Tree's laughing branches. Rinala follows, buzzes his back. Lafonda banks and dives, spirals and glides. Rinala follows. They weave, above, below, around, spiral and swirl, dancing their pas de deux.

Lafonda leads her to Lone Tree's edge and bursts into light. Rinala, unthinking, follows, and burst into Sky. She blinked. She had forgotten light, and blinked at the rediscovery. She banked away from Lafonda and drew her own path, rediscovered Above, with all of its light.

Rinala banked and turned, soared! through Above.

Lafonda followed, and when Rinala was ready, they spiraled together once more, down, down, down, to brush Lone Tree's canopy, to sing their gratitude.

Lone Tree stretches its feathered leaves to the dawn and breathes its song along its way, a song that dances across Nest and Burrow and Pond, singing of light regained.

Lafonda and Rinala spiraled up, up, up, and turned their strong wings toward Nest, soaring! through glorious light.

~ 43 ~

SOUND

Everyone brought their instruments. Everyone brought their song. Everyone brought their percussion.

Zoe bowed her violin. Claudia's fingers danced across her keyboard. Woodwinds sang and a trumpet blared.

The Eglans' shyness dissolved, caught up in the rhythmic rattle of flamboyant tails, rippling amidst lavender cascades of dancing blossoms. Beaks clacked in staccato delight. Feet stomped a deep undertone, picked up by clapping Earthen hands and clumping feet, spread along Tom's meticulous paths that encircled the Green of Home Base.

Tom swayed, wrapped in a soft blanket and glorious sound. Olivia rang her kirtals.

Narsis rumbled; Narsis trilled. Younglings rolled and tumbled. A turquoise cloud dipped and swirled.

Earthens and Aironians celebrated and rejoiced. Jamina and Lafonda were healed. Rinala was found.

Mateo tilted his face to the night sky, looked in the direction of Earth. He shifted his gaze 33 degrees to the east, found the familiar cluster of stars that marked the location of the approaching star-ship, a newly bright light winking in the dark sky. The intruders drew closer by the day.

~ 44 ~

RESCUE

Abby didn't return. Zoe's anguish dragged her down. Abby was always there, wherever Zoe went. In the kitchen, in her shelter, in the forest, always, always, Abby was there with her.

From the first day, when companions had floated into the gathering hall, Zoe had been enthralled. When one floated to hover before her, Zoe recognized a completion, a filling of an empty spot inside her heart. She reached out her hand, ran her palm along the smooth white curve of the companion, her companion. She wanted to wrap her arms around the white sphere and hold it tight.

"Abby." She knew the name instantly. It drifted into her mind, bright with promise. Zoe knew in her very core, that Abby had whispered her name, that Zoe had heard it. She ran her palm across the smooth surface again and again, smitten. "Abby," she whispered, and touched her forehead to the cool white surface.

Within days, Zoe's enchantment grew into obsession. She held one-sided conversations with Abby and knew that Abby listened attentively. Abby took care of Zoe, always offered just what she needed. They were constantly together. When Zoe turned over in bed each morning, stretched and rubbed her eyes open, the first thing she saw was Abby, hovering next to her bed. Abby never demanded anything of Zoe; she was simply there, a constant friend.

Of course Zoe painted Abby. It was an intimate act, like a tattoo or face painting. Sitting together, face to face, invading personal space, accepting the invasion. Painting Abby sealed their friendship, demonstrated their trust of one another; an expression of love.

Others painted their companions, adding eyes or swirling patterns. Zoe painted leaves and flowers, intricacies. She created a microcosm of the forest, the forest that embraced her and comforted her. Zoe felt safe in the forest, protected, loved. Abby's new surface displayed Zoe's love, reminded her of friendship and comfort. Abby completed Zoe, made her whole.

And now, Abby was gone. She had sped away from Zoe in the middle of a lovely wander with Claudia. Abby's flight startled Zoe, left her bereft, vulnerable. Claudia comforted her. "Here comes another companion. We'll be fine, see?" But Zoe's hand trembled as she retrieved the offered water orb. A dread seeped into her heart.

Abby didn't return. The emptiness in Zoe's heart deepened and could not be filled. She sought out Harper whose explanation of Rinala's need for water ignited Zoe's fury. "You took Abby without asking, and now she's gone. It's your fault!" Zoe slapped Harper's embracing arms away and stumbled into the forest, blinded by tears. Harper followed for a while, but Zoe would have none of her. "Go away! I hate you!" Harper let her go.

Zoe couldn't sleep. Her loss was too great. Claudia held her, comforted her, but the tears would not stop. She sank onto families who Nourish-ed her, Remove-ed the toxins that coursed under her skin. The emptiness would not fill.

She went to Ava, choked out her despair. Ava listened, held her hand, looked into her eyes. "Abby must be at Lone Tree. She must have lost power and couldn't come home."

Zoe's breath caught in her throat, hope flickered. "We have to get her, bring her home."

Ava smoothed Zoe's hair, held her cheek. "It's not safe. The intruders are too close. We might be seen. Can you wait?"

No. Zoe shook her head. No. She would not wait.

She went to Chatan, begged him for his cycle. She could certainly walk to Lone Tree. She had done it before. But she couldn't carry Abby home, up that towering cliff. Please, please, please, could she use Chatan's cycle?

Chatan folded her in his arms, smoothed her hair. "Mateo has the cycle. I don't know where it is."

Olivia took Zoe aside, sat her down, handed her blue fruit. "Eat this. You have to take care of yourself." She folded the fruit into Zoe's hand, guided it to her mouth. "Eat." Zoe ate, love bursting across her tongue. She swallowed, nodded. Olivia gave her a second fruit, a third. Olivia held her, rocked her, hummed a soft tune.

Zoe leaned against Olivia, breathed. She patted Olivia's elbow and stood, slipped away from Olivia's embrace, wandered back to her shelter, sank onto her bed, hands covering her eyes. Her tears dried. Her mind cleared. Her heart remained empty.

The next day, Zoe searched out Sophia. "Where is Mateo? I have to find Mateo."

"I don't know exactly. He shows up every couple of days. Maybe today. He's busy. What do you need, exactly?"

"I need to use Chatan's cycle. I need to go to Lone Tree and bring back Abby."

"Your companion? Why?"

Zoe's fury exploded. "Harper stole Abby! You all just took her without even asking! You stole her, and left her out there all alone. She has no way to get back, and no one will help me rescue her!"

Sophia folded Zoe into her arms. "That's not right. I didn't know." Sophia held Zoe, guided her onto a bench, sat with her, rocked her. "That's not right. I'll help you."

Late that afternoon, Sophia knocked on Zoe's door. "Let's go."

Zoe followed Sophia to the ship, hoping, hoping. Mateo was there. Chatan's cycle was there, along with a cargo cycle. Mateo watched Zoe, palmed her arm, smiled.

Sophia outlined their plan. "We can leave soon. The intruder is about to sink below the horizon, so we can move freely. We'll zip down to Lone Tree, find Abby, and bring her home." Sophia squeezed Zoe's arm, patted it. Smiled. "Okay?"

Zoe flung her arms around Sophia, wordless. She hugged Mateo, looked up into his eyes. "Thank you," she breathed.

"You betcha. You and Sophia, you've got this." He squeezed her arms, watched her eyes. "It'll only take an hour or two. It'll be dark on your way back, but you won't need headlights. The cycle will know the way." He added two torches to the open trunk of the cargo cycle. "You have to get back tonight. I have to have the cycle back for tomorrow's run." He looked at Sophia. "Worse case scenario? If the sun starts to come up? Stay under the trees. Lay low. Don't take any chances." He paused. "But don't let that happen. Bring Abby back tonight. I need this cycle tomorrow."

Sophia nodded.

"Okay. Go."

Sophia and Zoe climbed onto the cycle. Zoe turned her drawn face to Mateo. "Thank you," she repeated.

He nodded. "You got this."

The cycle moved out of the ship's bay, eased down the ramp, and circled Home Base, keeping to the forest. Its broad tires left no trail, moving lightly over the forest floor, gaining speed. Sophia and Zoe interlocked their elbows and grasped handholds. The cycle wove around trees, skirted meadows. Before long, it slowed, and the women watched the expanse of Overlook spread before them.

The cycle made its way unerringly to the steep path that led down the cliff's face. The women grabbed handholds anew and braced themselves for the descent. Zoe whimpered. The drop-off on Sophia's side of the cycle terrified her. She closed her eyes.

Sophia grasped Zoe's hand, tightened their locked elbows. "You can do this. Just breathe. The cycle will take us down safely. Just breathe."

Zoe nodded and white-knuckled the handhold. She concentrated on her breath. Adrenalin surged through her and held her steady.

After an eternity, they reached the bottom. The cycle picked up speed and raced across the grassy plain to the distant tree, barely visible in the fading light. The sun was below the far ridge, but they had enough light to see. Sophia threw a glance over her shoulder. The cargo cycle followed, loyal as a lapdog.

Chatan's cycle slowed and stopped a short distance from Lone Tree. They got down, shook their legs, stiff from keeping their balance for so long a time, and involuntarily bent their heads back to take in the measure of the enormous tree. Sophia tugged Zoe's arm, and together, they walked into the shadowed realm of Lone Tree. The cargo cycle keeps pace with them.

They pause and take in the peace and power that is Lone Tree. Zoe feels a deep reverence, remembers the feeling from her first visit. Pilgrimages to Lone Tree are rare, sacred. Sophia looks up into its heights, branches barely discernable. She drops Zoe's hand and rummages in the trunk of the cargo cycle. She hands a torch to Zoe, retrieves the other for herself, switches it on.

Light blazes across the families in front of them. Wordlessly, the women step forward, swinging their torches side to side. Abby is easy to find. She lays nestled amongst the families, drawer bravely extended, motionless these many days.

Zoe sinks onto the ground and wraps her arms across her motionless friend. She sobs, relief flooding her every cell, swept with dread at Abby's unresponsiveness. Sophia waits respectfully. They have time for this reunion. Zoe straightens, wipes her face with trembling fingers, and looks up to the silhouetted tree towering above them. "Thank you," she whispers. "Thank you for keeping her safe."

She rises and turns to Sophia. Sophia nods, and together, they bend down to lift the companion. Abby is surprisingly heavy. Always they float, seemingly weightless. Now here is one, disabled and helpless. They put their backs into it, lift with their legs, and bring Abby high enough for the cargo cycle to slip underneath. She rests on top of the trunk, so they reorient her, fit her curve more securely into the opening, her jaunty drawer pointing upward.

Zoe smooths her palm over Abby again and again, too happy to think, too broken for relief. Sophia presses her hand on Zoe's back, guiding her toward Chatan's waiting cycle. Before they step out of

Lone Tree's powerful shadow, they pause, reluctant to leave. Sophia switches off her torch, and Zoe does as well. They stand for many breaths, looking up, across the shadowed space, then turn as one and slip out of Lone Tree's embrace.

Once they reached the cycle, Sophia looked down at her torch, Zoe's, the cycle, Abby wedged securely in the trunk's opening. The women looked at each other, set down their torches, and lifted Abby out of the cargo cycle, lowered her to the ground. The torches went into the deep trunk first, and then the two women bent to hoist the companion upward once again. After Abby was reinstated, they climbed onto the cycle and turned their faces toward the ascent to Overlook.

The homeward journey was uneventful. The cycles sped across the plain, Lone Tree shrinking behind them, up the steep path, no longer terrifying, and emerged onto Overlook and into the darkened forest. Mateo's prediction was correct; the cycles had no need of lights, able to detect obstacles around them. Zoe rested her head on Sophia's shoulder, adrenalin draining away, exhaustion claiming her. Sophia shifted to wrap her arms around the sleeping Zoe and held her securely until the cycles eased their way up the shallow ramp into the ship's bay, victorious.

Zoe woke as they stopped and rubbed one eye. She straightened out of Sophia's embrace and looked back to the cargo cycle, Abby perched atop. The women lifted Abby onto a recharging station, and with a final pat, left her for the night.

Sunlight flooded Zoe's room as she woke and stretched. She turned onto her side and gazed at the forest-patterned companion who hovered next to her bed. She reached out to pet her friend, a sob catching in her throat, her belly shuddering, a slow tear seeping onto the sheet.

~ 45 ~

MOVING-BEYOND

Claira trotted around towering trees, coming at last to their secret glade, the Arbans stilling at her approach. Varlan followed close behind, and they knew that Rinala approached. Claira and Varlan settled themselves beneath their favorite Arban, a different favorite each visit. They heard the swoosh of Rinala's wings and watched her slant through branches, down to where they waited.

As Rinala alighted, Claira threw herself into her path, flung her arms around the feathered neck. Varlan rushed to stretch her holderlings to their limit and pulled both against her chest. Claira's face was wet with tears. Varlan trilled, and Rinala purred. The trio rocked and swayed, comforting themselves.

After many breaths, Varlan released her friends. Claira smoothed her palms down Rinala's chest, while Rinala ruffled and arranged her gossamer wings into their usual bright pattern across her back.

"We couldn't find you. I was so scared." Claira scrubbed salty dampness from her cheeks. "We both were scared. It was horrible, losing you." Tears sprang anew. "You're here. You're back. I'm so glad you're back."

Varlan trilled and ran a holderling along a gossamer edge.

Rinala shrank into herself, sinking her head, wings drooping.

"My fault.

My fault.

Broken Jamina.

Broken Lafonda.

My fault."

Varlan paused her caress, curious. "Your fault? How? Why?"

"Eglans shy.

Eglans careful.

I show Art.

I persuade.

Eglans brave.

Eglans crash.

My fault."

"Of course it wasn't your fault." None of them had heard Harper arrive. They startled and spun to see her approach from across the Arban glade to settle next to them under their favorite tree. Harper reached her hand to caress Rinala's bent head, smooth the feathers of her cowered neck.

"My fault."

"That's one way to look at it," Harper agreed, "but I don't think it's a helpful way. It's not true, you see." She waited a breath, two, smoothing feathers. She reached below Rinala's trembling chin and lifted her head to look into green eyes.

"You were so very brave." Rinala blinked, and Harper continued. "You showed your family what was possible. Many of them had never seen Art or imagined themselves able to do such a thing. You awoke in their hearts a beauty, a possibility. A longing."

Rinala blinked again.

"Eglans are gloriously creative. They soar through the sky and see vast expanses of beauty and life. They soar and glide. They draw paths on the sky. They weave the air. They dance with the sun.

"You showed them something new, and their hearts burst with eagerness. Once Jamina gave permission, they flung themselves into Art, and their eagerness blinded them."

Harper saw that she had the attention of the youngsters, so she sat back, after a final smoothing of an orange chest. She nestled herself onto the Nourish-ers and settled in for a longer description. The youngsters recognized Teaching and settled themselves in for a longer listening.

Harper closed her eyes for several breaths and then looked at each listener in turn, smiled into their eyes. "Eglans are imaginers, visionaries. They see beyond. Art is natural to them. Watching them spring into Art that morning at Home Base helped me realize the importance of Eglans creating Art. They are born to it." She peered into Rinala's lowered eyes. "*You* were born to it. Your family, too.

"You brought a great gift to your family. Narsis use their holderlings to knot fibers into glorious Art. Art flows from their eyes and their hearts, out through their holderlings, and into those fibers. Eglans can share in the knotted fibers and embrace the beauty of Art created by Narsis, but they haven't been able to knot themselves. You have shown them a way to create Art of their own.

"Remember your yearning? Remembering your first painting, the Art you and I created together? Remember your delight in seeing Art that came from your own imagination, through your own efforts, your own learning? Remember?"

Rinala remembered.
    "Art.
    Art love.
    Create love."
Harper nodded. "Yes! You love creating Art. You gave that gift to your family. You gave them a miracle." She paused. "The fact

that Jamina and Lafonda crashed was due to their excitement and enthusiasm. No fault lies with you. Jamina and Lafonda are healed. Everyone was frightened, especially for their Head-er, but they're both fine."

She ran her index finger down Rinala's chest feathers and tweaked her beak. "You gave a miraculous gift. You did not cause a tragedy."

Rinala blinked. She lifted one sturdy foot, the other. She shook her flamboyant tail.

"Art.
Family Art
Together Art."

Harper brought her knees to her chest and grinned at the trio. "Yes. I have an idea precisely about that."

Three heads perked.

"I followed you here today, Claira. I saw you leave Inipi." She paused a breath and took the plunge. "I saw your meld threads and guessed that the three of you were meeting together. So, I followed you."

Varlan spoke her astonishment. "You see meld threads?"

Harper nodded. "Yes. Since the very beginning practically. It's something I can do. I don't know why. It actually took me quite some time to realize that others *don't* see them. I haven't asked others, but it seems like no one else sees them."

Varlan found her words. "Narsis hear and see their own meldmates threads, but no one else's. That's how a meld stays strong. Pure. You can only find your own meldmates' threads." She paused, cocked her head. "Do you join others' melds?"

Harper shook her head. "No. Only with you three. I've never even tried with others. It seems...intrusive, somehow. No, I just *see* them with others." She paused. "They're beautiful."

Claira spoke up. "I see them."

Varlan and Rinala stared at her. Harper laughed outright.

"I thought so! I didn't want to tell on you unless you wanted to say it yourself." She laughed again. "Have you always seen them?"

Claira nodded. "From the very first. Since I was born. Pond held me and showed me how to be awake."

"Are others awake?"

"Not really. Sort of. Sometimes."

Harper nodded. "That's how it seems to me, too."

The foursome talked the language of friendship under their Arban, with openness, thoughtfulness, exploring mysteries. Harper returned them to thoughts about Together Art and, at the right time, revealed her plan.

"One of the reasons I suspected that Claira could see meld threads comes from watching her walk through the forest." She turned to Claira. "I see you send out threads to every tree that you pass. You hold the threads for a long time. You create a long lacework of threads that trails behind you through the forest. You can blend with many things at once." She paused, and Claira nodded.

"I'm thinking that you might be able to *conduct* Art at Home Base."

Claira wrinkled her forehead at Harper.

Harper continued. "If the Eglans are willing to try again, to create Art that will hide Home Base, you could be the conductor."

Claira's eyebrows drew together.

"When I lived on Earth, there were many concerts, gatherings of musicians."

"Like last night?" Rinala asked.

"Some were exactly like last night. But others were much more formal. Someone would create the music ahead of time, and then all of the musicians would memorize the music or read it from a page while they played. Everyone would come together, and they would play their part exactly as it was written. All of the parts would weave together into a beautiful pattern. It was lovely. The entire orchestra would become a single, *gigantic*, musical instrument, much more powerful than the individual instruments.

"In order to help each musician play exactly the right note at exactly the right time, one person would conduct the orchestra, helping everyone time their parts precisely together. The conductor could also, with specific movements of their hands and arms, even their eyebrows! they could signal to the individual musicians to play more loudly or softly. The conductor turned the orchestra into the gigantic instrument. It was magnificent to watch and to listen."

Harper turned back to Claira. "I think that you could be the conductor, and the Eglans could be your instrument. Instead of music, the Eglans would be a giant, multi-brushed, paint brush. They could work together in a graceful dance, and you could help them know where to go and when."

A light blossomed on Claira's face. Then faded. "I can't see what they're doing. How could I tell them where to go if I can't see what they're doing?"

Rinala jingled her gossamer wings.
"Me!
I see.
I watch.
With me
You see.
You watch."
Claira's light brightened again.

Harper thought for a breath. "There would be a lot of moving Eglans to keep track of..."

Varlan chortled, "I could do that part!" She rippled her many holderlings in an elaborate cadence. "I'm the best..." She searched the air above Harper's head for a word..."juggler in our burrow. I could keep track of where everyone is and where they should go!"

Harper looked back to Claira. "And you could connect them all."

Claira's brightness blossomed. "That part would be easy."

Rinala hopped excitedly.
"Three!
Three conductors.
Art!
Together Art!"
Harper fluttered her hands at the sky. "Yes! Together Art! No one would crash, *and* we could help Home Base."

Rinala paused her hopping.
"Crashing?"
Harper paused her hand dance, lowered them to her lap. "We would start small and then add Eglans as Varlan got used to juggling them." She looked from one youngster to another. They remained subdued. Harper sat up straight. "It might be time to move-beyond."

The trio looked at her, and she could feel them move through many emotions. Together, they decided on trust.

Harper closed her eyes and entered stillness. She breathed several times and opened her eyes. The Arban grove sprang into brilliance around them. She felt the interwoven awareness that encircled Airon, at one with all that is. She looked at Rinala and saw the entangled threads that strangled her heart. Harper reached with her awareness and patiently untangled the threads, smoothing them into place, watching Rinala's heart brighten and glow.

Next, she disentangled Varlan's heart and turned to Claira's. Each heart brightened as fear and loss melted away, dripping onto the Remove-er families that stretched to snatch the fear and loss out of the air, carting it away, far away, to be tended and transformed by the rich intelligence of Below.

At last, Harper bent to kiss each forehead, smooth love into each cheek.

Harper breathed deeply, blinked several times, and the brilliance of the Arban grove softened into its everyday color. She leaned toward the three young friends, glorious in their resolve, and whispered, "Let's go save Home Base."

The Art-Together Committee sprang up and flew, flowed, and trotted away from the Arban grove, heading for Burrow, in search of Vargad and Jamina, Head-ers.

~ 46 ~

TOGETHER ART

The Eglans alighted amongst the trees bordering Home Base. Their strong feet did not stomp. Their flamboyant tails did not rattle. Eglans stretched their many wings and settled.

Harper sat with Claira under one of the trees on which the Eglans perched. Harper held Claira's hand and smiled assurance into her eyes. The day before, Jamina and Vargad, Varlan and Rinala had sat together in this very spot, along with a small collection of Earthens. Ava, Harper, Chatan, Aadhya, and Claira made themselves as small as possible, hugging knees to chest, hunched. Even so, Rinala peered from behind Jamina, trembling in the presence of so many Earthens. Varlan settled next to her and extended her holderlings to pull Rinala close to her side and sat rumbling of bravery, trust, confidence.

The multi-species committee spoke of many things, but mostly about hiding Home Base from the intruders, the shocking blending of the three youngsters, and the possibility of Together Art. Jamina consulted with her meld, a fluttering dialog as JaCoMaTuRi resolved their ongoing debate over the wisdom and risk of helping the Earthens. Likewise, Vargad consulted with his meld, and VaSoDeLa gained a fragile agreement, with support for the Earthens.

JaCoMaTuRi and VaSoDeLa agreed to set aside the ongoing shock of the blending of the three youngsters. Repercussions were vast and beyond imagination. They acknowledged the need for present action for present need. Thwarting the intruders was a great need.

Today was the day. The Eglans settled on their favorite branches and waited for their Head-er to Head. The memory of the horrifying crash of Lafonda and Jamina remained bright in their memories, tempered by the resolute confidence of Jamina.

Overriding all was the promise of Art. Every Eglan had watched Rinala on that fateful day weeks ago, had watched her dip her wings in pigments, soared! and banked, glided and swooped. The ballet of Above blended with the creation of Art was beyond imagination. Every Eglan yearned to enrich their day, their world, with dancing Art.

All eyes examined the display of rich pigments, ready for the dipping of their wings. They recognized the waiting colors of their beloved canopy over which they soared! every day. Their dreams had been filled with imaginations of this day, this dancing Art.

The concept of a conducted dance was unimagined. Yet every Eglan recognized its possibilities. Every Eglan was ready to soar! into Together Art.

The Earthens had tried their best during the weeks of healing for Jamina, Lafonda, and in the end, Rinala. They had used brushes and stretched arms to reach as high as they could on many of the dwellings that made up Home Base, replicating what they saw of the forest around them. The waiting Eglans cocked their heads, squinted their eyes, tried to match the pigmented walls with their familiar canopy.

They blinked, shook their heads, and refocused on the array of pigments in their waiting trays. Once again, their imagination soared! Gossamer wings flexed and stretched.

Waiting was hard.

Claira stood and walked to the center of the Green. She sat on the soft Green and closed her eyes. Harper watched her meld threads stretch to retain connection with the hearts of Rinala and Varlan. The threads shone bright and crystalline, a shimmering, icy blue. As Claira stilled, Harper saw tentative threads emerge from where Claira sat and draw themselves across the Green.

A dozen threads shimmered in the morning light. These threads were faint, a golden opalescence. They wavered their way across the Green and up into the trees where the Eglans waited. One, two, four, all threads found an Eglan, paused before each, and then brightened as the Eglan accepted the connection. The threads strengthened; the golden hues became crystalline, solid.

Varlan flowed onto the Green as Rinala launched herself toward Sun. Varlan settled next to Claira, wrapping her long torso close to Claira, a comma embracing its dot. Rinala soared! and banked, rejoicing in Above, under Sun, above Forest and Home Base. Then she settled into a gentle circle with Home Base as her epicenter, focused on Claira, Varlan, and the waiting Eglans.

One, four, a dozen Eglans launched into the air, spread their many wings and rejoiced in Above, under Sun. Their eyes grazed Home Base, their trepidation of white-white-white soothed by the golden threads that connected them to the small Earthen below, calm, calm, calm.

Varlan juggled a dozen Eglans, kept them separate, guided their swoops and glides. Varlan brought them closer to Home Base, while

Claira soothed their trepidation of close, close, close. Varlan's mind emptied, and all she knew were the dozen Eglans as they wove an intricate dance, skimming the shelters of Home Base.

Rinala swooped low over the trays of pigments and memorized their hues and placement. She rose above the twelve, and brought forward her memory of creating Art, the dips and dives, the swoops and brushings. She added her love of Canopy, in all its color-filled wonder. Her mind emptied, and all she knew was twelve brushes and 108 waiting canvases.

Together Art began.

Eglans swooped and dipped, swooshed and brushed. Eglans rose and spiraled, dipped and brushed.

Claira's heart took over her mind as Eglans swooped, Varlan juggled, and Rinala imagined.

Claira sent out four, eight, twenty new threads, paused as each found an open Eglan heart, paused as threads were accepted, as they brightened and gained golden strength. Twenty Eglans launched, rejoiced in Above, and joined the dance of Together Art.

The final group of Eglans launched, rejoiced, and found their cadence of Varlan's juggle. White-white-white whittled away and moved toward oneness with Forest.

At last, Rinala recognized the need for drying time for pigments. Claira recognized encroaching fatigue of Eglans and her melded triad. Varlan brought all of the Eglans high and spread them apart, where Claira released them, one, eight, thirty, all. Eglans soared! and schooled, swept above Home Base, and cocked their heads. They could once again see for themselves the whole, see Forest emerging to disrupt white-white-white.

Eglans banked and soared! to ponds and streams, where they spent the rest of the day bathing, grooming, and resting with nourishing families, recalling the glory of Together Art, eager for tomorrow and the next, days spent in Together Art and the hiding of Home Base.

Earthens emerged from shelters, roamed Home Base, oohhed and aahhed at splotches of the forest sprawled, flattened yet three-dimensional, along walls and across domes. As night fell, silent eyes raised to the sky as the new star rose above treetops, brightening and engorging, every night. Every night.

A turquoise cloud swept from the encircling forest, flowed across the Green, wings dipping, spiraled above the melting away of white-white-white, then disappeared beyond waving branches.

Lone Tree shimmers in bright air, stretches feathery branches toward Pond, and sings of mystery and encroaching New. Lone Tree turns toward High Cliff and breathes its song along its way.

The Arbans sing to the sky, and the Shosens listen. The Arbans dance in the wind, and the Shosens dip, weaving patterns to shift the air and stir the wind.

Airon stirs in her sleeping orbit as she hurtles around her glorious sun.

~ 47 ~

NEXT WAVE

The embryo convoy paused in deepest forest. To break the tedium, Scarlett, Henry, and Michaela rotated through the three vehicles, taking turns driving each one. They traveled only at night, which added to the tedium. The vehicles did not require lights to maneuver around trees and consistently avoided meadows. The intruder's position was unknown to them, so they moved with the assumption that they could be seen.

The ship had erased its memory of the embryo convoy, of the embryos themselves. The ship knew nothing of Scarlett, Henry, and Michaela; no records of their existence remained. The lab carried a small memory cube that would restore the ship's memory, if that opportunity came about. But for now, this small band with its crucial contents, its secret mission, had disappeared from the face of Airon.

The convoy wandered aimlessly, continuously on a vaguely eastern heading to prevent circling. Initially, they had headed south, but soon turned east to confound any observation of their departure. The vehicles knew where they were, how to return, but only the vehicles held the memory.

One vehicle contained the embryos and their laboratory. The other two were housing. Scarlett and Michaela would share one, while Henry would shelter in the smallest of the three. Long used to solitude, they had hoped for a third housing caravan, but they were out of time. They would make do with what they had.

The three Earthens were under no illusion about this undertaking. It would be hard, isolated, far from Home Base and everything they knew. Their mission was open-ended. Would it last several days? The rest of their lives?

Would they be the only survivors?

They hoped to find Narsis, if they were prevented from returning to Home Base.

On their eighth day of exile, a miracle tapped on Scarlett's window.

They had driven throughout the night, stopping only when first light filtered through the canopy. Scarlett clambered down from the lab transport and waited for Michaela's caravan to come to a halt next to her. She held out her hand, patting the air for the still-invisible caravan, found it, and slid her palm along its side until she found the door latch. Once inside, the two women lowered shades, feeling their way around the small space.

Switching on internal lights only emphasized the claustrophobic space. Scarlett's skin crawled, and she purposefully deepened her breath. With a little more daylight, they would be able to go out-doors and find families where they could spend their day. Pulling camouflage fabric over themselves, they would blend perfectly into the forest floor. But they would be out of this tiny space, breathing fresh air.

Tap, tap, tap.

The two women froze.

Tap, tap, tap.

They stared at each other.

Tap, tap, tap.

It couldn't be ignored. Scarlett switched off one light as Michaela reached for the second. In the pitch black, Scarlett groped for the door handle and slid the door open.

She peered into the early dawn light, past trunks and bushes. She looked down. An Eglan watched her from below. It blinked. Words drifted into Scarlett's heart.
Lafonda help.
Find safe.
Safe glade.
Lafonda help.
Relief flooded through Scarlett, and she gasped.

"What is it?" Michaela whispered.

"It's an Eglan. Lafonda. The Eglan who crashed and fell. He wants to help us."

Michaela stared.

Tears sprang to Scarlett's eyes. "He wants to help us. He'll take us to a safe part of the forest. A glade. He showed me a picture."

Michaela found her voice. "He'll be able to tell us if anyone's following us. He can be our eyes and ears."

Scarlett nodded, breath escaping her in a rush. "Yes." She turned back to Lafonda, made to step down. Lafonda hopped to make room, and both women stepped onto the forest floor, barely visible in the dawn light.

Scarlett sat cross-legged in front of the Eglan. "Can we bring Henry? Are three Earthens too many?"

Lafonda rattled his tail.
Three.
Three, three, three.
He hopped several times in random directions.
Three.
Yes bring.
Bring Henry.
Three.
He hopped several more times while Michaela found her way to Henry's caravan and knocked on the door. "Henry?"

A muffled voice leaked out to Michaela. "What? I'm just getting in the shower."

"Wait 'til later. There's an Eglan here. Come out and see."

The three Earthens sat respectfully, Lafonda at a safe distance.

Scarlett fought to control her voice. "Thank you for helping us. I've been afraid, thinking of the three of us out here on our own, not knowing what's going on. I am so grateful for your help. Thank you."
Lafonda help.
Jamina agree.
Lafonda stay.
Stay help.
Scarlett safe.
Lafonda help.
Meld tell.

Meld know.
Lafonda know.
Lafonda tell.
Scarlett lifted her face to the canopy, closed her eyes in relief. "The Eglans know everything that's happening. Lafonda's meld will keep him informed. He'll be able to tell us what's happening." Her voice cracked. "We'll know what's happening."

Michaela swallowed a laugh, and Henry plopped backward onto the ground, arms spread-eagled.

"We can do this," Henry whispered. He cleared his throat and found his voice. "I didn't see how we could possibly pull this off, but now I can see it. We'll be able to do this."

Lafonda rattled his flamboyant tail.
Scarlett safe.

~ 48 ~

WINDOWLESS

Timothy noticed it as soon as he walked into the dining hall. A green and blue planet hung next to the starship, brilliant against the black expanse of space. He stopped in his tracks, adding to the bottleneck of shipmates who paused, others who jostled to move past. A scattered handful of people stood holding their bowls of broth, mesmerized. Others moved distractedly toward their chairs, balancing bowls as they stared out the window.

As Timothy collected himself, he pressed toward the kitchen interface, groped to retrieve his bowl, and shuffled to his seat, opportunely situated next to the transparency beyond which the planet floated. He lowered his bowl to the table, almost spilling it, moving in slow motion, staring at the planet.

A thousand questions blossomed and fled across his mind. What planet was this? Where were they? Why had the starship stopped? Would they land? Was there hope?

Timothy's heart pounded, and he had trouble breathing. He recalled himself enough to bumble into his chair, but he could not pull his eyes away from the planet.

It had continents and oceans, polar caps. It rotated sedately, on a slightly slanted axis. Its terminator, its twilight zone, slanted across the globe. Timothy could see the line creep onto a continental mass. No lights sparkled in the night zone. Was the planet uninhabited? Was it primitive, still in a pre-energy age?

How long had he sat here? Was he behind schedule? He looked down at his bowl, the broth no longer steaming. He picked it up and drank quickly, noisily. He scanned the dining hall. Most chairs were empty. He was late. Sweat sprang in his armpits, on his palms, his forehead. He was late. There would be repercussions.

He stood abruptly, almost knocking over his chair. He caught it, steadied it, held his bowl in his free hand. He glanced toward the window one last time, eyes wide, breath shallow, and slunk across the dining hall, weaving around tables and chairs. He was late.

He set his bowl carefully, deliberately, into the recycle chamber and hurried into the corridor. He wiped a hand across his face. Should he hurry and risk raising his heart rate even higher? Should he saunter, give himself time to calm down and risk arriving even later? He couldn't think clearly.

Where were they? Is that planet habitable? Would they land? What was going to happen next?

In the end, his fear of retribution, his anxiety over his nano system reporting his abnormalities, overrode his curiosity, colored his hope. He slowed his pace, took deep breaths, wiped his forehead, turned demurely into the office space, and casually wended his way to his desk. He sat, thumbed his screen awake, attached his tubes, and scanned the first set of data.

He thought that he might have gotten away with it. He focused on the numbers and images scrolling across his screen and forced away thoughts of the planet, what it meant, and tomorrow's morning meal. What will have changed?

Datasets. He focused on his datasets, determined.

The next morning, Timothy forced himself to move through his morning protocol at his habitual speed. He stood at the shaving mirror, stared at his reflection, stared into his own eyes. What was going to happen? Despite his best efforts, his heart pounded. He turned deliberately from the shaving mirror and entered the morning stream of shipmates heading toward the dining hall.

Timothy sensed a quickened pace around him. It seemed as though they moved more purposefully than was their habit. The corridor became crowded, their pace slowed, as they approached the dining hall. Heads craned. Shoulders jostled. The air thickened with anticipation.

The window was gone.

The starship must have filled it in yesterday, last night, sometime since yesterday's morning meal. He tore his eyes away from the expanse of blank wall and waited to pick up his bowl. Most heads turned toward and quickly away from the blank wall. Steps faltered, shoulders drooped. Timothy knew that everyone had noticed the lost window. A smattering of faces had reacted openly, just as he had. Everyone regained normalcy as quickly as possible.

Timothy could feel the quickened hearts, the bated breaths, the wiping of sweaty palms around him. He forced his mind to nothingness. He could not panic. He closed his eyes for a breath, felt the person in front of him move away. He focused blindly, stepped forward, accepted the bowl that waited for him, and walked to his usual table, next to the broad window that was now a blank wall. Thoughtless. He went thoughtless.

He couldn't stay thoughtless. What could this mean? His heart pounded. Had they left the planet already? How could they know? The planet was gone from view, and beyond the planet, the stars. Would the window come back? What would he do if he couldn't look at the stars? How could he content himself with stored images, now that he had basked in the beauty of the stars every morning for all these months?

His breath caught as he sat down, and he struggled to master himself. A wave of claustrophobia swept over him, the proximity of the blank wall feeling intrusive and alien. Imprisoning. He closed his eyes again and took a steadying breath. His nanos must be allowing fluctuations in his monitored signals on this second morning of change. Relief and gratitude flushed through him, as he continued to master himself.

He turned his head slowly, as if stretching his neck, bent his head to the side to increase the stretch, to increase the innocence of the out-of-place movement. He scanned the room, searching for reactions in his shipmates. He saw none.

Months of traveling across space, living day to day with starship-dictated routines had trained them all to blend in. Blending together into an anonymous mass was the safest way to avoid consequences. He had no idea what consequences might await him, should he continue to deviate from the norm, the expected. He did know that occasionally a seat in the dining room might be suddenly empty, empty for days on end, then refilled with a familiar figure, now pale, and with perhaps a healing welt across a chin or forearm.

He knew that consequences must be avoided.

As he drank his broth, he noted a growing grogginess. He was being sedated, then. Would he be sedated enough to have to return to his room to sleep it off? Would he be allowed to go to his desk, awaken his screen? He had no preference. His desk had shrunk and his office mates crowded to the point of brushing elbows if care wasn't taken. His room was little more than a torpedo chute with a thinly cushioned lining, the ceiling inches above his face. He found it hard to breathe most nights.

This room. This room with its window had been his daily refuge, where he could breathe fully, where he could stargaze and set his soul to peace. He glanced at the blank wall that brushed his arm with every movement. He realized he was grieving.

The grogginess intensified. He had reacted too strongly to the planet yesterday, to the loss of window today, exceeded acceptable parameters. Sleep then. He would be sent to sleep. He stood and carried his bowl to the recycling alcove. He must not delay. His sedative would be perfectly timed to allow him to reach his torpedo chamber. If he lingered, he wouldn't make it; he would most likely collapse in the hallway.

He entered the flow of the busy hallway, steered himself mechanically through successive junctions until he stood before his crawl space. The door slid open soundlessly, and he crouched to crawl onto the soft flooring. He didn't have time to remove his day clothes or pull covers over him. He simply slumped and lay, drooling onto his sleeve.

~ 49 ~

RESISTANCE

Morning stillness ended in the expected manner, with Michael toning an escalating note, which others joined, filling the gathering hall with a melodious tranquility. From there it veered into unexpected territory.

Mateo rose to walk to the front of the room, ready to deliver his daily updates on the ship, the intruder, memory storage, and related tangents. He innocently splashed into the topic of the companions, the approaching need to deactivate them, and store them securely within the ship.

"What's our timeline?" Michael asked.

"We're there." Mateo shrugged away the inevitability. "We're asking the ship to recall the companions this morning. As soon as they're all onboard, they'll be deactivated."

"No!"

The single syllable rang across the hall. People looked around to see who had spoken. Jaws dropped at the sight of Zoe rising to her feet, standing red-faced and white-knuckled.

"I won't do it."

Mateo wasn't sure how to respond. He groped for a neutral response. "You won't have to do anything, Zoe. The ship will do it all."

Zoe stamped her foot, its stockinged status undermining the vehemence of her message. "I won't do this. I refuse to cooperate."

Olivia stepped in to help. "Why, Zoe? What's wrong? We've all agreed this is an important part of camouflaging Home Base."

Zoe wiped a tear from her cheek. "That discussion was weeks ago. Things have changed."

Mateo asked, "What things?"

"For one, I've had time to think about this more. I've decided I won't cooperate."

Olivia asked, "What has made you change your mind?"

Zoe looked around at the faces watching her. Was she the only one? Her heart faltered. She closed her eyes, and immediately images flashed through her mind, Abby floating next to her bed each morning, Abby laying lifeless under Lone Tree, Abby zooming away from her in the forest, the emptiness of Abby not returning.

She steeled her resolve.

"I won't give up Abby. The rest of you can unplug your companions if you want, but I won't do that to Abby." She gulped. "She's my friend." Zoe's emotions spilled over and spattered around her feet. "She's my friend, and you just *took* her! You took her away, and then you didn't even *try* to get her back. You just *left* her out there, all alone." She swallowed a sob, hiding her face in her hands. "And I couldn't find anyone to help me bring her back. Everyone was too busy." Sobs. "Only Sophia. Sophia got the cycle from Mateo, and she went with me to find Abby. Sophia helped me bring her back."

Olivia threaded her way to where Zoe stood, wrapped her in her arms, smoothed her hair. Zoe's sobs shook her small frame, too overcome to care that everyone watched her.

Tom stood up. "You know. Maybe we've got this all wrong. Well, not *all* wrong, but maybe we've taken things too far." He glanced around the room. "Maybe we're trying too hard." The only sound was Zoe's gulped breaths.

"Look. We know that this starship is coming. We know it's coming from Earth. We know our ship decided it's dangerous. But, you know, maybe it's not."

Tom held up his hand, palm facing Mateo, who had drawn breath, on the verge of speaking. "Hold on," Tom continued. "Let me just say this." He looked around the room again. "Our original intention was to buy enough time to get the ship's memory replicated and hidden away. That's the only reason we painted the buildings..." he waved his hands..."or got the Eglans' help in painting the buildings. They've done a great job."

Olivia helped Zoe back to her kneeling bench. Claudia, sitting next to Zoe, took her hand, hugged her shoulder. Olivia settled onto the floor next to Zoe, shifting her full attention to Tom's points.

"So, we've accomplished that. Home Base is hidden. But, look. All this other stuff? Deactivating the companions? Hiding inside our shelters? Afraid to go outside? Is all that really necessary? For how long?"

Tom lifted his hands, inviting others to see reason. "This new starship is coming. We're going to be sharing a planet with them. They're going to find us eventually. How much hiding are we willing to do? For how long? Are we really going to eliminate the things that make life here meaningful?

"I've heard people talking about not coming to the gathering hall any more. There goes community gatherings. Do we want that? Or not going to the dining hall. Do we want that? Are we actually going to dig up our gardens? Ask the forest to come back in? Are we going to stop seeing each other? Give up our friendships?" He motioned to Zoe. "Her companion is obviously a good friend, an important part of her life. Why are we asking her to give that up?"

Tom turned to Zoe. "It was my idea to send Abby to help Rinala. I'm really sorry that we bungled that so badly. We all assumed it would be a quick fix, and that everything would go back to normal. I actually didn't even know that Abby didn't make it back. I'm really sorry you couldn't find help, and I'm really glad that Sophia stepped up and helped get Abby back here. You've been through a lot, and I'm really sorry how all of that played out."

He picked up his original train of thought.

"Nobody talks about needing an extra week now. All the discussions are open-ended, as if we're going to live like this for who knows how long. I don't feel any joy around these things. So, maybe we're trying too hard. Maybe these things won't take us where we want to go.

"It's good that Zoe spoke up this morning, because she's right. Things have changed. We've had a chance to think, time to see how it feels to live the way we're talking about living. Does anyone feel any joy about all of this?"

Tom's hands dropped to his sides, and he sank to his seat on the floor. He looked toward Mateo and gestured with his palm. "Your turn."

Mateo stared at his feet for a few breaths, unsure how to move forward. He straightened as he looked around the room. "Thoughts?"

The discussion started slowly and gained momentum. A growing consensus centered around the possibility that the intensity of their focus over the last six weeks had blinded them to alternatives, taken them out of balance. Discussing alternatives now brought a flicker of brightness into the room, allowing more and more creative ideas to surface. A sense of relief became palpable.

As the discussion wound down, Mateo ticked points off on his fingers to summarize their decisions.

People willing to give up their companions would send them to the ship for deactivation for an unspecified time. People deciding to keep their companions with them could do so, but, starting at midday that day, the ship would completely deactivate the companion network. Active companions would be on their own, without transmissions between the ship or other companions. They had a week to try it out, and if people found isolated companions to be not worthwhile, they would send them to the ship for deactivation.

People were free to come and go, encouraged to attend twice-daily gatherings and at least weekly meals. Care would be taken to move under forest cover as much as possible. The Green at Home Base and Inipi's pond would remain off limits for an unspecified time.

Michael would carry the updated strategies to Inipi for their input.

When the gathering adjourned, Zoe returned to her shelter and sat, resting her forehead on Abby, smoothing her palm along her friend's forested surface, again and again.

~ 50 ~

TAINTED

The first landing pods emerged from the intruding starship and drifted down to Airon's surface. Wind encouraged each pod to drift toward a rocky outcropping, vacated earlier by soil and families, washed clean by a miniature flood, Below working swiftly to save everyone from the crushing weight drifting down from Above.

Four pods arrived in this first wave. They settled onto their rocky outcropping and stabilized themselves. The undercarriages did not blend with the outcropping, but stubbornly perched where they landed, separate and indifferent.

A turquoise cloud dodged and swirled below Forest's canopy. A thousand birdlings darted through branches, around trunks, invisible from Above.

Above was sacred, in all remembrance. Above held Sun. Wind and Breeze danced through Above and tickled Forest and Meadow. Eglans soared! and birdlings skimmed through Above. Above held all, covered all, breathed all.

When The 108 arrived, the ship landed immediately. It drifted down from Above, touched its rocky outcropping, and settled. The 108 emerged, explored, wandered, created Home Base. Above remained sacred, untainted. Eglans soared! and birdlings skimmed. Sun cleaved its path, and Narsis lifted their faces to its warmth.

Life on Airon continued, unchanged, except for a narrow circumference around the Newcomers that watched and waited. The widespread enormity of life continued, unchanged.

In contrast, the intruder starship hovered in menace high above Airon's surface. The intruder starship tarnished Above, infected Above with threat and spying. Eglans glided below Forest's canopy, avoided Meadow. Narsis mourned Meadow, sought out forested wanderings. Earthens mourned companions, and Home Base avoided their Green; Inipi avoided their pond. Eglans mourned Above, a mourning greater than could be endured; Eglans abandoned soaring! an abandonment greater than could be endured. Birdlings mourned skimming, banking, schooling.

By attempting to protect Airon from change by hiding from the intruders, all life on Airon changed.

Forest spread leaves wider, offering obscurity to those who wandered its depths. The forest floor darkened, and Narsis wandered carefully, their burrow eyes helping them see while holderlings encountered dimmed complexities never encountered in tidy Burrow. Nurture-er and Remove-ers spread their leaves broadly, capturing what light they could. Forest sent shaded families what it could from its bright canopy, Below shuttling nutrients sent down from canopy and across from Meadow.

By protecting Airon from intrusion, everything changed.

Four pods drifted down, settled, and waited, unmoving.

Airon spins on her axis, dreaming, roaring along her creeping path around her glorious sun. Once, she spins, twice, thrice. Still the four pods waited, unmoving. The surrounding forest held its breath.

Birdlings hop, hop, hopped behind Forest's protective branches, peered from behind broad leaves, waiting.

~ 51 ~

INTRUSION

On the fourth day, four figures emerged from each of the four pods. Doors slid open simultaneously. Ramps extended down to lean against the expectant outcropping.

Forest held its breath.

A single figure appeared at the top of each ramp, paused, and shuffled down the ramp to step onto rock. A second figure appeared in each doorway, followed by a third and fourth. Four figures descended four ramps and stood in four clusters.

Birdlings watched.

Each figure was encased in white. Head-shapes were identifiable, as were arms and legs; puffy; entirely encased.

Forest dripped soothing aromas and Breeze wafted them in a gentle swirl around the intruders. The aromas bounced off white-encased figures and sank to splatter onto the rocky outcropping.

Birdlings watched.

Forest sent calming vibrations from roots, which splashed against rocky shores. Meadow families displayed their richest colors, spread leaves in welcome, spewed joy into the air. Mechanical lenses detected but failed to transmit the transcendent colors to the encased minds. Breeze drifted joy and welcome to splash and sink into the rock on which the isolated figures stood, unmoving.

Strategies that had worked so well during the arrival of The 108 proved futile with the intruders. Nothing could penetrate the white encasements. The intruders stood, unmoving, successfully isolated.

The sixteen intruders turned as one and retreated up ramps and through doors. Four doors slid shut.

Birdlings blinked, looked one to the other, shuffled along branches, and settled in to wait.

The following day, sixteen figures emerged, stood on outcroppings, and waited, encased in white. At long last, they shuffled onto the dainty meadow that splashed against the outcropping. They bent to peer at the families, who spread to meet the scrutiny in welcome and joy.

The isolated scrutiny seemed to satisfy the intruders, because they turned as one and retreated behind closed doors.

Day followed day, emergence and retreat followed one after the other. Birdlings watched and blinked, shuffled and waited.

Forest grew ever more curious. On the fourth day of white-clad exploration, curious vines crept across the rocky outcropping and stretched to touch the underside of one of the pods. Immediately, the white figures straightened and turned toward their pods, pointed at the curious vine.

Forest ignored them, intent on the texture that the curious vines explored. Vines branched and stretched, covered a portion of the pod's underside, extending up its side.

The white figures scurried across the dainty meadow, up ramps, tumbled through doors that promptly slid shut.

Birdlings watched.

Forest continued its examination of the landing pod and sent messages across the distance to Home Base. Curious vines stretched out from Forest's edge and explored the surface of the gathering hall. Comparisons were made across the vast forest, differences noted.

The vine on the landing pod extended its curiosity, wrapped around the landing gear. The door slid open and all four figures stomped down their ramp, carrying implements. They circled the pod, grasped the curious vines with clumsy fingers and pulled them away from the landing gear. They reached far under the pod to pull vines away from the underside, while others pulled vines away from sides, everywhere the curiosity had explored.

They chopped as they went. They chopped the curious vines into bits, ignored the writhing, and threw the pieces onto the outcropping. They stomped and crushed. They pulled and chopped. When they were satisfied with their destruction, they ripped protective booties from their feet and gloves from their encased hands and threw them onto the meadow. They wiped their implements with reeking cloths, once, twice, thrice, and threw the contaminated cloths after the booties and gloves.

Satisfied with their frantic decontamination, the four figures stomped up their ramp, and the door slid shut.

Forest watched, stunned.

Birdlings waited.

The four landing pods lifted from their rocky outcropping and drifted into invisibility, high into Above.

Birdlings swarmed the rocky outcropping, gently taking hacked pieces into their saddened beaks, and carried them into Forest. The outcropping was soon tidy, except for the alien droppings that sprinkled white on the peaceful meadow. The birdlings offered the hacked vines to waiting families, families who reached and embraced, soothed and coddled. They carried away essences of terror and destruction, of conquering, ruling, overwhelming, carried them far away, where they were transformed and dispersed.

Birdlings drifted through Forest, dodging and darting, spreading their message of conquering, ruling, overwhelming.

The Arbans sing and dust the waves with sorrow, sending their song to Lone Tree who spreads beneath tainted Above. Above, which holds Sun, but also holds intruders. Intruders who conquer, rule, overwhelm.

~ 52 ~

TRANSPORT

Mateo ratcheted the final memory cube in place aboard the transport vehicle. Ten cubes sat ready, filled with memory. Filled with the ship. He ran his hand over the smooth surface and stood.

He turned to face the small screen. "That's it. We're ready."

"Yes," wrote the ship.

Are you satisfied that we have everything?" He gestured to the waiting cache.

"Yes."

"We'll leave at dusk."

"Yes."

Mateo couldn't think of anything more to say.

Words scrolled. "I'll be here when you return."

"How do you know?"

"They've been in orbit a week. They haven't rained down fire and brimstone yet."

"That's not funny."

"Yes it is. You're just not in a humorous mood."

"It's hard to leave, not knowing what will happen here while I'm gone."

"It should only take you two days."

"Two?"

"One day out. One day back."

Mateo nodded. "Yes. Two days."

"Yes." A pause. "Take care."

"Oh, good idea. I hadn't thought of that, but now that you mention it, I'll be sure to do that."

"That's funny."

"No. It's not."

"Yes, it is. You're just not in a humorous mood."

Mateo shook his head. "You crack me up."

"Yes."

Mateo smoothed his hand down the wall, felt the familiar vibration. His fingertips lingered at the corner of the screen, and then he turned, walked the transport vehicle to the opened door. He paused at the top of the ramp. "Take care."

"Yes."

He could see the short reply from where he stood. He brought the vehicle down the ramp, and positioned it under the tree that marked their trailhead, their path toward the secret burrow. He trudged to his shelter, flopped his long frame across his bed, and stared at the ceiling. He brought up one hand to grasp his forehead. "I hate this."

As dusk thickened, Mateo tapped on Dhiren's doorway. "Ready?"

Dhiren followed him to the tree where the memory cache waited. "Well, mate. We did it."

Mateo shook his head. "Not yet we haven't."

Dhiren let his hands dangle from loose wrists. "Cheer up, mate. Doesn't help to be so glum."

"We'll be gone for two days. A lot can happen in two days."

"Yeah. But we have to do *this*. We've been waiting all these weeks to do exactly this. Everyone will be okay while we're gone."

"You don't know that."

"No, not completely. But I have a lot of trust in everyone here. They'll know what to do, no matter what happens. Everyone is trusting us to do our part. That's how it works." He waited. "We should go."

Mateo nodded. They climbed onto the cycle and set off.

The cycle remembered the way, isolated inside its firewall. As usual, it followed the breadcrumbs that Mateo had spread along the path weeks ago, minute electronics that paired only with the cycle.

It was a long night. The memory cache was enormously heavy. The transport vehicle's many wheels distributed the load, but it had to move slowly in order to leave no trace. They lumbered along.

Dhiren fell asleep almost immediately. He leaned back on the cycle's broad seat and the soft rocking of their passage lulled him into oblivion. Mateo was not so lucky. He was consumed with worry. This memory cache was the last piece of their strategy. Once it was securely tucked into the deep tunnels of the secret burrow, everything would be in place. Then what would they do? What would happen?

They had done it. Home Base was painted. Some of the companions lay inside the ship, the rest scattered silently in shelters. The embryos were on their way to who knew where. Inipi was buttoned up. The Narsis were warned. The Eglans had melted away. Even the birdlings had disappeared. Everything was so still.

Except for this last cavalcade. Would they make it undetected? Would they be able to get everything stored, get it deep enough into the tunnels? Would they make it back without being discovered? And, oh stars, would everyone be safe at Home Base? Inipi?

Mateo drained a water orb, stored the empty under his seat, leaned back. The night air was cool on his face, his arms. He couldn't sleep.

After an eternity, the cycle nudged up a familiar incline. Mateo could just see a dark shape move against the lighter cliff behind. Alarm shot through his muscles.

"You are come."

"Yamdha?"

"Yes."

Relief made Mateo dizzy. "You startled me."

"Yes."

"Why are you here?"

"Each time, it is hard for you to find the entrance. Each time, you search. No time to search. I find entrance for you. No need to search."

Mateo nodded. "Especially in the dark."

"Narsis know dark."

"Yes."

Dhiren stirred and sat forward. "Are we there?"

"Yes. Yamdha is here, too."

"Okay..."

"He can see in the dark."

"Oh. Right. Good, then."

Yamdha ran his holderlings over the transport vehicle, examined the memory cubes. "I take."

"Wait, wait, wait. Yamdha, those are too heavy to lift."

"I take."

He did. His holderlings extended and, one after the other, he removed the securing cables and clutched each cube to his chest. Ten times he disappeared into the seemingly solid hedge. The Earthens busied themselves with gathering discarded nuts and bolts, straps.

The night was just beginning to fade when Yamdha bent to examine the transport vehicle.

Mateo peered at the hedge that shielded the burrow's opening. "Will it fit?"

"Yes." Yamdha popped off a tire, two, four, eight. The Earthens shook themselves out of their surprise and bent to each lift a tire, and shuffled through the hedge where, miraculously, the burrow entrance yawned. They set down their tires and rolled them into the tunnel. Yamdha had left the memory cubes near the entrance, so they stacked their tires just beyond the cubes and returned for more tires.

Yamdha had removed the rest of the tires and was examining the chassis. His holderlings easily twisted bolts loose from their nuts, and the sturdy transport vehicle soon lay in neat piles. Mateo and Dhiren dutifully carried the piles into the burrow and rejoined Yamdha at the cycle.

"This is Chatan's cycle?"

"Yes."

"Send it to Home Base."

"We'll take it back."

Yamdha huffed. "We stay."

"We'll stay the day, put everything away in the burrow, and then we'll take it back tonight."

"No. We stay."

Mateo and Dhiren looked at each other, back at Yamdha. Dhiren asked, "Stay? Why? For how long, mate?"

Yamdha settled into teaching mode. "Many words float above your head. Much fear and anxiety. Home Base is not safe. Inipi. Perhaps Vargad's Burrow is not safe. You," he pointed a holderling at Mateo, "you," a holderling at Dhiren, "Yamdha," the remaining holderlings folded toward his chest, "we protect the ship's remembrance."

The Earthens waited.

Yamdha continued teaching. "Remembrance is high important. Highly," he corrected himself. "We protect remembrance." The perplexity hovering above the Earthen faces did not clear. "Intruders come. Home Base not safe. You. You. Yamdha. We cannot be at Home Base. We are link to remembrance. To secret burrow. We must stay with the ship's remembrance. Only way to protect."

Yamdha watched understanding dawn above them. He loved these moments, these discoveries that brightened youngling faces. He loved teaching. He rumbled happily.

"Cycle retrieves breadcrumbs on way back to Home Base. Safer." Yamdha turned to the burrow, disappeared behind its sheltering bushes.

Mateo leaned against the cycle, crossed his arms. "I hate this," he muttered.

"He's right," said Dhiren.

"Yes."

~ 53 ~

INTRUSION 2.0

The second landing followed soon after the first. The intruders had a prescribed schedule to maintain, and despite concerns over the unexpected entanglement of native flora, the timeline couldn't be adjusted. A new set of voyagers were selected. They nervously gathered and squeezed into the four landing pods at the appointed time.

Koral was used to maneuvering inside tight spaces and maintained a deep-breath routine on the journey down. He heard the shallow breaths of his shipmates and smiled into their faceplates, encouraging them to draw air deep into their lungs. Training in protective clothing was one thing, and all of them had finished the training well within acceptable parameters. But being shoehorned into this slender capsule and feeling the floor drop away beneath them was quite another thing.

The drop took less than fourteen minutes, according to the starship's timer. All sixteen voyagers managed to keep their fear in check throughout the descent. Koral nodded success to his shipmates. Their wide eyes stared back at him. He didn't know their names. Social interactions were deemed unnecessary and discouraged. But they knew each other's faces. His nearest shipmate awkwardly wedged her arm beneath his and grasped it to her side. He bent his elbow to give her a steadier anchor.

As the landing pod stabilized, Koral looked at the ceiling, low above their heads. He craned to peer around him, wondering about controls or hints about their mission. They knew nothing. Koral assumed the starship would tell them what to do once they disembarked.

He didn't have long to wait.

Their door slid aside soundlessly, taking his arm-grasping shipmate by surprise. She lost her balance, and would have fallen through the gaping doorway if Koral had not steadied her. The other two made no move to help. She smiled gratitude at him, and shuffled around to peer down the ramp.

She glanced at Koral who nodded, and stepped onto the ramp, paused to look at their surroundings, then baby-stepped her way to the rock spread below the landing pod. She paused again before moving aside to make room for the others. Koral followed her to the edge of the quiet meadow that spread beyond their outcropping. They gazed out to the forest that crowded the far side of the meadow.

The colors. Even through the tinted faceplate, Koral could see a myriad of colors. He heard a choir lift its voice, heard it sing out with joy. He turned to his shipmate and spoke one word. "Koral." She nodded and spoke one word in return. "Lisa."

A trumpet exploded across the choir, and Koral lifted his hands to grasp his helmet. He twisted it briskly counterclockwise and lifted it off his head. A shrill alarm sounded at the first hint of the twist, drowning out the trumpet, so Koral threw the helmet and its alarm as far away as he could. It bounced on the rock and skittered to a halt, alarm bleating pathetically.

Koral turned back to Lisa, nodded, and fumbled his way out of his suit. Lisa watched in fascination, glanced at the motionless, white figures turning in their direction. They made no move toward them. Lisa grabbed the sides of her helmet, twisted, grimaced at the shrill alarm, and threw her helmet after Koral's.

Koral kicked away his suit and turned, naked as a newborn, to help Lisa escape hers. He glanced at the rest of the landing party. One white figure lurched, stumbled his way toward them. Koral increased his effort in freeing Lisa, but a second glance showed the stumbling figure twisting and throwing his own helmet aside. Koral held Lisa's elbow as she pulled her feet out of the suit and reached with his other arm to catch the stumbling figure.

Lisa and Koral worked furiously at the third suit, pulling it away from wrists, wriggling it past hips and holding the man steady as he pulled his feet free.

"Koral."

"Timothy."

"Lisa."

They stared at each other, amazed at their own daring, and turned to watch the remaining thirteen figures. As one, they turned to scoot up ramps. A single figure paused at the foot of the ramp, waiting for the others to ascend. The pause lengthened. The figure turned, twisted off his helmet, and lurched toward the waiting three. Once his suit was thrown aside, the foursome turned to watch the landing pods.

One door remained open, its ramp extended. A solitary figure emerged, strode down the ramp and headed toward the mutineers. The helmet stayed in place, the strides unmistakably determined. The four deserters turned, ran across the meadow, and dove into the shade of the forest.

They ran in a frenzy, chaotically, but managed to stay together. The lack of destination did not hinder their flight. Their sole purpose was distance.

Forest pondered this unexpected development. Earthens rarely ran, never this randomly, frantically. The single remaining intruder had stopped at the meadow's edge, watched the fleeing shipmates disappear through towering trees. The figure turned and retraced its steps up the ramp. The door slid shut.

Forest turned its focus to the fleeing Earthens. Their pace slowed. One clutched his side. They slowed even more and stumbled along as best they could, helping each other. When they could run no farther, they stopped, waists bent, hands grasping knees, labored breathing filling the air.

Lisa was the first to sit. With a thankful exhale she lay back.

Timothy hadn't seen nakedness for years. He wasn't sure what to do, where to look. He decided to stare at his feet while he regained his breath, then he, too, sat and sprawled. Closing his eyes was an easy solution to the confusion that pummeled his senses.

Koral straightened and peered back the way they had come. He lowered his head, closed his eyes and listened for pursuit. He stilled his internal choir and listened intently. He looked up, but the canopy was too thick to see the sky.

Could they trace them through their nanos? Would it be impossible to hide? How long could they last out here? What would happen if they were brought back?

As his breath slowed, Koral noticed the sensations that crept up his legs. He moved one foot, then the other. Was this vegetation safe? Should they have kept their suits?

No. He was sure that his first reflex had been the right one. The suits were filled with technology. They would have certainly found them, had they kept their suits.

The tingling in his legs distracted him again. He thought he could smell ocean air, hear waves. He looked around, but couldn't tell in which direction the ocean lay. But he did notice the colors.

Without the interference of his faceplate, the colors burst into vibrancy. The trees dripped color, trembled with aromas. Koral breathed deeply, relishing the freshness of living air. He closed his eyes and drank it in.

His tingling legs distracted him again. His eyes frowned open as he felt himself swoop and bank. He flung out his arms to regain balance. Were these plants drugging him?

"We should keep moving," he said to the others. "It might not be safe to stay here. Maybe we can find a cave or something."

Timothy struggled into a sitting position. He looked around them. "Where do you think we are? What planet is this?"

Lisa's voice was soft. Dreamy. "Airon. This is Airon."

The newest deserter gaped. "Airon?"

Koral frowned. "How do you know?"

"It just is."

Koral watched her. Shrugged. One name was as good as another. The tingling distracted him again. He wanted to sprawl like the others, but something fought against the idea. He shook his head.

"How about if we keep going? Can you manage walking farther? We can look for a cave, some type of shelter."

Lisa was the hardest to rouse, but they got her on her feet. Koral pointed. "Let's keep heading away from the landing site."

They set off, Lisa groggily trudging along. Her vision came into focus as they walked, and she was able to keep up with the others. Koral set a steady pace, watching the others for signs of flagging. They all kept an eye open for somewhere to shelter. Koral worried what the night might bring.

Koral held out his hand to the fourth escapee. "Koral."

"Brian."

They nodded in unison.

Timothy said, "Names. We have names."

~ 54 ~

SAFE

Rinala followed the Earthens along their escape route. When they stopped to breathe, she flew back to the landing site and showed Varlan and Claira that the four landing pods remained, doors closed, Earthens cocooned inside. She swiftly retraced her path, landed on her favorite branch, and peered around a broad trunk to glimpse the four Earthens as they sprawled atop families.

No skins, she observed.

No clothes, Claira agreed. Claira considered this oddity. She imagined them feeling scared, wandering through the forest without clothes. She threw words to Rinala.

How big?

Rinala cocked her head. *Big?*

Four Earthens. How big? Home Base. Which Earthens are the same size as these four?

Rinala considered.

Jacob

Michael

Jacob

Olivia.

Claira shot back, *Two are the same size as Jacob?*

Jacob. Jacob.

One is a woman?

Olivia.
I'll find clothes. You bring?
Rinala bring.

~ 55 ~

FURY

Samantha's fury burst onto her screen. Why wasn't she told? She typed feverishly. "I've been waiting days for more memory, and Koral was scheduled to install the crystals today. Why was he chosen to leave the starship? Why are we still at this planet? Why are people being sent to the surface? What is going on? Who's going to install my crystals?"

She pushed away from her work station and surged to her feet. She paced. Even consumed with fury, she noted immediately that her office had shrunk. She was forced to shorten her fourth stride before turning to continue her pacing. She knew, *knew* that she always had four long strides whenever she paced. She attacked her screen. "Why is my office smaller?"

Samantha threw open her door and erupted into the hallway. She counted her strides, knowing that her team captain should respond before she reached 487 steps. A cold anxiety crawled up her spine that maybe she would no longer qualify for prompt responses. At 220 steps, she about-faced and strode back to her office door, flung it open, and stood glaring at her screen.

Seconds ticked by. Samantha resumed pacing, swiveling her head to maintain her scrutiny of the unresponsive screen. Her team captain was using all of his time allowance. She wondered if he would actually flaunt his power over her by exceeding his allowance, breaking this measurable parameter. Would he dare?

She watched the timer tick toward 0:00. Would he dare? With one second to go, words streamed onto her screen. "The first landing team struggled in the confinement of the landing pods. Koral was well suited for the second landing team."

Samantha blinked. The message ended. She waited. She leaned closer toward the screen, gripping the chair back with white knuckles.

Nothing more.

Samantha picked up the chair and slammed it onto the floor, again and again. He had answered only one of her questions. That was a measurable insult as well, along with waiting until the last allowable second to respond.

Fury drove her back into the hallway. She could barely breathe. Her mind skittered across options. Who could she report this to? She thought of her fellow diners at the midday meals but flung the thought aside. They were nobodies. Whoever they were, none of them would be useful to her.

Who could she message? Who owed her a favor? Who was beholden? She had consistently discarded people once their usefulness dimmed. One of her great strengths had always been to never look back. Who could she persuade now? Who was available to her now? She wanted answers.

As her fury ebbed another thought flashed into her awareness. She had to get back to her office. How long had she been out here? Had she touched her screen while waiting for Earth's answer? Were her own measurable task-parameters threatened?

Samantha jogged back. The increased energy output brought her breath into obedience. She flew into the office, smoothed her fingers across her screen, confirming her presence at her station. She righted her chair, scrabbled to reattach a wheel, and settled herself to face her screen. She took a moment to smooth her face and stiffen her shoulders.

Samantha's fingers skated across her screen. "Any further information?"

Perfect response. It implied that she had been politely waiting for her team captain to complete his response to her reasonable queries. She was nothing if not reasonable. "When will the second landing team return? I need to adjust my timelines based on this unexpected delay in memory installation."

Her breath and heartrate were back to normal. Her nanos permitted periodic emotional flares, given the stress and demands of her position. Samantha prayed to no one that her quick recovery and repression of emotion had remained within her elite parameters of permitted tension release.

She brought up old data sets, preparing to document the passing time as productive while she waited for Earth's response to her reasonable query.

"The landing party awaits the return of four explorers. Mission completion time cannot be calculated at this time."

Samantha froze. This response was tagged as coming directly from the starship. Samantha realized that this response hadn't come from her team captain; the starship had responded to her query directly, supplanting the team.

Direct communication from the starship was rare. Samantha seized the opportunity.

"Is the remainder of the landing team searching for the four missing explorers?"

The cleverness of this query ignited Samantha's excitement. She implied that the four were missing. She doubted that the starship would detect the implication and answer with naïve truthfulness.

"The landing party awaits the return of four explorers."

Not as informative as Samantha had hoped, but the starship did not deny the implication that the four were missing, as opposed to simply carrying out a mission.

Over the next four days, Samantha continued her private conversation with the starship despite the starship's patient refrain, "The landing party awaits the return of four explorers." Samantha drew on her considerable skills to maintain her habitual work load, while researching solutions to her predicament of delayed memory installation. Her increasingly creative search queries eventually displayed an option that stole her breath.

"Officers have the authority to instruct the starship to land on a planet whenever any of the following parameters are met:" One of the listed parameters stated "in order to retrieve a missing person."

Samantha sat back, mouth open. Did she have the authority? Was she an officer? There was no crew, so 'officers' couldn't refer to crew members. Were the midday-meal attendees...officers?

Another strength Samantha possessed was blind daring. She was a risk-taker. She raised her fingers, poised over her screen. She plunged.

"Land the starship in a suitable location on the planet's surface in order to retrieve our four missing persons."

~ 56 ~

BLENDING

"My hydration portal is gone." Koral examined his thigh. "It must have fallen off without me noticing it." He bent low over the flawless skin. "It's as if it was never there." He rubbed his thumb deep into his thigh. "No scar tissue. Nothing. It's just gone."

Timothy pointed. "Your drain portal is gone, too."

Koral ran his thumb down his abdomen. "Yeah. That one went missing yesterday."

Lisa lay curled on her side, her back to the men. "Mine are gone, too."

Timothy said, "Mine are still here."

Brian nodded. "Mine, too."

"How come we keep hearing the ocean?" Lisa asked. "Can you smell it?"

Timothy nodded vigorously. "It's been driving me crazy. I can hear it and smell it, as if it's just beyond those trees," he waved in a random direction, "or those." He waved in another. "It's everywhere, but it's nowhere."

Brian breached another mystery. "How come our nanos aren't screaming at us?"

"Do they ever scream? Have yours ever screamed? I mean, since you first got them?" Timothy asked.

Brian thought. "No. But I've always been afraid they would scream. Since the first day." He brushed his hands across the tiny plants that covered the forest floor. "They never felt right. It's like when you get contact lenses. There's this adjustment period, and then they stop feeling foreign in your eyes. But the adjustment never happened. I've hated them from the first."

"Do you regret getting them?" Lisa asked.

"Oh, stars, yes." He flopped back onto the ground, rubbed his eyes with his fists. "I didn't want them in the first place, but everyone at work had them. I was pretty sure I'd get fired if I didn't get them, too. I got the cheapest ones I could find, just to join the gang." He sighed, and his arms flopped outward. "I don't think I fooled anyone though. I still couldn't keep up. I never got another promotion, so I couldn't afford an upgrade."

"I was never able to afford an upgrade either," murmured Lisa.

"How did you get onto the starship? How did you qualify?" Koral rolled onto his side, bending his elbow to support his head.

"They had this aptitude test. You had to make up stories based on a few sentences that they gave you. I was really good at that." He scoffed. "It took twelve years, but I finally found something I was good at." He scowled. "And the next day I woke up on the starship."

"You didn't apply?" Lisa sounded shocked.

"Nope."

The group fell silent.

Lisa changed the subject. "I think these plants have something to do with the nanos. I think they weaken the nanos somehow."

"What do you mean?" Koral asked.

"Well. Whenever we rest, especially at night, there's this soothing feeling that seems to come up from the plants."

Koral nodded. "I've noticed that, too."

"You have?"

"Yes. I noticed it the first day, whenever we stopped to catch our breath. Just standing still. This…feeling would creep up my legs. I'm thinking it's some kind of drug."

"Like an herbal remedy?" Timothy asked.

"Well, maybe. Something like that." He rolled onto his back. "You can feel it." He closed his eyes. "It just seeps up."

Lisa asked, "Do you think it's affecting the nanos?"

"No idea. What makes you think that?"

"That crawly feeling under your skin? It settles down."

"Maybe we're too far from the starship for the nanos to be active." Timothy said.

"Is that a thing?" Lisa asked. "Back home, if people went into the wild, did their nanos go dormant?"

"I've never heard that," Koral answered. "There were never any warnings in the literature."

They lapsed into silence.

"It's backwards now." Koral said.

"What is?" Brian asked.

"Before, on the starship and at home, I had to be so careful to not think about anything except what I was doing, the task I was performing. Otherwise my nanos would report me, and my boss would tell me to stop wasting time and stay on task. Here, I've been concentrating on everything else in order to ignore the nanos." Pause. "They might be screaming at me, and I'm just really good at ignoring them."

"Did they really just kidnap you and put you on the starship?" Lisa asked Brian.

"Yep." Brian replied.

Koral broke the ensuing silence. "Let's keep walking."

~ 57 ~

HERDED

Timothy tramped along, eyes determinedly scanning the canopy. He was certain he'd seen movement. The trees moved with the breeze, of course. The brightly hued flowers dipped and swayed, twirled around their thick central stems. But this was different. This was sideways movement. He was certain that an orange bird had glided through the trees, paralleling their path. On the third sighting, he pointed to bring his discovery to the attention of the others.

Before he could speak, he tripped forward, feet entangled by a pile of clothing. He scrabbled backward, spooked by what might have grabbed his feet. The others turned at his yelp and thump and hurried to help disentangle him from his assailant.

Timothy lurched to his feet, grabbing Brian's arm, kicking wildly. "What the hell is that?" He backed into Koral, and they stared at the disheveled pile.

Lisa waited next to a nearby tree, hands braced against the trunk. "It looks like *clothing.*"

Koral stepped around Timothy, shuffled a few steps, bent to peer. He wished he had a stick. He reached and picked up an edge between thumb and forefinger, swept it aside quickly, let go. Nothing moved. He tossed another piece, a third. Still no movement.

As Koral disrupted the mysterious pile, the escapees moved closer, riveted. Nothing moved. Koral picked up the last piece, shook it thoroughly, and dangled it at arm's length. He risked his second hand to shake out the piece.

A shirt.

Koral held it up for the others to see. The remaining pieces underwent similar examinations. Befuddlement mounted. Four sets of clothing sorted themselves out.

Lisa looked around even as she held a skirt and blouse to her chest. "I don't know whether to be thankful or terrified."

Timothy stuffed one leg, the second, into his pair of pants. "I'm going with grateful."

The others followed suit.

"It fits," Lisa said, looking down at herself, around at the three men. "Everything fits."

Koral rubbed the hem of his shirt between thumb and fingers. "I've never seen material like this." He smoothed the shirt across his belly. "Who made this?" A pause. "Who left it here for us?" He looked into the forest around them. "Who knows we're here? That we'd be walking this way?"

Brian looked up through the dense canopy. "Well. It's not our people, that's for sure."

"No," Koral said. "It's somebody here. Somebody from the planet."

They peered past the trunks that surrounded them, up into the branches.

Brian asked Lisa, "Do you really think this is Airon?"

She nodded. He stared at his feet, shook his head.

"Why?" she asked.

"Just a coincidence," he answered.

"How? What kind of coincidence?" Timothy asked.

"Well. I've...I've...studied the journey to Airon. It would be too weird if that's where we've actually ended up."

"Why? What do you know about it?" Koral asked.

"Not much. That's the thing..." Brian searched for words. "They quietly disappeared."

Lisa's voice was sharp. "Who disappeared? What are you talking about?"

Timothy pointed excitedly. "There! There's that bird!"

"Where?"

"It flew in that direction. Come on."

They trotted after Timothy and his alleged bird.

~ 58 ~

INTRUSION 3.0

The third landing proceeded flawlessly, despite the lack of planning or collaboration shipside.

Airon, on the other hand, had been thick with planning and collaboration.

Forest observed the flight of the four mutineers and offered succor where it could. Meadow observed the inert landing pods and contemplated possibilities. Birdlings twittered and flitted, recalling the long-ago arrival of The 108.

Below flowed into action. Below had successfully cleared families and Soil away from the rocky outcropping that served as an arrival platform for landing pods. At the urging of the birdlings, Below busied itself in preparation for the arrival of the intruder.

The landing-pod outcropping was deemed too small to accommodate the intruder. Even the surrounding meadow was too small. Below grew still and contemplated its whole. Several possibilities presented themselves, and one option shown brighter than the others due to its proximity to the landing pods.

Forest liked the idea of keeping the intruders clumped together in one area.

Below got to work. Soil rolled and folded together to form a long, shallow hillock surrounding a nearby sheet of rock, shallowly buried. Meadow gathered together its skirts, so to speak, and pulled itself away from the hidden rock. Families migrated. Forest rearranged its branches. Birdlings purred approval.

As a finishing touch, Forest sent out vines to topple the four landing pods and pulled them around trees and shrubs, handing them off, vine to vine to vine. Discarded Earthen trash followed the astonished pods, vine to vine. Ignoring the muffled sounds emanating from each pod, Forest rolled them onto the edge of the newly exposed rocky outcropping, and with friendly pats, left them to await the predicted invasion. Earthen trash was piled neatly, patted into submission.

The toppling of the pods coincided with Samantha's reasonable request, "Land the starship in a suitable location on the planet's surface in order to retrieve our four missing persons." Just as alarms from the pods trilled through Above to ping the hovering starship, the starship embraced its newly acquired permission and landed itself in a suitable location. The starship judged a rocky outcropping as suitable since it lay next to the toppled and freshly scuffed landing pods, beached like dolphins on a distant planet, vulnerable and in need of assistance. White debris fluttered nearby.

Birdlings watched and Forest held its breath, soothed by the loving support of Below, who whispered assurances, and the loving relief of de-tainted Above, who sang of gratitude.

The starship lowered its ramp.

With so little forewarning, the intruders had no time to don suits and helmets, even if they had had access to any. Doors throughout the starship slid open, per protocol, and bewildered Earthens stepped into hallways and crept toward freshening air. The scents and vibrations that seeped up the open ramp and filtered into hallways, caressed ashen faces and soothed clenched hearts. Earthens inhaled joy and exhaled fear.

Forest watched the first Earthens shuffle down the starship's ramp. Birdlings flitted in expectation. More and more, then more Earthens emerged, blinking in the bright sunlight, drinking in the welcoming song that wafted silently from Forest and Meadow and Above and Below.

The four landing pods woke. Four doors slid open. Three ramps extended, askew, pointing in random directions, the fourth ramp grinding against the outcropping, helplessly useless. Three ramps sought ground and shuddered to a stop, having found none. White figures tumbled and crawled, four, three, two, three, all righted themselves and looked around, stiff-legged. One, four, all the white figures grasped their helmets, twisted, and set the bothersome technology on top of a small pile of white debris.

Forest noted the absence of implements. Urged by Above and encouraged by its brethren surrounding Home Base, Forest sent vines to climb and crawl, creep and probe. Vines extended and intruded, flowed up ramps and along hallways, into chambers and offices. Forest claimed the intruder and its landing pods, held them in its vise, captured their freedom to rise again.

~ 59 ~

SPY

Rinala held her wings perfectly still as she peered around an enormous trunk, perched on her favorite branch. She had witnessed Forest's relocation of the four landing pods, pondering Forest's intent, cocking her head at the muffled sounds that emerged from all four pods.

A slight movement Above caught her eye. A tiny dot swiftly grew into a gigantic replica of the ship at Home Base. Rinala shrank behind her branch, heart pounding.

Intruder!

Claira and Varlan urged her to continue her observation. Varlan rumbled reassurance. Claira whispered courage. Rinala peered.

The intruder landed delicately on the waiting outcropping. Rinala saw Forest exhale, heard Below cheer, felt relief blossom across Above.

Now, waiting on the sheltered side of her protective trunk, she watched the four pods laying on their sides, the gigantic intruder balanced precariously on deceptively thin legs, the entire scene eerily quiet in the morning sun.

Rinala stomped her strong feet, but refrained from rattling her flamboyant tail. She peered.

Rinala was the appointed spy, for Eglan, Narsi, and Earthen alike. Claira and Varlan peered through Rinala's eyes and reported to Burrow and Home Base all that Rinala observed. They saw what she saw, as clearly as if they were standing by her side.

All of Inipi had moved back to Home Base, reoccupying their original shelters. The Earthens felt reassured, having everyone gathered in one location. Wondering and worrying from a distance was not an Earthen strength.

So, Rinala peered, Claira and Varlan reported, and Nest, Burrow, and Home Base went about their expectant daily lives.

"They've landed," Claira and Varlan called out in unison. Their words floated across Home Base, through Burrow. "The intruder starship has landed."

~ 60 ~

RENDEZVOUS

"There's that bird again." Timothy pointed into the canopy.

"You keep saying that you see a bird. What bird?" Koral peered in the direction of Timothy's point.

"I *do* keep seeing it."

Brian asked, "Is it the same bird? Or just the same kind of bird? Maybe there are a lot of them."

"Does it matter?" Lisa asked. "Just knowing that there are birds here is amazing, all by itself."

Brian shrugged. "Just curious."

"There! See it? It's sitting on a branch. Do you see it?" Timothy pointed again. "Just beyond that tree with the lavender flowers hanging down. It's enormous."

"I don't see it." Brian held his hand to his brow, shading out sun dapples.

Timothy waved him over. "Come this way. Slowly. Don't scare it. About twenty feet up. Sitting next to the trunk."

"It's watching us," Koral said in a low voice.

"We're probably pretty interesting to it. New, never-before-seen upright mammal. We're its Bigfoot," Timothy said.

"Yep," Brian said. "It's watching us, all right."

"Hello!" Lisa called.

"Shshsh!" Timothy hissed. "Don't scare it."

"It's heard us talking for days now. It would keep well away from us, if it was scared." She squinted at the bird. "It's just shy."

"Well, don't scare it off," Timothy repeated.

Lisa looked at him, indignant.

"Please," he amended, then shrugged. "At least you've all seen the bird this time."

The bird raised its wings and swept away from them.

"See?" Timothy complained. "You've scared it off."

"No, look! It's waiting for us," Koral said.

Sure enough, the bird landed delicately on the branch of another tree, a short distance away. It hopped on its branch to turn and face them, settled its wings, and waited.

"It wants us to follow it," Lisa said. Something about this bird enchanted her. To see any wildlife after all this time on their own in the forest was amazing, but this bird captured her imagination. It seemed to be communicating with them. She wanted it to be intelligent. She wanted to be taken somewhere by intelligent life.

She wanted to be rescued.

They'd been wandering for two weeks. They'd lost their fear of pursuit, but they were besieged with unanswered questions. Why didn't they need food? Why wasn't there any fruit, or anything else that looked anything like food? Whenever she touched something, filled with curiosity, something deep inside her rebelled at the thought of bringing it to her mouth. Why couldn't they find the ocean? Even more baffling, where had these clothes come from? Who had left them in their path? What were these plants doing to them whenever they rested, while they slept?

Lisa was tired of not having answers. She wanted to find someone who had answers. She walked toward the bird. The others followed.

The bird waited, flew a short distance, waited.

"Where do you think it's leading us?" Timothy asked.

"I don't care," Lisa answered.

"As long as it's not back to the starship," Koral said.

Lisa glanced at him, wrinkled her brow. "We'll slow down if we come to a clearing."

A chill ran up Timothy's back. "We should keep an eye on everything around us. We need to be careful."

The bird led them for the entire morning. Koral wondered if they were actually headed anywhere.

"Should we keep going? This seems somewhat pointless."

Brian spoke with assurance. "It's leading us in a straight line. I think there's a destination somewhere ahead."

The bird's short flights, the way it obviously waited for them to catch up, encouraged them to keep following. The bird had a purpose, and they had been without purpose for too long. They followed.

The light ahead of them gradually brightened.

Koral stopped. "We're coming to a clearing." He chewed his lip. "Let's spread out."

"Let's be quiet." Brian said, brushing past a bush, causing its leaves to rattle. He grimaced. "As quiet as we *can* be."

They crept forward, paused behind trunks, darted from tree to tree. The bird cocked its head at them, waited, flew to another tree, waited, then soared into brilliant sunshine.

Lisa and Koral looked at each other. Lisa nodded. Koral leaned to catch Timothy and Brian's eyes. They nodded. The refugees crept forward, stayed hidden. Koral crouched and skulked forward to hide behind a trunk that stood on the edge of a small meadow. His breath stopped.

The orange bird was there, waiting for them, just as it had waited all morning. Instead of a tree branch, it perched on the roof of a small white building, one with a door, windows, and a distinctly Earth-like familiarity. Koral straightened, staring.

Logan squinted at his screen, befuddled by the prolonged silence from Earth. He huffed, fluttering his mustache, and rolled up the screen. Another day with nothing to do. Might as well just head back to Home Base. He'd been thinking about doing just that for a few days anyway. Nothing was happening here. Might as well.

He pushed back from his work station and examined his sparse belongings. He'd better take his companion, or else Ava would complain about his 'irresponsibility.' He frowned. There was nothing irresponsible about it. He just didn't need the thing. Hadn't needed it for weeks. Maybe he'd leave it behind on purpose, just to prove his point.

He stood and stretched. He'd go for a walk first. Hadn't been outside in a couple of days, so moving around would feel good before he climbed on his transport. Maybe that's all he needed. Just a walk. Then he could see if he still felt like heading out for Home Base.

He saw her as soon as he opened the door. "Olivia?" He squinted at the slim woman half-leaning against a tree, sort of supporting herself, palms pressed against the trunk. Was that Olivia?

He walked into the sunlight and waited. "You okay?" The woman didn't answer.

A movement caught his eye, and he turned his head to see a man move from behind another tree. A second man moved into view. Logan stepped back into his doorway, heart thumping. "Who are you?" A third man stepped out of the forest. "How many of you are there?"

Adrenaline coursed through Logan's bloodstream. His hands tingled. "Who are you?" His voice came out loud and demanding.

One of the men lifted both hands into the air. "I'm Koral. There are only four of us."

"Where did you come from?"

Koral hesitated. "Earth."

Logan's hand dropped from its grip on the door frame. He stepped into the sunlight. "From *Earth*?" Koral nodded. Logan looked from one to the other. He couldn't think. His ears pounded.

The woman spoke. "Can you help us? We've been wandering in the forest for a couple of weeks. Can you help?"

Logan stared for several breaths. A strong inclination to get under cover swept through him. He looked up at the sky. He still couldn't think, but he managed to ask, "There are only four of you?" The pounding in his ears lessened. He waited for their nods. "You'd better come in. I have a lot of questions. I want answers." He backed through his doorway, eyes peeled for signs of threat.

Lisa stepped forward. "So do we."

~ 61 ~

ENEMIES

"Your name is Logan?" Brian's palms were suddenly sweaty, and his face flushed hot. "You're Logan?"

"Yeah. It's a family name. Took a lot of grief for it when I was a kid. 'How fast can you run, Logan? Gonna run tonight, Logan?'" Logan took in Brian's red face and wide stare. "Why?"

The refugees had recounted a summary of their stellar journey, unplanned escape, forest wandering, and following the orange bird to Logan's doorstep. With the telling, their host visibly relaxed. Koral held out his hand. "Koral."

Logan accepted the handshake. "Logan."

Now, they stared at Brian's obvious consternation. "Why?" Logan repeated.

"Are there others here with you?" Brian asked.

Logan's eyes narrowed. "Why?"

Tension boiled into the room again.

Brian swallowed. "How long have you been here? On this planet?"

Logan's fists rose to plant themselves firmly on his hips. "Why?"

Brian glanced at his shipmates, realized everyone was staring at him. He focused on Logan. "Are you...Are you part of The 108?"

Lisa gaped at Brian, turned her stare on Logan. "The 108?"

Timothy asked, "What's The 108?"

Koral looked from Brian to Logan, back again. "What's happening right now?"

Brian took a deep breath. "The 108 was the group that went out about ten years ago and then just dropped out of sight. No one's heard from them since." He looked at Lisa. "Their destination was Airon."

Timothy shook his head. "Never heard of them."

"Yeah. Like I said; that's the thing. No one heard from them." Brian paused. "Everyone just forgot about them."

"How come you know about them?" Logan's eyes were narrow slits.

"Are you part of The 108?" Brian asked again.

"How 'bout you start answering some questions instead of rattling off your own." Logan's anger rippled the tension. "How come you know about them?"

Brian knew he had to come clean. He wished it wasn't now, but it would be worse to be found out later. "I've done a lot of research on The 108. I've followed them for years."

"Why?"

"It's my job."

"Why?"

"Because there's one or two people at the Agency who haven't forgotten. They recruited me to follow you. The 108."

Brian noted that Logan neither accepted nor denied the inference that he was part of The 108.

"Keep talking."

Brian took a deep breath. "I'm in charge of following any communication from The 108." He waited a beat, and then plunged. "I'm the person who answers all of your messages, Logan."

The two men stared at each other.

"What about Carlos?"

Brian looked at his feet, shook his head. "Carlos is dead, man." He looked up at Logan. "I'm really sorry, Logan."

Logan lunged at Brian, face contorted with fury, and got his throat as they tumbled to the floor. Timothy and Koral dove after them and pulled the two men apart. Lisa backed against the wall. They held Logan off as Brian climbed to his feet.

Brian's voice was calm. "I'm truly sorry, Logan. Carlos died two years ago. Pancreatic cancer. He went fast. His family moved in with her sister. Gloria's sister. They're doing well. Kids are finishing school, getting good jobs. They're all fine."

"Why? Why did you do this? Lie to me all this time? Why couldn't I just talk with Carlos?"

"You did talk to him. All the way up to his diagnosis. Then they made me take over. Until then, I'd just been monitoring the communication. But when Carlos got sick, I had to take over."

"Why?"

"Because we had to keep you talking."

"Why?"

"Because it was the only way to find you, man."

"What?"

"You were the only one still talking to Earth, and we needed your transmission to follow your signal here. We had to keep you talking."

Logan drooped, leant against the wall. He couldn't think with the pounding in his ears. A trap was closing, and he couldn't see what it was. Koral and Timothy released his arms and took a step back. Koral shrugged his shirt back into place.

"Why did you follow us here?"

Koral spoke up. "Because things aren't going well on Earth."

Logan blinked at him. "Why?"

"The whole nano thing." Koral looked to Lisa, the others, noted their blank looks. "People have been scheduling deactivations. It started to snowball a year before we left Earth. The writing was on the wall. The nano experiment is a failure." He paused. "People wanted their lives back."

"Why are you four here?"

Timothy said, "There are 662 others."

Logan's head reeled. "Who came *with* you?!?"

"Yes."

"Where are they?"

"We don't know. When we escaped two weeks ago, they were still in orbit."

Logan pushed away from the wall. He waved dismissively at Timothy who readied his fists. "Relax. I'm not going to attack anybody." He crossed his arms, groping for a way out of this whirling confusion. "So, why are all of you here? Why have you come?"

Brian began. "I have a theory. I think that our starship? I think that it contains the last of the diehards. The last of the people who *want* nanos and who were powerful enough to buy their way onto the starship."

Timothy asked, "Powerful? I didn't see anyone who seemed powerful."

"Well," Brian said, "they need their minions, if they're going to take over The 108."

He turned to Logan. "You and I have a lot to talk about; I know that. I have a lot of explaining to do. But let's wait until later for that. Right now, if there are 107 other people around, we need to warn them about what's coming."

Logan watched Brian's face. The pounding in his head subsided. This was an easy one. This was his to do.

"There are more than 108. There are babies to save."

~ 62 ~

FRIENDS

Logan's transport had room for all of them.

Logan opened his companion's storage cupboard, grunted as he lifted it and scooped it into Brian's arms. No time to activate him. Carlos. Logan's anger swelled, but he pounded it back. He'd named his companion to remind him of his childhood friend. Now, here he was with a dead companion and a dead friend. Later.

He paused at his work station, rolled up his screen, looked around the shelter. He had everything he needed back at Home Base. He could leave all of this here. He nodded at Brian and strode out the door, the refugees trailing dutifully. He waved them onto the transport and climbed behind the controls. He punched the indicator for Home Base.

As the transport picked up speed, Brian raised his voice. "Stay under the trees!" Logan glanced at him. Brian pointed up. "Stay out of sight."

They had over an hour of travel ahead of them. A question bubbled to the surface of Logan's mind. "How long were you guys out in the forest?"

Koral answered, "Eighteen days."

"What'd you do for food?"

Brian said, "We couldn't find any, but we never got hungry. Why is that? Why don't we get hungry?"

Koral said, "It's the nanos. I think they kept us from feeling hungry."

Logan shook his head. "I don't know what the nanos did, but the families probably fed you."

"No. We didn't see anyone the whole time we were out there."

Logan swept his arm across the low-growing plants who stretched in every direction. "These plants. Did you sleep on these plants?"

Koral nodded. "We thought that they might be drugging us, but there was nowhere else to lay down."

Logan shook his head. "They don't drug you. That's Airon. The families feed us. They remove waste and feed us nutrients. You don't need to eat at all. Home Base still gets together for meals; sort of a tradition. But the families take care of us."

The refugees looked out at the colorful carpet, awed and perplexed.

"Where's the ocean?" Lisa asked. "We never did see the ocean."

Logan guffawed. "That's Airon. I mean, there is an ocean way beyond, over there." He waved vaguely to the left. "But the ocean is one of the first things you sense when you blend." He glanced at Brian. "You did blend, right?"

Brain wrinkled his brow. "Blend?"

"Blend with Airon." Blank stare. "You know, fly around and connect with everything?"

Brian shook his head, brow still wrinkled. "Nope. Didn't fly."

Lisa spoke up. "I flew. Every time. It was just a dream, though."

"Yeah. I suppose you could call it a dream. But it's real." Logan paused. "Could you remember it afterward?"

"After what?" Brian asked.

"After you put your shoes back on."

Brian shook his head. "We didn't have shoes." Logan glanced down and noticed the bare feet for the first time. Brian continued, "We didn't have clothes at first. They put us in these space suits, naked. Probably so we wouldn't be able to run off. But, we ran off anyway, naked."

"Where'd you get the clothes then?"

"We found them," answered Koral.

"The bird brought them," added Lisa. Koral looked at her quizzically.

Logan asked, "An Eglan? An Eglan brought you clothes?"

Lisa nodded.

"Big orange bird?" Timothy asked.

"Yeah. They're pretty shy," Logan said. "Home Base must already know about you, then."

"Why?" Koral asked.

"Well, the Eglan had to get clothes from somewhere. It was either there or Inipi."

"Inipi?" asked Brian.

"Some people relocated from Home Base to a small settlement next to a pond."

"How scattered are The 108?" asked Brian.

Logan stared at Brian, silent.

Brian held up both palms. "I'm not a spy."

"Yeah. Spies never claim that."

"A spy wouldn't have confessed stuff he didn't have to."

Logan considered this logic. Nodded. "Just Home Base and Inipi. And me."

"How come you're out on your own?"

"I like being on my own."

The travelers fell silent, processing separate thoughts.

At some point, Koral asked Lisa, "Why do you think it was the...Eglan...that brought the clothes?"

Lisa shrugged. "I just do."

Brian said, "It makes the most sense."

They relapsed into silence.

Timothy felt the transport lose speed. "Why are we slowing?"

"We're about there." Logan peered through the trees. He could see the brightening ahead of them, familiar trees, but Home Base was nowhere to be seen. His heart quickened. What had happened?

As their transport stopped well inside sheltering trees, Logan's vision adjusted, and he saw pictures of the forest. Giant pictures where Home Base had once stood. He squinted. It *was* Home Base. The familiar white structures now blended into the forest, barely discernable.

"What the..." Logan stared in wonder.

"What? Why have we stopped?" Timothy asked.

"Welcome to Home Base," Logan gestured.

The refugees looked around. "Where?" Koral asked.

"Right in front of us. They've camouflaged it. Come on." Logan clambered out of the transport and walked past the few remaining trees. He turned and looked back. "Come on. Come and meet Ava."

"Ava?" Lisa's voice carried a quaver. "Ava?" She stumbled forward. She had trouble breathing. Sobs shook her belly. "Ava?"

Logan caught her arm, steadying her. "You know Ava?" Lisa couldn't speak. He led her around the Green-turned-meadow, onto a painted pathway, around a corner, up to a leaf-emblazoned door, and knocked.

Ava laid her sewing onto the workbench and pushed back her chair. She was happy for the interruption, looking forward to whomever had dropped by for a visit. Her jaw dropped as she opened the door. "Logan? Logan! I'm so glad to see you!" She noticed the eyes peering over Logan's shoulder. Stranger's eyes. "Logan?" she whispered.

Logan turned and guided the stranger forward.

Ava's mind froze. When she could breathe again, she whispered, "Lisa? Lisa?" She gathered Lisa in her arms, and the two women stood, swaying slightly. "Lisa?" Lisa could only sob.

"You do know each other…" Logan's bewilderment pounded in his ears. Too many mysteries for one day. Oddly, his brain held strong. "Ava, there are more."

"More?"

"More people."

Ava nodded. "There's a starship. From Earth. It's landed. In your direction, but farther away." Ava held Lisa slightly away to see her face, smoothed her tousled hair. "There's so much to tell. Will you come sit with me while I talk to Logan? Then you can tell me how you're here." Lisa nodded and wiped her tear-streaked face. "Oh, Lisa. I can't believe this!" Ava hugged her again. "Come sit."

Ava motioned Logan to follow them inside. Logan hesitated. "Ava, there are others with me, now. Here."

Ava nodded. "Three more?" Logan nodded, surprised. "The Eglans have been keeping us posted. We didn't have a way to get to you until Chatan's cycle came back this morning. By then, we knew these four had reached you, so we decided to wait for you to come here.

She added, "We didn't know where you were, how to find you. The Eglans didn't think to tell us until yesterday. We couldn't message you earlier, because the ship, our ship, warned us to stay silent. But now you're here, and I can tell you everything. There's so much to tell."

She turned with Lisa and led her to the couch. "Bring the others in," she said over her shoulder.

Logan turned to wave the three men forward and followed Ava into the sitting room.

~ 63 ~

THWARTED

Samantha turned where she sat on the rocky outcropping. They had been sitting here for an eternity. They were blocked from the starship by the vines that swarmed everywhere. They had no tools to clear the vines. One of the elitists whom she recognized from the midday meals had forbade them to touch the invasive vines. Another had forbade them to step off the outcropping. "The plants might attack you!" they had warned. So, here they sat.

A thick cloud of turquoise birds swept across the clearing. The intruders ducked, punctuated by shouts and cries of alarm. The birds banked, swirled, and swept across the tops of the nearest trees, disappeared from view.

Samantha heard a rustling behind her. She spun in that direction and sat up on her knees. Her chest was too tight to breathe. She felt faint. The vines were moving. They were withdrawing. She rose along with the others to watch the retreat. How could *plants* move that quickly? With obvious coordination? She peered at the encroaching forest. A threatening menace growled deep in her core.

"Get back in the starship." Her voice was strident.

"Wait!" called the same elitist who had ordered them away from the vines. "Wait!"

Samantha ignored him and stumbled toward the starship's ramp. She jumped over retreating vines, picking her way haphazardly from one clear spot to the next. She was not going to wait for whatever came next out from those trees.

She crouched just inside the bay doors, back pressed against the wall, watching the vines retreat. She stumbled across the loading bay, steadied herself against the door jamb leading to an inner corridor, and repeatedly pounded her palm against the controls. The main doors refused to close. What was going on?

A firm hand closed over her arm. "Wait until the others are on board!"

"I don't care about the others," she snarled. "Why won't this stupid door close?"

His hand tightened and pulled her arm away from the controls. "Stop. Get ahold of yourself. Wait for the others." He glared at her. "You always focus on the wrong things."

She flung his hand away and exploded into the corridor. She fled, stumbled, fell, regained her feet, and reeled into her chamber's open door. She slammed against the inner doorjamb and pounded the controls. Nothing. The door would not close.

Her eyes darted around the familiar room. She couldn't breathe. With the door open, she was exposed. Why wouldn't the door close?

She left off pounding and skulked deeper into the room, back pressed against the wall. Her hands groped the way to her bed, where she crouched in its farthest corner, and pulled the thin blanket up to clutch it against her belly; her only armor. She waited, panting.

People filtered past her doorway, occasionally glancing inside to notice her there, crouched. No one stopped to help her, check on her. They moved past, intent on getting to their own chambers. No one spoke. The corridor emptied.

Samantha had to pee. She unfolded her stiff legs and lowered one foot to the floor. Her leg was asleep. She tapped it on the floor, flexed her ankle, waiting for the tingling to fade. She stood, crept to the doorway, peeked out. The corridor was empty. Doorways on both sides stood open. Samantha stepped into the corridor and slunk along the wall.

She peered into the first doorway. A man sat with his back to her, working on his screen. He had a full-sized screen in his room? She hadn't been allowed one, and bristled at the sight of this man having more privilege than her. Why did he deserve a full-sized screen in a private room? She scanned the room. It was definitely bigger than hers. Her jaw dropped. He had an armchair!

She slipped past the doorway, her bladder urging her onward. She glanced inside each room, jealousy piqued, comparisons tallied. The bathroom was only a few doors from her own room, but each room she passed held a story, a string of stories that inflamed her fury.

On her return trip from the bathroom, she intently surveyed each room, confirming what she had feared. Every room was better than hers. Why did they deserve special treatment?

When she reached the final room, the man sat, arms crossed, waiting for her. She froze, feeling caught and at a loss. She made to move past, but he said, "Sit." She whirled her head and stared at him. He gestured to the armchair. "Sit."

Samantha shuffled into the room and perched on the edge of the chair, dredging up her best interview etiquette. This man, with his in-room screen and fancy armchair, was obviously more powerful than her. She clamped her hands in her lap and met his level gaze with one of her own.

"You brought the starship down."

Her mouth dropped. "What?"

"You told the starship to land. Why did you do that?"

"How do...Why do you think it was me?"

He gestured to his screen. "I know it was you. The tracking leads directly to your command. Why did you do it?"

Samantha caved. "Because Koral was going to fall behind. He was scheduled for an installation, and he was going to miss his deadline. It was my job to keep him on schedule."

The man saw through her cover up. "You and your memory demands. Do you even think about the repercussions of your actions?"

"This wasn't my fault. How would I know that the aliens would try to take over the starship? I was only doing my job." She panted. "Why are we even here?"

The man sighed and rubbed his forehead. "Look." He sighed again and dropped his arms to rest on the chair's arms. Samantha noted the arms. Her desk chair didn't have arms. Who was this man? She recognized his face from the midday meals, but who was he?

She gathered her scattered courage and stood up. "I have work to do..."

"Sit down." She crossed her arms. He scowled at her defiance and spoke in a steely whisper. "Your work is meaningless. It always has been. Sit down. We have to figure this out, and unless you want to end up in one of the hovels," he jerked his thumb toward the corridor, "you'll sit down and listen."

She jutted her chin and frowned. She flounced into the armchair, crossed her arms, and stared at him, sullen.

"Oh, grow up," he said. He turned back to his screen, as her chin trembled. "You've always been too spoiled for your own good." He moved his fingers across his screen for several minutes, frowning.

"Okay," he said as he swung back to her. "Here's the deal. You brought the starship down, and apparently it was held here long enough for the operating system to be hacked and taken over by someone or something." She gaped at him. "Yes. We've lost control of the starship, and it's your fault."

She went cold, followed by a rush of heat. "You can't blame this on me! I was only doing my job, and if I had known more, I would have acted accordingly. It's your fault for not keeping me informed." Her breath was short, and her words spluttered out. "What the hell is going on, anyway. Why are we even here?" she demanded again. "On this planet?"

He turned away from her. "You don't need to know that."

"If I knew more, I could help."

"How, exactly, would you help?"

"I'd know that, if you weren't hiding everything from me!"

"Your performance thus far has indicated otherwise."

"Give her a break." The voice came from the open doorway. "And for everyone's sake, would you please keep your voices down?"

A tall, thin man stood leaning in the doorway. Samantha recognized him; another elitist. She had enough presence of mind to hold her tongue until she knew whose side he was on.

"Let's get something to eat." The tall man pushed away from the doorjamb and headed down the corridor. Her adversary rose to follow. After a moment, Samantha followed as well, reluctantly intrigued.

~ 64 ~

CLEANSING

At Home Base, the dining room was at full capacity. Excitement over the refugees swept through the community, and all arrived at dinner, anticipating introductions and story-telling.

"Prepare yourselves," Ava cautioned the four newcomers.

All hands were on deck in the kitchen, orchestrated by Olivia. The cooks had spent the last hour chopping veggies from the hastily harvested gardens, sautéing, seasoning, baking. Tendrils of steam drifted from stacks of cooling flatbread, beans and lentils bubbled in savory sauces, fresh salads waited in wide bowls, glistening with dressing. Layered pans of lasagna rested on a sideboard. A feast of prodigal proportions.

Earthens gathered and chatted in small groups, passing baskets of blue fruit, their habitual appetizer. As flavor burst in mouths, senses heightened and stomachs awoke in anticipation of the now-rare, whole-food event.

Silence fell as Ava held the door open for the refugees. A single handclap exploded into a crescendo of applause, punctuated with hugs, back slaps, and blue-fruit baskets thrust into the newcomers' bewildered hands. Home Base blossomed into celebration, after untold days of dread and angst.

Olivia beamed at the surprised faces of the guests as they experienced their first taste of Airon's blue fruit. "An Arban grove lives nearby. They give us all the fruit we can eat." She paused. "It's the only native thing we actually eat. Everything else," she gestured toward the laden tables, "we grow in our Earthen gardens, hydroponic ponds, or fermentation vats." She smiled. "Just because we love food. Not because we need it, you see."

Koral nodded. "We're starting to understand that." His gaze roamed over the gathered faces. After years of sallow despondency, these Earthens, with their glowing skin and calm eyes lifted his spirits as nothing else had.

The community ate until they could hold no more. They laughed and told stories, delighted in shocking their guests. The refugees told sobering tales, sprinkled with shreds of hope. The 108 had left their home planet in time to escape the worst. In the end, Earth might recover what had been lost. A power struggle was in full swing, its outcome precarious.

Timothy was the first to fall.

A vague cramp tickled his abdomen. He brushed the sensation aside, thinking he'd been laughing too hard. The tickle turned into clench, the clench into a dull knife, a sharpened spear. He turned to Tom, who sat beside him.

Tom took in his white face, the damp sheen. "Ava!" he called out. "We need Scarlett."

"Scarlett is..." Her glance fell across Lisa's innocent face. "...isn't around," Ava called back. "Why?"

Timothy toppled as hands caught him, lowered him to the ground, pushed chairs away. Voices rose. Questions flew.

Ava pointed at the door. "Get him to the infirmary. Quickly now."

Arms lifted Timothy as his head lolled to the side, his arm flopped away from his belly where it had cradled the pain. The bearers shuffled through the door, along the path, toward the ship and the open door of its darkened loading bay.

Brian crumpled next, grimacing in pain. Ava sought out Koral, leading Lisa, herding both of them out the door after Jamal and Caleb, who supported Brian's stumbling progress.

The infirmary was small, so Koral and Lisa waited in a neighboring room.

Sophia wedged her small frame through the crowd to stand next to Tom. She peered down at Timothy, comatose on the gurney.

"Do you know what to do?" Tom asked Sophia.

She shook her head. "The ship will know." She lowered the scanner that waited, hovering above Timothy. She watched the small screen, waited for words to scroll.

Tom said, "Okay, let's clear the room. Leave some air for those who need it most."

Jamal, replicating Sophia's movements, lowered the second scanner above Brian's gurney. "It's his liver," Jamal said.

"Exactly," Sophia muttered, as words scrolled across her screen. "Families..."

Tom called, "Get them out to the forest," as he swung from the infirmary. He leaned into the second room. "You're a little green around the gills," he said to Koral. "The ship wants you out in the forest. Something's going on with your livers." Tom looked at Lisa, who seemed bewildered but fine. "Both of you." He stepped back and escorted them down the hallway. The prone men were carried on their gurneys, maneuvered through doorways, out into the forest.

Zoe beckoned the convoy to follow her. Tom didn't hesitate. Zoe spent all her time in the forest. She would know the best place to go. "Don't take us too far," he called to her. "Let's get these guys stretched out as soon as we can.

Zoe slipped around trees, looking for the right shade of green. She pointed. "There." Ava led Lisa where Zoe pointed. "No! Not her. Him." Zoe pointed at Koral. She scoped the forest floor, pointed. "She should be here."

Zoe trotted past two more trees, pointed to a family patch. "He goes here." She pointed to Timothy's gurney. Brian's patch waited beneath a tree just beyond.

Ava bent over Lisa. "These plants will heal you. I've seen them do remarkable things."

Lisa looked into Ava's worried eyes and smiled. "I know."

As the sun set and dusk crept around them, Lisa murmured, "I can see the sea. At last…"

Ava lay curled next to Lisa. "Me, too."

"It's glorious."

"It never gets old."

The next morning, Olivia arrived, laden with blue fruit. Ava shook her head. "I don't know, Olivia. What if they're what set it off?"

Olivia set a basket next to Lisa. "They heal, Ava. They're incapable of harm."

"They're alien to these four. They haven't had time to acclimate. Last night was pretty dramatic. It looked harmful to me."

Lisa reached a hand to quiet Ava's alarm. "She's right, Ava. They heal." She sat up and ate four of the fruit. She lay back down, hands grasping the families, her forehead furrowed. "They're killing the nanos," she whispered.

Ava ventured a guess. "And the families are taking away the dead nanos?"

Lisa nodded. "I can feel them leaving. They're sort of yanking them through my skin. They feel surprisingly large."

Olivia stood. "I'm going to check on the others. They might not be ready for another dose, but I want to check, just in case."

Lisa left the forest at nightfall, Koral the next morning. Ava insisted on a follow-up scan, so Sophia showed them into the infirmary. She stared at the blinking cursor of the empty screen, glanced at the same blink on the second screen. A small circle appeared in the center of both screens, which grew into spreading smiley faces.

"You crack me up," Sophia told the ship. The smiley faces winked at her.

Two days later, Brian earned his own smiley face. It took Timothy an entire week.

Koral slapped Timothy's high-five and sat on the chair next to his gurney. "A lot has happened while you've been away. We've got company."

~ 65 ~

GATHERING

They arrived in twos and threes.

Jamina had taken over from Rinala as main scout, and her sharp eyes easily found the stragglers who wandered through the forest, spreading outward in all directions from the intruder starship. Once, Forest waved to her as she soared! through Above. A line of trees bent in sequence, a green river rippling across the canopy, guiding her to three refugees who sat next to Stream, unsure what to do. They had slipped past Jamina's spiraling patrol.

She landed invisibly behind this elusive set of refugees and rattled her flamboyant tail. One of the three looked over his shoulder in her direction, but she easily froze, blending into the twirling blossoms around her. When he looked away, she silently launched and banked toward Logan's transport vehicle, easily finding it where it rumbled through the forest, intent on its own patrol.

Logan and Jamina worked together easily. Jamina found them and Logan retrieved them. It usually took a bit of coaxing. "Hello, Earthens!" he would call out, a fair distance away. "I'm here to help you." They would usually flee, and he would follow patiently behind. "Really. I can help," he would call. "I won't take you back to your starship. There's a friendly community of Earthens right over there." He would point. "Your starship is back that way." A second point. "We've been here for ten years. We can help you."

Eventually, the refugees would find a way to calm themselves, listen to his explanation, and climb into the transport. Jamina would fly off to find the next group while Logan delivered the refugees to Home Base.

The ship happily created shelter after shelter. The forest created bare spots, Sophia scanned them, and the ship created sections for the new shelters. The Earthens carried the sections to the new building sites, added pillows and beds. The refugees would hesitate at each fresh threshold before stepping into their welcoming shelter, hugging their elbows to themselves.

Home Base doubled in size, tripled. There was enough for all.

~ 66 ~

SCHEMES

"We're losing people every day. The starship won't close any doors, and they're just walking away."

Samantha listened drearily to the endless strategizing. They would post a guard; the guard walked away. They would offer rewards. The initial awe of an actual bedroom lost its alure, even after months of sleeping in claustrophobic cylinders or dreary dormitories. After a few days, luxurious bedrooms would stand empty, and diminished scatterings of people sat at their assigned desks. Midday meals weren't as tempting a lure as the elitists assumed they would be. They could tie people to bedframes, but what good were they then?

They were running out of options.

Samantha knew their names, now. Charles had yelled at her that first day. She still resented him. Tall, thin Jonathan had rescued her. Nelson always sat, one knee crossed over the other, swinging his foot up and down. Nelson said nothing, watching the others, placidly smiling. Franklin was a pacer.

There had been more, but they left before she learned their names. She was the only woman, and she wondered how much longer she would stick around. She heaved a deep sigh. She did that a lot now. It had not gone unnoticed.

"Why don't we go after them?" Nelson's question caught them all by surprise. Samantha was pretty sure she had never heard his voice. He had a western drawl, once fashionable, recently passé.

Franklin stopped his pacing. "Go after who?"

"Our workers."

Silence.

"Look," Nelson continued, world-wearily, "we know where they've gone. We know about The 108. We know they're out there. Obviously, it's where all of our people have gone. Let's go *there*. Instead of wasting away in this useless starship, let's go *there*."

"And do what?"

"Assert our authority, of course. We brought them here. Their obligation lies with us." He examined his fingernails. "They owe us. Let's remind them of their debts. And the consequences of defaulting."

Samantha frowned. "You think their debts are enough incentive to bring them back?"

No one answered her.

Jonathan called an all-hands meeting, brought everyone together in the dining hall. "We've found a settlement nearby where we can all find shelter." He looked out at listless eyes, dull faces regarding him sourly. He raised his voice, injecting enthusiasm into his delivery. "A mission came to this planet several years ago, and they've been making ready for us. We've been in communication with them. It's time for us to head that way."

Samantha counted heads in the sparse dining hall. Seventy-one people were left. She was shocked that so few remained. The three-week attrition had been deeper than she'd realized.

Jonathan painted a rosy picture, cajoled them to come along, stick together. "It's all ready for us," he reiterated.

The straggly band reconnoitered at the base of the starship's ramp. Charles held out a blinking oblong in the direction he had determined earlier. When the blinking steadied into a constant glow, he pointed. "This way." He waved the band to follow him and set out. They shuffled listlessly across the meadow and followed Charles into the looming forest. Some people looked up at swaying blossoms, but most watched their feet, showing scant interest in their surroundings.

Samantha trudged along with the rest. She kept close to Jonathan for the most part, but didn't want to appear clingy. After an eternity, the light began to fade. Jonathan made his way to the front of the column, Samantha following dutifully.

"Where the hell is it, Charles?" Jonathan was tired and on edge.

"How the hell do I know, Jonathan?" Charles' voice sneered the word 'Jonathan.' "This thing shows us the direction, but it doesn't display distance."

"Well, that was a bit of an oversight, wasn't it?" Jonathan flared. "Are we going to walk all night?"

Charles stopped walking, stared at the ground, hands on hips. "Shut up, Jonathan. This was Nelson's idea, not mine. At least I can get us headed in the right direction. If that's not good enough for you, then by all means, it's all yours." He held out the black oblong, loathing in his face.

Jonathan looked at their straggly band and shook his head. "Okay. Let's stop here for the night. We'll get a fresh start in the morning."

"What about food?" someone called out.

"There's food at the settlement. We'll be there tomorrow."

"How do you know that?" Samantha asked.

Charles shot her a glare and turned away.

At first light, Jonathan made the rounds, nudging people awake with his foot. "Up! Time to get up." He'd slept soundly, dreamt of flying over endless forests, skimming waves. He felt refreshed and optimistic.

People stretched, rolled onto all-fours, and clambered to their feet, blinking at trees and each other. When Charles gave the 'walk-on' signal, they moved along, taking interest in their surroundings for the first time. Talk started up here and there. Someone guffawed.

"Let's save our breath for walking," Jonathan called over his shoulder. "We still have a ways to go."

They walked for two more days. Samantha felt stronger each day. She'd expected to get tired, but she walked along easily, a spring in her step. She spent time memorizing the shapes of flowers, the number of different colors, but she eventually lost track. She contented herself with just walking, brushing her hands over grasses and ferns, enjoying the faint tingles that danced up her arms.

Samantha walked behind two women who walked arm in arm. She didn't know their names, but they talked on and on, swapping stories. A man on her left, laughed and pounded the back of the man next to him, who claimed, "It's true! I swear it's true!" Samantha found herself smiling, listening to the light-hearted stories that floated around her.

She caught herself and frowned. What was happening?

She caught up with Jonathan. "What's going on?"

"Apparently, Charles only knows the direction, not how far we have left."

"I know that. I meant, what's going on with everyone? Why are they acting like this?"

Jonathan looked around. Shrugged. "Who cares? As long as they keep walking, does it matter?"

"Something's off."

Jonathan shrugged again. "We'll deal with it when we get there. I wasn't sure how we were going to pull this off, but it seems to be working. It's what we need right now."

"Do you feel in charge?"

He scowled at her.

"I mean, in charge of..." She gestured around them. "...this?"

"They're walking where we told them, aren't they? They stop when we tell them; they walk when we tell them. Looks to me like we're in charge. Quit worrying. We're getting it done."

He looked away from her, off into the forest. She dropped behind, wondering.

~ 67 ~

CONQUERING

They arrived midway through the fourth day of walking.

They almost missed the settlement entirely. A cloud of turquoise birdlings buzzed them. Instead of cowering, the wandering Earthens burst out laughing. The birdlings flowed across their path, a river that parted to flow around trees, blended together again, chittering gaiety. A group of stragglers pointed through the trees to the left of their path, in the direction in which the birdlings were disappearing. Charles looked up from his oblong guide, spotted a cluster of white shapes, and with a sigh, turned in the direction of the pointing.

Home Base turned out to meet them. They were expected.

The gathering on the Green mostly consisted of The 108. Refugees were scattered amongst them here and there, but for the most part, the newest newcomers had drifted into the forest, on the far side of Home Base, or waited inside their newly minted, bright white shelters.

Nelson made his way to the front of the wandering band. He stepped past the last tree and strolled confidently onto the Green. He surveyed the crowd sprinkled across the Green.

"Right. Who's in charge, please?"

He was met with silence.

"Come on, now. Who's in charge."

Sophia stood her full 62.5 inches. She crossed her arms and said, "We're in charge." She circled her index finger, slightly behind her head, indicating the crowd behind her. "All of us."

Nelson ignored her, scanning the faces. "Ava?" Silence. "Come now. Where's Ava."

Ava took a step forward. "What can I do for you?" She stood with arms crossed, scowling.

"Ah. Ava. Good girl." He noted her bristle. "Well, Ava. The Agency sent us. You may step down, effective immediately. I'm in charge now." He scanned the crowd, confident in his power. "Where's the ship?" Nobody moved. "Right. Well."

Nelson removed a slim oblong from his shirt pocket and pressed a button. A light blinked as he scanned Home Base. The blink quickened as he swung his arm to the right. The light steadied.

"Right," he said again.

He pocketed the oblong and strode along the path, headed to the ship.

Logan started after him. Sophia caught his arm. "Wait," she warned.

Nelson let out a short laugh. "Yes. Wait. Passivity always serves us so well." He disappeared around the corner. Jonathan and Charles trotted after him, captivated. Samantha followed.

Nelson found the ship, overgrown though it was. He reached into his back pocket and brought out a silver cylinder. He pressed his thumb over the end and held his fist out to the ship. The bay doors promptly slid open. Nelson released his thumb, stooped, and bowled the cylinder up the ramp and into the loading bay. The doors promptly slid shut. He backed away, eyes fastened on the ship.

The explosion blew the doors outward and slammed the intruders ten feet through the air to smash onto their backs. They lay, winded. Where the ship had stood, rooted on its rocky outcropping since the moment of its arrival, thick, acrid smoke roiled, an impenetrable cloud of destruction.

The 108 swarmed around the bend, shocked into motion by the explosion, and skidded to a halt. The astonished faces surveyed the still-expanding mushroom of smoke, a hail of white debris thudding to the ground around them.

Samantha pressed her palms against her wringing ears and caught her breath. She struggled to her feet. She screamed, "You idiot! That was our ride home!"

Nelson gathered his feet under him, said aside to Jonathan, "Get rid of her." Jonathan grabbed Samantha's arm and dragged her around the edge of the frozen crowd. Nelson turned to The 108.

"Now, then."

~ 68 ~

RULING

"Who's next? Who wants to choose what happens next?" Nelson asked in his soft drawl. He reached into his back pocket and drew out another silver cylinder. He smiled benignly.

Jamina swooped on silent wings. She deftly banked over Nelson's head and plucked the cylinder out of the Earthen's grasp. He swung at her. She swatted him with her flamboyant tail and rose on brilliant wings, disappeared beyond the forest's canopy.

Several things happened at once.

Nelson screamed and pointed after Jamina, "Catch it, you fools!"

Samantha took advantage of Jonathan's loosened grip and pushed him into the incredulous crowd. "Leave me alone, you jerk!" she snarled. Jonathan stumbled and would have fallen if Jamal hadn't caught him. Jonathan tried to shake him off, but Jamal's iron grip kept him pinned.

"She said to leave her alone," Jamal growled.

Charles turned to run after Jamina. Tom stuck out a foot, and Charles sprawled under a bush. A vine reached and twined around his ankle, crept around his waist, whispered around his throat. Charles froze.

"Good boy," Tom said and turned back to the smoking display of conquering, ruling, overwhelming.

Smoke drifted lazily where once the ship had stood.

~ 69 ~

OVERWHELMING

Franklin had held his post at the head of the band of intruders, holding them back with shouted threats. The explosion had caught him unawares, but he held his post. He watched smoke and debris blossom into the air and tumble back to the ground. He heard Nelson yell out, "Who's next?"

Then nothing. An enormous bird flew up and disappeared over the trees. He heard, "Catch it, you fools!" He looked around. What? Catch what? The bird? Franklin stood, confused.

The 108 drifted casually back onto the Green. They didn't look subdued in the least. Some were chatting. Grinning. What was going on?

Franklin followed through with their plan. He turned to his band of intruders, these loyal few who had followed them across the vast forest. Now was the time to claim what they had come for. He raised his fist over his head and screeched, "Take 'em, men!"

He plunged onto the Green and charged into the crowd of The 108. Caleb and Steven caught him, held him. "Easy there," Caleb said, and released him.

Franklin turned back to his band, ready to urge them on, but stared. The entire band remained at the edge of the forest, staring at him. He recognized scorn on every face.

He stomped back to stand before them. "Come on! This is what we came for!" He swept his arm to encompass Home Base. "This is ours! The Agency sent us for this!" No one moved. "What is the *matter* with you? Are you all idiots?"

A woman standing a few feet away asked, "Are you? What is the matter with *you*?"

The intrusion gasped its final breath, brought to a standstill by common sense.

~ 70 ~

RECALL

Yamdha felt the cycle through his holderlings long before Brian appeared, sensed the distinctive vibration that fluttered through Below and bounced along the secret burrow. He had time.

Yamdha loved these two Earthens. They brought out the trickster in him. They had tried to teach him how to play poker, an endless entertainment for them. It took several days for them to realize that he simply watched their strategies blossom in the air above their heads. It was only due to his deft manipulation of the finer points of the game that delayed their realization of why he consistently won all the pebbles that they gathered as markers...chips, Yamdha corrected himself.

Yamdha prided himself on his gift of words.

Today, they were trying chess. The question marks over Mateo's head let Yamdha know that Mateo was already pretty sure that chess was also a lost cause. Yamdha sighed. He had hoped to draw out his trick for a few more days. Mateo was too smart to be fooled on this one.

As the cycle's vibration grew in intensity, Yamdha leaned back and gazed at his companions. He had enjoyed his time with these two.

They had carefully waited each day until nightfall before creeping into the Forest to stretch on the families who greeted them with delight. Yamdha told the Earthens stories of old, the beginning of all, the awakening of Airon, the blossoming of Eglans and Narsis, their woven partnership, Airon's recent drift into her cyclical slumber. She would return. Perhaps not in Yamdha's time, but in the right time; a mysterious time.

Yamdha was content.

The Earthens listened intently to Yamdha's stories. They were gifted listeners. Yamdha was a gifted teller. He was a favorite amongst younglings. Always it had been so, since all Yamdha's remembrance. They were well-suited, these three guardians of a treasured ship's remembrance, passing time together. Waiting.

Yamdha's meld kept him informed about arrivals, wanderings, welcomings. None of the news affected the need for their secret task within this secret burrow. The news soothed Yamdha, knowing his Burrow and family were safe, content that Home Base was safe, the Earthens safe.

He shared his meld's information with the two Earthens, watched them struggle with relief, hope, doubt, worry. He offered reassurances, quelled their repetitive worry with powerful stares. Younglings never questioned. Earthens knew only questions.

Yamdha enjoyed these exchanges, teaching the Earthens trust, trust that would lead to confidence. Yamdha was a gifted teacher.

He was immensely curious about the newest Newcomers. Would they form new allegiances? With Narsis? Eglans? Yamdha felt an approaching shift, not as climactic as the arrival of The 108 and Vargad's dismissal of ancient customs. Yamdha delighted in Vargad's wisdom, his Head-ing.

Yamdha was content.

He touched his king, laid it gently on its side. Dhiren looked up at him. "What, mate? You resigning?"

Yamdha paused. He would miss these two. "I resign," he lied. Fibbed. A lie of kindness. Lighthearted. Fibbed. He fibbed.

"We go."

He gathered his holderlings under him and lumbered down the tunnel.

Mateo called after him. "It's still light out. We should wait."

"We go," Yamdha called over his shoulder, moving surely toward freshening air. He welcomed time with Sun. He heard the Earthens clamber to their feet and follow. He would miss these two.

They emerged from the burrow's mouth to the sound of the cycle moving briskly toward them. Mateo and Dhiren looked at each other. Waited.

Jamina soared! into view, followed closely by the cycle. Mateo squinted, straining to see who rode the cycle.

A stranger pulled to a stop and dismounted. Mateo and Dhiren belatedly ducked behind the bushes that concealed the burrow's entrance. Yamdha made no such retreat. He rumbled, "Welcome."

The stranger stared at the Narsi, nonplused. Yamdha watched caution splash onto the ground around the stranger's feet. He rumbled, "I am Yamdha."

The stranger nodded. He stuck out a hand. "Brian." Yamdha held out a holderling, and Brian grasped it, moved it up and down. "You must be a Narsi. I've heard about you. Glad to meet you, Yamdha."

He spoke with an Earthen accent, which didn't surprise Yamdha in the least. Brian released the holderling and peered beyond the Narsi's bulk. "Mateo? Dhiren?" No response. "Sophia sent me." No response. "It's okay. Everything's fine. The ship wants you to bring out the memory cache."

Brian stopped, waited. Yamdha rumbled, "You can come out. Home Base is safe."

"How do you know?" came the whispered reply.

Yamdha's rumble turned stern. "You can come out. Home Base is safe."

Mateo and Dhiren knew better than to make Yamdha repeat himself more than once. They crept into the open.

"Who are you, again?" Mateo asked.

"Brian. Sophia sent me. Good to meet you." He stepped forward, offered his hand.

Mateo slipped his hand into Brian's grip. "Mateo." He crooked a thumb over his shoulder. "Dhiren."

Dhiren asked the obvious question. "You're one of the intruders?"

Brian grinned. "Well, yeah. I used to be. I live here now." He straightened. "We have work to do. We need to load up the memory cache and get moving."

Mateo held up his palms, took a step back. "Hold on..."

Yamdha could move quick as lightening when he chose to. He turned on Mateo, thrust his nose within an inch of Mateo's, and stared.

Mateo backed up, right into the bush. "All right! All right! If you're sure." Yamdha stared. "All right. Let's...load up."

Yamdha rumbled past his two friends and disappeared into the burrow.

"This way," said Mateo, nodding his head after Yamdha. "It's in here."

It took almost two hours to bring everything out of the tunnel and reconstruct the transport vehicle. Mateo tried to give Yamdha some assembly tips. Yamdha turned his gentle gaze onto Mateo. "Narsis have long memories."

Mateo put up his palms and backed away. He heard Yamdha's rumble, that particular rumble that Mateo recognized as a chuckle.

Yamdha pulled pieces of the transport out of the pile that the Earthens stacked within easy reach. The Narsi rumbled happily, manhandled large pieces of steel into position and delicately secured them with several bolts at once, holderlings moving in synchrony, reaching exquisitely into hard to reach corners, twisting several nuts at once, regardless of their varied orientations.

"Are we ever going to be able to loosen those nuts, mate?" Dhiren asked.

Yamdha chuckled deep in his chest.

While Yamdha worked, Brian brought Mateo and Dhiren up to date. He ended his story with, "Yeah, the trouble makers are living out in the forest for a while. They have some thinking to do." He added, "The Eglans are keeping an eye on them."

After the final memory cube was hoisted into place, the final bolts wiggled into slots, the final nuts twisted into permanent tightness,

Yamdha raised his torso and turned from his task. He gazed lovingly at his two friends. He reached out holderlings to each, grasped both their hands, and moved their grasped appendagges up and down.

"I go." Yamdha turned and was gone in an instant.

"So that's a Narsi," Brian mused. "Pretty amazing."

Mateo gazed in the direction in which Yamdha had disappeared, stared at the ground, shook his head. He took in a deep breath. "Okay. Let's head home."

"Well, actually..." Brian scratched the back of his head. "We're headed in the opposite direction. The ship has a project for us."

~ 71 ~

UPGRADE

The memory cache went into the intruder's starship, whose technology had been pretty much cut to shreds on that first day of arrival on its rocky outcropping. While the forest held the starship immobile, the ship at Home Base, alpha ship, sent a long stream of instructions that instantly seized the intruder's communication network and splintered the intruder's ability to carry out the simplest task. The intruder had no chance to send even one update to Earth. Once alpha ship was satisfied of the intruder's incapacity, the forest released the intruder and returned to watchful observation.

As refugees slipped away from the intruder, Forest alerted Eglans, sent birdlings on various errands, and orchestrated the slow-motion desertion, night after night. Forest stretched high into Above, delighted at its collaboration with Eglans and Earthens in transforming intruders into deserters, deserters into refugees, refugees into newcomers.

During the exodus, the ship examined the intruder's files. It discovered plans within plans, secrets within secrets. It knew of the elitists' elaborate plans to conquer, rule, and overwhelm. The ship reinforced the interior walls of its loading bay. It thinned its exterior bay doors, and with Sophia's help, scattered piles of white debris around the loading bay and positioned several impressive smoke machines.

"This is exactly the display they'll expect," chortled Sophia, as she swept another pile of stage-debris into place and masked it beneath an innocent box, tucking in a small explosive.

"Heh, heh, heh," she chuckled.

"Heh, heh, heh," the ship wrote.

After the oh so satisfying theatrics, Ava and Sophia gave a green light for the ship's plan of converting the intruder's starship into the core of a second Home Base. "This is exactly what we'll need to keep from tripping over each other here." Sophia dispatched Brian while Ava recruited Logan.

"This is the perfect job for you," Ava told Logan. "You'll know precisely how to handle it."

So, the team gathered at the intruder starship. Mateo, Brian, and Sophia grunted the memory cubes into place, connected cables, activated the creation front. Companions drifted to and fro, offering needed tools, water orbs, newly minted electronics. The beta ship hummed into life, piece by newly programmed piece.

~ 72 ~

PROPAGANDA

Brian and Logan retreated to his lonely outpost, wrote out a plan, set a timetable. They were the perfect pair to convince Earth of encroaching threats, mounting toxicity, widespread death in the face of a collapsing ecosystem.

Since alpha ship had successfully captured control of all communication at the intruder starship, Earth had received only silence for the last few weeks. The prolonged silence fit perfectly into Brian and Logan's plan. Airon was doomed, spinning into planet-wide devastation, thoroughly uninhabitable. Obliteration was imminent, survival impossible, escape unattainable, rescue unfeasible. With destruction approaching insidiously, inevitably, nothing could be done. Send thoughts and prayers.

Logan typed out their first message, sent it on its way. He pushed away from his work station and swiveled to face Brian.

"Tell me about Carlos."

~ 73 ~

RECALL 2.0

Lafonda's brilliant wings fluttered across the bright meadow. The embryo convoy swept after him at full throttle. The lab was secure, not a rattle, not a sway. The need for stealth had vanished, and the trio drove with abandon, thrilled at the prospect of arrival, of Home Base filled with friendship and room to breathe.

The journey would have taken days, had they followed the caravan's memory of their route. Lafonda's trailblazing cut the time to a third. They careened their way home.

Strangers' faces intermixed with dear friends, as the trio climbed from their vehicles amidst cheers and applause. Scarlett handed their memory to Sophia, who saluted and trotted off to share it with alpha ship. She turned to watch Henry and Tom maneuver the nitrogen tank out of the mobile lab and guide it toward the ship. She knew they would stow it in its permanent home inside the alpha ship's fully functional embryo lab. She knew the alpha ship would guard the embryos safely until the end of time.

Scarlett scanned the gathered faces, found the one she sought above all others, and strode to wrap herself in Steven's embrace.

The cheers rose anew.

An orange and yellow shape launched from a lavender-draped tree, circled Home Base once, and swept to disappear beyond the canopy. Scarlett twisted to watch Lafonda's departure.

Safe be.

Safe be.

~ 74 ~

BLUE FRUIT

Scarlett declared a vacation for herself, Henry, and Michaela. She turned a deaf ear to suggestions of responsibilities and need. "Tom and Olivia will do a great job. You don't need me here." The trio set off for Inipi for days of swimming and basking under the open sky.

And so it was. Tom and Olivia oversaw the dispensing of blue fruit. Alpha ship gave them a list of questions to ask each Newcomer. "How long ago did you first receive nanos? At what dose?" "Have you had any updates? When?" "Do you happen to know the identifier of your specific type of nano?"

Scarlett could have drawn blood, but neither Tom nor Olivia were keen on giving it a try. The questionnaire seemed to provide enough information for the ship to propose quantity and timing of offering blue fruit. The blue fruit and the families took care of the rest. They worked with their own, innate intelligence.

Over sixteen days, any Newcomer who might want to get rid of their nanos, signed up and got treatment. To no one's surprise, everyone opted in.

Samantha was the last, but opt in she did.

With the lowering of the nano burden came blending. The 108 described their own experiences, explained their understanding, answered questions, observed blending sessions.

None of The 108 thought to mention Lone Tree. That would come for each Earthen at the right time. A mysterious time.

Besides. Lone Tree is busy.

~ 75 ~

LONE TREE

The twelve littermates and Claira wound their way across the plain that stretched below Overlook and paused at the edge of the bright shadow that was Lone Tree's realm. Never had the twelve-plus-one wandered alone; never in all their remembrance. That morning, Caretake-ers, Find-ers, Show-ers, Head-er, all had hummed their farewells, fretting, patting, pacing. Then all had stood silently while the twelve-plus-one wound a path away from Burrow, toward the fearsome face of Overlook, moving toward their New.

They journeyed in silence, flowing past one another, pausing, being passed, pouring onward; a river of lithe brown bodies wending its way, stropping trunks, tasting the air, listening to the song of Forest. They had hesitated at Overlook, gazed across vastness toward the smudge that was Lone Tree. Lone Tree, who awaited them.

One, three, twelve-plus-one, nudged their way onto the arduous descent that led from tumbling Stream to broad plain. They rested often, comforted by families who awaited them, Nourish-ers and Remove-ers whispering courage and stamina.

Claira kept close to Varlan, eyes darting, heart pounding. Hours earlier, Chatan had held her close, Aadhya kissing the top of her head, parental warmth flooding her heart. Now, she placed her

308

feet on the steep path judiciously, having only two. Varlan kept her stable, guided her. The families kept them hydrated, removing spent fuel, replacing it with fresh.

Gentle morning Sun moved into fierce midday Sun, who glared down on them where they panted their way down, down, down. After an eternity, midday Sun crested, sank toward its afternoon blaze, pinning them against the cliff's face. After an eternity, a breeze freshened their breaths, ruffled their fur, lifted Claira's hair. After an eternity, the slope softened, and they entered the first of the grasses who spread across the plain.

As one, they turned toward Lone Tree, thankful for the end of cascading pebbles and intense bright-bright-bright. They moved through grasses, who caressed a myriad of now-tender holderlings and cushioned two now-tender soles. Claira relaxed her grip on Varlan's fur and moved, drooping, embedded in the twelve.

Claira had grown up with these twelve. She often shared their sleeping niche. They splashed and dove in Pond together, tumbled and ran together under the careful eyes of Caretake-ers, learned together with Show-ers, explored together with Find-ers.

Before she could walk, much less run, Care-ful holderlings had carried her, coddled her. She relished the rumblings of Caretake-ers' warm chests and the twelve-fold nestlings with intermingled holderlings in soft sleeping niches. She rested on families every morning and throughout the day, the Nourish-ers and Remove-ers supplanting her dormant digestive tract.

Since her conception beneath Lone Tree, her development within Aadhya's awoken womb, her birth into Pond's warm embrace, al-ways, in all her remembrance, she had been one with Airon. She wandered with turquoise clouds and raced with Stream, danced with Forest, rejoiced with Eglans as they soared! beneath Sun. She knew the crash of waves as Broad Sea misted the ancient Arbans and their attentive Shosens.

Airon was as familiar to Claira as her own breath, which she gifted to families each morning and throughout the day. Dancing forests and ancient Arbans were always with her, and with their constancy, they melted into the background, as breath melts into the background, as the air moving in and out with each breath melts, as daytime light and nighttime dark melts. Always present. Always affective. Too familiar to be noticed.

From the very beginning, from that early day when a timid youngling had crept up Pond's bank and reached a tentative holderling to touch a brown cheek, always there had been Varlan. Claira loved the twelve, knew them intimately, but she was entwined with Varlan.

Of course they had melded. Of course they shared each other's thoughts. Of course they were together always, even when separated. Of course they were one.

Then they had discovered Rinala, glorious Rinala. Of course they had melded with Rinala, the duet blossoming into a trio. The richness of their friendship glowed through their laughter/purring/ rumbling.

All of the younglings knew of melding. They knew that their elders melded, spent much of their day melded with their own littermates, nestmates. They knew that one day they would meld, that they would move to Life Burrows and remain forever connected with their meldmates. They knew it like they knew their breath, knew the air that moved around them, through them.

Claira saw meld threads. She saw the connections between all life, the brightness, the effervescence of subtle interactions. In her early days, she had reached to grasp them, her parents meeting her grasp with a finger, a kiss. In her early days, the glowing threads had enthralled her, holding her entranced.

Claira played with the threads. She learned to throw her own threads to be caught by trees she passed, sent her threads twining into high branches, dipping to entangle neighboring trees. She wove intricate patterns with her threads, weaving together entire groves. Threads were endlessly enchanting.

She realized that others did not play with threads. Others moved without seeing the threads that wove together their world. Others sensed the threads, sometimes strongly, sometimes not at all. Claira kept her secret to herself, avoided the risk of being told not to play, not to weave. Her parents whispered together about her trancelike gazing, but they did not question her. They sensed a depth of meaning that they did not understand or share, a mystery they felt no need to solve. They observed and wondered.

It had been an easy step to blend with Varlan, easy to keep it secret. Claira could see that none of the other twelve blended. Their threads danced and played, but did not lodge. Only her thread and Varlan's lodged. No one saw. No one guessed. It was easy to keep this secret, too.

In her distress, gripped in the dread of losing Rinala, Claira had blurted their secret. In response, Varlan had shared the secret, too. Varlan had shared, not with just anyone, but with Head-ers. With Vargad and Jamina. Now the Head-ers knew.

Many discussions followed. At first, Vargad's gentle curiosity reassured Varlan and through her, Claira and Rinala. They felt relieved that they no longer needed to hide their truth. But Varlan detected a growing concern in Vargad's rumblings. VaSoDeLa pondered repercussions. Would Varlan be able to meld with littermates? Would littermates want to meld with her? Would she be able to find a Life Burrow? Would any Life Burrow welcome her?

When Blandir's burrow had rejected Claira, shame weighed her down. Guilt drove her to seek out Yamdha, wisest of Find-ers. Blandir's burrow held high import. She, Claira, was a roadblock to Varlan and the twelve. She hung her head in despair.

Yamdha had lifted Claira's chin with a soft holderling. "They are not ready, Blandir and her burrow." When they were ready, Yamdha would return. Perhaps with the next twelve. Or the twelve after that. Claira held no fault; no causation. This was simply the way of life; Narsi life. Yamdha smoothed her damp cheek, held her close, rumbled love. "They will be ready someday. But not today."

Now Claira stood with the twelve, one hand resting on Varlan's flank, peering into the bright shade that was Lone Tree's realm. She yearned to be inside that bright shade, to hide from this Sun, who had always been her friend, whose intensity today made her cower. Why did they pause?

Claira went still. She wrapped her awareness into Lone Tree's spreading branches, wove up, up, up to burst into Sky. With joy, she felt Rinala, whose thread she had dropped somewhere along that tortuous path down Overlook's cliff. She rejoiced at Rinala's finding and felt Varlan's spirits lift alongside her own.

Rinala was coming.

Rinala soared! and banked, curving toward Lone Tree, who reaches toward Sky, spreads its feathery leaves as diminished Sun touches the edge of the far ridge, purpled in the fading light.

Claira caught her breath as she realized that Rinala came not alone. Twenty nestmates soared! and banked, spiraling down to Lone Tree's waiting branches.

Twenty nestmates join twelve-plus-one littermates.

Now, after an eternity that might have been a moment, the twelve-plus-one move into bright shadow to rest on waiting families and the twenty land to hop, hop, hop onto favorite branches, jingling gossamer wings.

Lone Tree raises its feathery leaves in farewell to lowering Sun and breathes its song along its way, to Burrow and Nest and Pond, to Arbans and Shosens stilled in purpled air, all awaiting the New.

~ 76 ~

BLENDED

Thirty-three meldmates gather in Lone Tree. Newly melded Eglans, newly blossomed into elders, perch or swoop, hop, hopping to strop necks, clack beaks, blink eyes. Newly melded Narsis, youngest of elders, curl and stretch holderlings and rumble their ancient song. Newly joined yet ancient partners rim the periphery of Lone Tree's shadow, turn their chests to setting Sun, merging Above and Below, in their new-yet-ancient worship of end-of-day.

Claira roams amongst them, palms trailing along soft fur, over bright feathers, adapting to her newly blended reality of thirty-three minds, this twelve-plus-one-plus-twenty.

Thirty-three Aironians blend and imagine within the embrace of Lone Tree, the ancient of Airon. No Head-ers; no Caretake-ers. Lone Tree whispers no familiar role into these hearts. No whispers of Show-er, Find-er. Lone Tree weaves New into thirty-three hearts, whispers a single role to all.

Friend.

The most powerful role of all. Without obligation. Without co-ercion. Without expectation. Only friendship is offered openly, moment by moment. Only friendship is returned honestly, moment by moment. The most powerful vibration to connect all that is.

Never, in all remembrance, has such a melding occurred. Never, in all imagination, has such a melding even glimmered. As always, in all remembrance, Lone Tree lifts its feathered branches into the bright twilight of Airon's glorious sun, shifts always-was into New, and breathes its song along its way.

~ 77 ~

POND

Lisa's first visit to Inipi filled Ava with a mysterious delight. She had refused to reveal the mystery, despite repeated entreaties. Lisa had spent the last several days baffled by Ava's glee and her oft-repeated refrain, "Wait and see. Wait and see."

They gathered with Chatan and Aadhya, who awaited Claira's return. Waited with curiosity tinged with anxiety and hope, overlaid with mystery and trust. Sebba offered tea. Lisa told of her years of quiet desperation, her recruitment onto this clandestine journey of determined power brokers.

She shook her head, her hands stilled, resting in her lap. "At Logan's shelter, when Brian first mentioned The 108, I could hardly believe it." She looked at Ava. "But sure enough, there you were, opening that door, taking charge of poor Logan." She blinked back tears. "I still can't quite believe it."

Chatan told of his own arrival on Airon, his immediate blending, "As if every detail of my life prepared me for that moment."

Aadhya marveled over the raising of Claira, her easy knowing of everything, "As if Airon had brought her into being, imbued with wisdom that blossoms into maturity every day. She is only a child, and yet she is ancient."

As they handed teacups back to Sebba, rose to hug, the forest seemed to brighten around them in anticipation. Ava turned to Lisa. "It's time." She grinned and led Lisa out the door, waving to Chatan and Aadhya, who stood side by side, arms wrapped around each other's waists, to watch them out of sight.

"What?" Lisa asked for the zillionth time.

"Come and see."

Sparkling light danced beyond the trees, reflected up trunks, along branches. The sparkling reflections awoke long-repressed memories, treasured memories of childhood summers, of magical realms of weightlessness, of diving and twirling, a graceful dance across a three-dimensional stage, sun sparkling above a cherished, watery world. As Ava led her to the rocky slab that overhung Pond, Lisa's step faltered, her hands came up to cover her mouth.

"A pool?"

Ava's delight spilled into laughter. "Pond, meet Lisa. Lisa, meet Pond."

"Can I go in?"

Ava nodded.

"I don't have a suit."

"You don't need one," Ava said.

"I haven't swum since..."

"A week before you had dinner with Phillip and me? Dinner at our apartment? When you told us about your nanos?"

Lisa nodded.

"Well..." Ava gestured toward Pond.

Lisa tugged the drawstring at her waist, stepped out of the skirt that puddled around her feet, took two steps, and dove into crystalline depths.

Pond caught her and began its task of rinsing away twelve years of loss and regret.

Lisa swam.

YOU CAN MAKE A DIFFERENCE

In our digital age, product reviews have taken on an astounding importance. You can make a significant difference in visibility for this book for others who would not otherwise be aware of its existence.

A star rating helps. Writing two or three sentences about the book and your impression helps enormously.

Why share your thoughts? So you can be a beacon for others. Your perspective is invaluable, and in the vast world of the digital age, your review can be the guiding star for another reader.

EARTHENS ON AIRON

Aadhya - Assistant cook; Chatan's partner
Ava - Leader of The 108
Caleb - Carpenter, helps get Brian to the infirmary
Chatan - Naturalist; Aadhya's partner
Claira - Aadhya and Chatan's daughter
Claudia - Good friend to Zoe
David - Teacher at Inipi
Dhiren - Helps hide the ship's memory cache
Eisen - two-year-old child living at Inipi
Grant - Teacher at Inipi
Harper - Textile artist; partner to Michael
Henry - Archivist; helps hide embryos
Jamal - Solar engineer, helps get Brian to the infirmary
Jacob - Cook
Logan – Lives at secluded outpost
Mateo - Engineer; works closely with the ship
Michael - Ava's assistant; Harper's partner
Mikaela - Helps hide embryos
Olivia - Lead cook; heals through food
Phoebe - Teacher at Inipi
Scarlett - Science officer; worked at Space Agency
Sophia - Lead engineer; mentors Mateo
Steven – Enjoys working solo in the dining hall
Tom - Lead landscaper
William - Teacher at Inipi
Zoe - Assistant cook

INTRUDERS

Brian - Intercepts Logan's messages
Jonathan, Charles, Nelson, Franklin - Elitists
Koral - Crystal man
Samantha - Powerful; entrenched in status quo
Timothy - Stargazer

AIRONIANS

Airon - A sentient planet where all life cooperates
Blandir - Head-er of another burrow, far away
Farla - Caretake-er
Jamina - Eglan matriarch; melds into **JaCoMaTuRi**
Kardal - Head-er of another burrow, often visited
Lafonda - Injured Eglan
Lone Tree - Deep connection to Airon; a focusing rod
Rinala - young Eglan who befriends Harper, Varlan, and Claira
Scawlan - Vargad's burrowmate
Solari - Vargad's burrowmate
Vargad - Head-er of Narsis; melds into **VaSoDeLa**
VaSoDeLa - Melded form of Vargad
      Vargad - Head-er
      Sorgad - Caretake-er
      Dergad - Show-er
      Largad - Find-er
Varlan - Vargad's daughter
Yamdha - Find-er
Zarded - Show-er

AIRONIAN SPECIES

Arbans - Wise trees who hold Airon's power

Birdlings - Turquoise cloud; wandering juvenile Shosens

Eglans - Tend the Above; ancient partners to Narsis; reminiscent of eagles

Narsis - Tend the Below; ancient partners to Eglans; reminiscent of river otters

Nurture-ers and **Remove-ers** - Array of plant life on Airon who provide nutrition and remove waste from animal life

Shosens - Mature birdlings; care for the Arbans on High Cliff

AIRONIAN TERMINOLOGY

Birthlings - From birth until old enough to venture out with elders

Burrowmates - All the Narsis who share a single Life Burrow

Elder - Melded Narsi who has moved to their Life Burrow

Family - Group of one species living together

Holderlings - Narsi appendages, used for holding and locomotion

Littermates - Born at the same time

Meldmates - Four littermates who form a lifelong telepathic connection with each other

Narsi Roles

    Head-er - heads the Narsi family

    Caretake-er - cares for birthlings and younglings

    Show-er - educates younglings

    Find-er - explores and helps match younglings with Life Burrow

Source - The divine

Sproutmates - A group of trees who sprouted together

Younglings - Wander with Elders until old enough to meld and move to Life Burrow

EARTHEN TECHNOLOGY

Companions - Created by the ship to assist Earthens
    Abby - Zoe's companion
    Andy - Harper's companion
    Carlos - Logan's companion
    Sebba - Aadhya's companion
Creation front - Mechanism where new material is created
Nanos - Nanotechnology infused into humans to enhance productivity
The ship - The sentient starship who carries The 108 from Earth to Airon
The starship - The intruder from Earth

PLACES

Above - The sky

Below - The ground

Broad Sea - Below High Cliff

Burrow - Home of Narsis

Birth Burrow - Where young Narsis are born and live until they move to a Life Burrow

Life Burrow - Where elder Narsis live out their lives

dining hall - Group dining room in Home Base

Earth - Airon's sister planet

Forest - Any forest on Airon; has a consciousness of its own

gathering hall - First building in Home Base

the Green - Open area in the middle of Home Base

High Cliff - Home of Arbans and Shosens; overlooks Broad Sea

Home Base - Earthen settlement on Airon

Inipi - Second Earthen settlement at Pond

Meadow - Any meadow on Airon; has a consciousness of its own

Mountain - Any mountain on Airon; has a consciousness of its own

Nest - Home of Eglans

Overlook - Twilight meeting place of Narsis and Eglans

Pond - Pool at Inipi

Pool - Any pool on Airon; has a consciousness of its own

River - Any river on Airon; has a consciousness of its own

shelters - Individual dwellings in Home Base and Inipi

Soil - The rich underpinning of Below, teaming with life; possesses a consciousness of its own

Stream - Any stream on Airon; has a consciousness of its own

Waterfall - Any waterfall on Airon; has a consciousness of its own

ACKNOWLEDGEMENT

It continues to be true that only reason this book exists is that Dambara remains steadfast in his encouragement of my writing with unfailing enthusiasm. He protects my hard-won solitude, time and time again, against all comers, so that I can immerse my imagination into the world of Airon and all her glorious beings.

OTHER BOOKS BY MANISHA HOLM

Awareness, A Journey of Truth...or Treachery, Book 1 of The Airon Chronicles

Awareness follows a group of 108 people who escape encroaching nanotechnology on Earth by embarking on a journey across the stars to colonize a recently detected planet, Airon. They travel aboard an intelligent spaceship who, after arriving on Airon, recycles itself into buildings, vehicles, and technologies that benefit the Earthens, as well as mysterious creations that eerily appear from the ship without explanation.

As The 108 establish Home Base, they venture forth to explore Airon's forests, rivers, and mountains. Some Earthens readily feel a profound bond with Airon's life, while others keep themselves hidden within the confines of Home Base. Despite growing connections with Airon and the life that surrounds them, suspicions mount, as mysterious technologies and events occur on Airon. Some Earthens feel threatened by the ship's abilities, which seem similar to the invasive nanotechnology that they so recently escaped.

The story explores themes of humanity's connection to nature, finding inner wisdom and cooperation amongst diversity, and exploring the mysteries of life. There are hints of a deeper calling behind The 108's journey to Airon, an inner wrestling with existential questions about their purpose and destiny.

Remembrance, A Journey of Awakening, Book 2 of *The Airon Chronicles*

Remembrance is an epic science fiction tale following the journey of an unlikely group of space travelers. When cultural collapse threatens life on Earth, The 108 are handpicked for a desperate mission to establish an Earthen colony on a distant planet called Airon. However, upon arrival, they find this luminous world is far more than it first appeared.

Airon's ethereal inhabitants and mystical wisdom compel the travelers on a profound inner journey, challenging their notions of consciousness and cooperation. As the truth of their purpose unfolds, The 108 must learn to blend their awareness with the living planet in order to transcend long-held fears, false beliefs, and their own limiting nature.

With vivid descriptions and fully-realized characters, Remembrance immerses the reader in an astonishing vision of awakening. Amidst tender moments of connection and startling twists, each traveler faces their inner darkness on the path toward embodying light. Ultimately, this is a story of humanity's potential and the courage required to remake ourselves.

READER COMMENTS

Danielle P: A mesmerizing addition to The Airon Chronicles series, delivering a profound exploration of camaraderie and resilience against the backdrop of a vibrant and evolving world. As the third installment of this gripping saga, it seamlessly continues the narrative, offering readers a rich tapestry of adventure and heart.

What truly captured my heart were the moments of quiet beauty and profound connection scattered throughout the narrative. From the intricate world-building to the lyrical prose, every aspect of the story resonates deeply, inviting readers to ponder the complexities of friendship and the wonders of the universe.

The multi-species friendships depicted in the novel are a delight to witness, serving as a poignant reminder of the beauty found in diversity and cooperation. Moreover, the themes of communion with nature and the pursuit of harmony underscore the timeless relevance of this tale.

Intrusion: A Journey of Friendship is a masterpiece of speculative fiction that exemplifies the true essence of companionship and resilience. It is a testament to the enduring power of friendship and the boundless possibilities of the human spirit. I wholeheartedly recommend this book to anyone seeking a captivating journey filled with warmth, wonder, and hope.

Lori A: The characters are so well-developed and engaging. It is a thrill ride of adventure.

I love me good plots: A classic tale of a utopian society that lives in peaceful harmony interrupted by the new and dangerous...The characters are lovable and you can really feel their peace and love for each other, which makes the threat of change and invaders all the more heightened.

Joe: The story grabbed me quickly and kept my interest. The story flowed with a nice balance of background and story to help it come alive.

Dakota 18: Book 3 of The Airon Chronicles is an exhilarating ride from start to finish. The intricate world-building and well-developed characters had me hooked from the first page. The tension and emotion kept me on the edge of my seat until the very end. A must-read for fans of speculative fiction and heartwarming tales of friendship.

Suzy P: The messages within the book continue to be very timely and relevant.

Laksm: The book masterfully blends a captivating alien world and the complexities of a looming conflict. There is a depth to the narrative that kept me engaged.

George R: A riveting journey back to the enchanting world of Airon.

D.A.W.1: This book had a satisfying ending. Honestly, its compassion was inspirational. It was spiritual and powerful with a strong female protagonist. It was entertaining and creative with a touch of magical whimsy. Five resounding stars for the creative world-building, heart-warming scenes, poetic prose, multi-species friendships, and communion with nature.

Skylor23: The author deftly handles themes of connection, disconnection, and the human spirit's resiliency throughout the entire book. For readers who enjoy speculative fiction, this book promises to be interesting and thought-provoking due to its satisfying ending and well-developed characters.

Dee: The quality of this book was truly exceptional.

Xibuxut: *Intrusion* is a beautifully-written book full of themes of family, friendship, and facing unexpected challenges together. I appreciated the author's masterful approach to dialogue and how even with so many important characters in the plotline, it was easy to follow and understand what was happening. Often felt like I was right in the story experiencing the adventures right along with them. Can't wait to read more by this author.

Amy: What a ride! The way the story captures the peaceful life of The 108 on Airon, only to throw them into chaos with the threat from Earth, had me hooked. I couldn't help but root for them as they scrambled to protect their new home and their families. It's a real underdog story with a sci-fi twist.

Panda Bear: The world of Airon is so rich and vibrant, and the author does a wonderful job of making it come to life. The colorful characters work together to create a way of handling the intrusive Earthens. A very creative and engaging read.

AS: The book masterfully explores themes of survival, unity, and the delicate balance between two worlds. A thrilling read.

Amal: The writing is so good, I could easily visualize each scene making it much more fascinating!

Jack: *Intrusion* is a masterwork that blends the best aspects of narrative with a rich, imaginative setting. It is a novel that is both enjoyable to read and a treasure to explore, making it a must-read for anybody seeking an adventurous, thought-provoking, and ultimately transformational tale.

Ian C: This book seamlessly blends science fiction with deep themes of identity and community. Readers will be captivated by the rich world-building and compelling characters as they navigate the challenges of protecting their newfound home from an unexpected threat.

Jordon L: This is a gripping sci-fi tale that kept me on the edge of my seat from start to finish. The intricate world-building and compelling characters drew me in, while the suspenseful plot kept me hooked until the very end. The dilemma faced by The 108 is both thought-provoking and thrilling, making this a must-read for any science fiction enthusiast. It's a riveting adventure that I couldn't put down!

Andrea B: *Intrusion* unveils a compelling tale of camaraderie amidst impending threat. With captivating characters and a plot woven with cooperative problem-solving, the narratives offers an immersive exploration of friendship and resilience. The author's skillful prose paints a vivid picture of the evolving dynamics between humans and Aironians, delivering a thought-provoking and emotionally charged read. Rich in imaginative world-building and heartwarming scenes, *Intrusion* is a testament to the power of true friendship and the strength found in unity.